Now it is the time of night
That the graves, all gaping wide,
Every one lets forth his sprite
In the church-way paths to glide.

- A Midsummer Night's Dream

D1378018

TRUSSVILLE PUBLIC LIBRARY
201 PARKWAY DRIVE
TRUSSVILLE, AL 35173
(205) 655-2022

Summer Gothic

A Collection of Southern Hauntings

EDITED BY
JARED MILLET

PRODUCTION COMMITTEE
INGRID SEYMOUR   SEAN DeARMOND
LARRY HENSLEY   HEATHER LEONARD

TRUSSVILLE PUBLIC LIBRARY

Summer Gothic © 2012 Jared Millet

The Reproach © 2012 Ray Busler
Beachfront © 2012 Sean DeArmond
Fourth of July © 2012 Margaret Fenton
Summer Forever © 2012 J. M. Gruber
The Haunted House © 2012 Larry Hensley
Earl and Bubba Save the King © 2012 Louise Herring-Jones
Dead in Me © 2012 Teresa Howard
Wayward © 2012 Megan Ingram
All the Good I Could © 2012 Suzanne Johnson
Family Ties © 2012 Joan Kennedy
Feral © 2012 C. M. Koenig
The House Near the Covered Bridge © 2012 Mary Brunini McArdle
Hurricane Season © 2012 Jared Millet
Shades of History © 2012 Lin Nielsen
The Exorcism of Mary's House © 2012 Jessica Penot
Sugar Baby © 2012 Lindsey Robinson
The Beaky Bunch © 2012 Ingrid Seymour
The Colors © 2012 Julia Jones Thompson
The Apparition © 2012 Bret Williams
The Ghost of Bear Creek Swamp © 2012 Tracy Williams
Nancy's Jog © 2012 Larry Williamson
My Best Girl © 2012 Michael P. Wines

Introduction © 2012 Sean DeArmond
Cover Model: Haleigh Huggins

ISBN-13: 978-1470092108
ISBN-10: 1470092107
First Printing: March 2012

All Rights Reserved. No part of this book may be copied, reproduced, or transmitted in any form without express written consent except in the case of brief excerpts used for review purposes.

This is a work of fiction. All persons, locales, organizations, and incidents are products of the authors' imaginations or are used fictitiously. Any resemblance to actual persons, places, or events is purely coincidental.

TRUSSVILLE PUBLIC LIBRARY

Contents

INTRODUCTION

Sean DeArmond

Night has fallen. Work is done. The woods surrounding us loom overhead, blocking what light the moon reflects. Perhaps a little too closely, the sounds of the wilderness challenge our notion that we are the apex of the animal kingdom.

But we have a campfire, a decidedly human metaphor of comfort and promise that the darkness holds no cause for alarm. Sleep will come soon enough, and day will follow as it always does. But for a moment, we have nothing to do except simply to be.

I guess we have to talk about something.

Ghost stories are probably as old as tribal society. History cannot identify how and when the ghost story became a standard format for people to swap, but the notion is probably related to us learning about ourselves. We understand that we're mortal and our time on this world is finite. Ghosts, by definition, require an ongoing existence beyond death. This comforts us. Some ghosts act as wizened sages who can guide us from beyond. Others regress to more selfish motives, demanding we finish whatever business they left undone.

We may not have all had the experience of encountering a ghost, but everyone knows what it feels like to be haunted. Guilt, regret, isolation, obsession – all these can be projected onto our shadowy apparitions. All of us intuitively understand this, which allows everyone at the campfire a human connection.

From a storyteller's perspective, ghosts are a gold mine. Enough themes appear so as to create a basic genre without having to describe the gothic castle every time, and there are very few rules. Ostriches don't bury their heads and reading in the dark won't hurt your eyes, but in *my* story apparitions are purple and they sound like vacuum cleaners and no one can argue with me about it.

Ghosts can take any role we need. They hire you to kill your uncle, they trick you into a duel with your estranged father, they fight you for territory, they warn you about your doom, and sometimes they just want to be your friend. They're benevolent, critical, terrifying, humorous, murderous, helpless, and heroic. They're ambiguous enough to be versatile but not so much as to be incomprehensible. Ghosts serve as ambassadors into the unknown, and ghost stories offer a taste of 'anything is possible.'

So welcome to our campfire. Grab a marshmallow and find a pleasant spot on the ground, because it's time once again for our long, glorious tradition of telling ghost stories.

Now, who wants to go first?

My Best Girl

Michael P. Wines

Jolene loved the summertime. She had more visitors then than during the other seasons. The heat and humidity didn't bother her; she hardly noticed them any more. The old thermometer hanging from a rusty, bent nail pushed the mercury to ninety-eight. That was just fine by her, the hotter the better. Everything wanted a cool place to get away from the scalding Alabama sun. Having been a true Southern woman, if Jolene liked you, she'd take care of you. Her home was a first-rate shelter, welcome to any creature that didn't try to take it all for themselves.

A family of jays nested under an overhang that would have fallen off decades ago had Jolene not protected it from years of corrosion. She loved the songs the birds sang, not to mention that the jays ate all kinds of bugs that tried to bore into the walls. She could take care of the bugs on her own, but she always rewarded help. Every time a rat snake caught the baby birds' scent, it found itself misdirected and lost once it started getting close. No guest in *her* home would be neglected. The weenlings would grow enough to take care of themselves shortly. They always had, anyhow, and Jolene reckoned they always would.

She was glad spring had passed. It brought too many storms. Most of her energy was spent defending her little shack against the weather. A few times she even tussled with twisters. She got beat pretty bad at first. It wasn't nearly as harsh as the whoopins her papa used to give her. Getting a bloody lip, a cuffed ear, or even a broken arm from her daddy hurt more than anything a cyclone could dish out. Tornados weren't personal. They just came through like a drunken freight train, and all she had to do was convince them to go around.

Nowadays there wasn't much home left to protect. Four crooked walls of ancient barn wood, a holey roof, and a rickety door covered a dirt patch big enough to shelter the moonshine still that had rusted to dirt years ago. The field it sat upon nestled between a pasture and a hardwood gully on what once was a proper plantation homestead. The main house burned during the war. Jolene wasn't ever partial to it anyhow.

But she loved that old shanty. As a girl, she'd visited with a mama cat and her constant stream of kittens that lived there. There were so many she couldn't keep all the names straight. For a while her daddy didn't mind, since they kept the mice out of his drinking corn. Then he caught her giving old mama cat some cream. He drug a howling Jolene by her hair with one hand and the sack of yowling furballs in the other, and he made her watch as he sunk the sack in the creek.

"I work too damn hard to waste good milk on some damn cats."

Daddy had too much of his tonic that night. The milk was going bad anyhow. That old cat must have hexed the place; the mama never came back and another hadn't been seen since. Jolene heard them squawking at night, down in the gully sometimes. She always felt worse about what he did to those kitties than what she did to him a few years later. Besides, he deserved it.

That was all so long ago, she hardly thought about it anymore. It seemed like a thousand seasons since she played with that tabby. She let some coons nest in the rafters for a while, but they were too messy and didn't appreciate a good cuddle, so Jolene settled for the jays, lizards, bats, and even an occasional opossum to keep her company. They all ate bugs, which was fine by her.

Sometimes people came poking around, but they never stayed long. On the patch where the big house stood, a few trailers moved in. They stayed mostly to themselves, but they put up electricity poles. Jolene didn't like those, not at all. They buzzed something awful. She had to bring tree branches down, swallow a few up with sink holes, and even guide a twister through to take the blasted things out. It took her half a year to get rid of the first batch, but them idiots kept putting them right back up. Finally, they put them far enough away that they didn't hardly bother her any more.

The trailers were allowed to stay on account that she was so lonely. Kitties liked people, and she hoped the hex would wear off eventually. These folks were different than the ones she knew before. They were almost fun to watch sometimes, and they didn't seem nearly as mean as she was accustomed to, either. The men let the women and kids talk whenever they wanted. Heck, she thought, the men couldn't shut them up if they tried. They dressed funny and talked even funnier. The girls wore britches as much as the men, but thankfully the men hadn't taken to skirts just yet.

Late one night, the stars were shining and the moon was peeking through the trees. A man stumbled out of the closest trailer dragging a beat-up old guitar and a half-full bottle of whiskey. Jolene watched him stumble about for a while, mumbling.

"I was just trying to sing my songs, damn it," was one of the few understandable statements he repeated between hiccups. He fell several times, letting his face take the brunt of the fall instead of landing on his guitar or bottle. Both seemed equally important to him.

Jolene considered making him go away, but she was bored and kind of lonesome. It'd been so hot out lately that even the lizards were hiding for most of the day. So she watched him. *What harm can a drunken idget do with a guitar and a bottle?*

Besides, that guitar reminded her of her mother. People always said Mama's singing was so sweet, it could make the devil give penance. A couple of songs always calmed her daddy when he was in one of his moods. Too bad she died when Jolene was shorter to the ground than a worm's butt. Maybe things would have been different.

The man eventually made his way toward Jolene's shack. His sweat-stained shirt and faded blue jeans acquired a few grass stains along the way. His boots brought their own.

"It's too damn hot to be outside," he slurred between gulps. "I'm going to sing my songs whether she likes it or don't. Jimmy crack corn and I don't care about her needing to sleep."

Jolene swung her door open slowly as he approached. She didn't want him putting any pressure on the delicate hinges. She rearranged a few boards so the moonlight shone through to a spot on the grass-covered floor. A few other adjustments, and a slight cooling breeze blew through to make the short grass sway invitingly.

"Don't mind if I do," the man said, plopping down on the patch Jolene prepared for him. She'd opened her door for a few other people she deemed harmless over the years. Most of them ran off quicker than a jackrabbit with its tail on fire. Apparently this one was drunk enough not to question the mysteriously opening door. That was fine. Jolene knew mean drunks and this pathetic creature was not part of that posse.

He struggled with which of his two prizes he needed to tend to first. His drooping head looked between the bottle and guitar for several seconds of considerable contemplation. Finally, he gulped down a powerful plug of whiskey and set his bottle aside. His voice twanged as he spoke like the old six-string he plucked not quite into tune.

"What to play?" he asked, as if expecting an answer from his imaginary audience. "All I know are country songs. So, how abouts one of them?"

Odd, she thought. Maybe he could tell she was there, listening. Some of her other visitors could tell, but that was because she made it known. This guy just started yakking like he knew her. That tugged on her mischievous side. She hadn't gotten a good scare out of someone in a while. Maybe she'd let him get comfortable for a bit before she played him like a drum. She had nothing but time.

"What song to play? Oh, I got the one, jus' the one. *My Best Girl.*"

Jolene listened.

He tossed back another swallow of drink, coughed twice, concentrated on his fingers, and finally began. The strings vibrated in a sad, tinny thrum. He sang like he talked, with a knowing drawl, but somehow sounded more lonely and heavy.

As he plucked the strings, Jolene shifted her house subtly. She liked the song so far and didn't want to scare him off just yet. The acoustics sharpened and the moonlight fell onto the guitar strings. She lit up his face to show a gritty little bit of handsome under his greasy mop of hair.

He opened his eyes between verses to look at the frets, but when he sang, his eyes closed and he belted the lyrics to the sky. Jolene just knew he was singing to her. This was different from the songs her mama sang. They were always about the Lord and praising and hoping. This song wasn't hoping. This was pain and loneliness. This was for Jolene. It had to be. That tune reminded her of something, but she couldn't quite grab hold of it.

Jolene felt lonelier than ever, but somehow a little better at the same time. At least someone knew how she felt. He sang her sadness. He crooned her loneliness. She'd been there so long that she didn't know anything else. It was quiet and safe, but most of all, it was hers. She never had anything that was *all* hers until she was dead.

Now, this bard, this roughly beautiful boy, had come into her home and heart. The more he sang, the more she swooned. He visited every few nights, carrying his whiskey, guitar, and sweet sorrow. Every steamy summer evening, he started and ended with *My Best Girl*. There were a few songs between, but none of them made her dusty walls shudder or her clay foundation shake like that one did.

One night in what must have been early August, her visitor fell asleep in the middle of a song. He and his bottle tumped over like the world's saddest dominos. She reset his whiskey and straightened him out so he wouldn't wake with a crick in his neck. She directed a cool breeze over his sweat-soaked skin and rested his head on her softest grass patch. Once she felt he was comfortable, she watched him for a long while.

Jolene ran her invisible fingers through his hair as he slept. It was greasy and sodden but still managed to smell good. It reminded her of the kittens. She found herself cuddling up under one of his arms, resting her spectral head on his muscular chest. Jolene listened to his heartbeat and would have wept, had she been able to.

He rose with the sun and staggered out of her arms, bleary-eyed and confused, bottle and six-string in tow. The kittens hadn't let her hug on them long either. It made the time she had with them that much sweeter.

Before he strutted through her door, she'd spent too many years lonely and angry. Jolene had considered fading to nothing for a while, but just couldn't let go of her little home. Even summertime had been picking at her with boredom. But who would care for the baby jays or chase off the twisters if not for her? Folks had lived for years with less of a reason, or no reason at all, for that matter. So she stayed the course, and finally he came for her.

He visited a dozen more times and even slept there once again before he broke her heart.

She'd been waiting, as always, for him to liven up her quiet summer night. He'd been singing to her about five nights a week lately. Jolene relished every simple second of it, until he brought *her*.

He sauntered out to her shack after sunset but before the moonrise. The air was heavy and hadn't shrugged off the day's heat yet. Usually he came around midnight and usually there wasn't anyone with him. This time was different. It'd been easy enough to let him in, knowing she could scare him out whenever she wanted. But how was she supposed to scare off one and not the other? She held the door closed as he tugged on it drunkenly. He handed his bottle to the woman to get a better grip on the door.

"I swear it never sticks. Hell, it's usually open. I guess the wind swung it closed."

"Come on, Johnny," the woman said. "I don't much like it out here. This dirty old shack creeps me out." She wore a dress no bigger than a wash-rag and had straw-colored hair springier than a hog's tail. One hand carried Johnny's bottle, the other held a massive cup brimming with red wine.

"I'm telling you, I sound a lot better out here. Just let me play a song and show you. Damn, girl, one song ain't going to kill you."

"But there's bugs out here, and my hair's already poofing up cause of this dang old heat."

Johnny, his name was Johnny. Jolene was reluctant to let *her* in, but had to allow it this one time. She didn't want to miss out on her song. The pressure on the door eased and Johnny fell back on his butt as it abruptly swung open.

"Dang it!" he said, dusting the red clay off of his already dirty jeans. "There now, come on in. It's always cooler inside."

Jolene hoped she was his sister, had to be. Who else would he bring out here to her home? As the woman crossed through the door, Jolene was reminded of the last time there were two others in the shack with her. It'd been so long ago. She never forgot that damn yellow-toothed sheriff and his deputy, but sure enough tried.

Johnny started singing. The beauty of it pushed the painful memories to the side for a while, like always. Johnny's sister even shut up when he started playing, thankfully. He didn't start off with *My Best Girl*. Maybe he was saving that one just for Jolene.

She pushed a slight breeze over him as he sang. She didn't direct much of it at the girl, though. Her comfort was of no importance.

Johnny played for almost an hour. The air had cooled and the moon rose from trees topping the lonely gully. "One more song," he said. It was *My Best Girl*. He sang like the stars were listening and took a pull off of his bottle when he was done.

The girl sat silently for a moment, then said, "I thought I was your best girl." Before Jolene could react to that, the hussy crawled over to Johnny with a troublesome look in her eye. She kissed him right there, on Jolene's floor, in Jolene's house. And Johnny kissed her back.

Jolene screamed like runaway barge hitting a mountain side. Rage, memories, and the need for vengeance rushed out of her like a stampede. She slammed the door shut.

"I'm his best girl! Not you. This is my house. Not yours."

"What the hell was that noise?" Johnny asked, pulling away from *her*. "It sounded like a damn freight train."

Jolene was betrayed.

It hurt more than watching those kittens sink.

It hurt more than the time her daddy came to her room.

He'd been sipping from his jug all night. Her bedroom door swung open. His silhouette menaced her wall. He carried that damn old clay jug and told her something. He said, "You're my best girl." She'd forgotten that part.

He set down that jug and started to fiddling with his britches. Jolene knew something bad was going happen. He wasn't ever nice to her, especially when he was drunk, so she picked up that jug. It must have weighed ten pounds, half empty. She knocked him on the head. Spirits flew in all directions from the busted crock and his bleeding scalp. He fell into a puddle of himself and never got up.

A few days later, the sheriff and his man showed up, looking for her daddy. They found him just like she left him. It wasn't hard to figure out what happened. They caught up to her in that shed, the only place she ever felt safe. At first they didn't see her, but then that yellow-toothed creep spotted her and yanked her out of her hole by a handful of hair. Jolene bit into his arm like she was the mama cat protecting her babies.

He hit her so hard her neck broke, and that was that.

They buried her on the spot, next to that rusty still. She should have run off instead of hiding. Instead, she hid in this barn, this busted up, musty, old, cat-abandoned shack. It felt safe, but nowadays all the protecting was done by Jolene. She hadn't thought about how strong she'd become over the years. She didn't need this hut anymore. It needed her. Maybe she could still leave. The realization hit her like that bastard sheriff.

It was her turn to hit back.

Two-timing Johnny and his hussy ran about, hollering like kittens in a sack. His guitar got stomped to bits and his bottle busted in the tumult. The strumpet's red wine spilled down her chest like blood as they frantically searched for a way out.

Jolene focused her rage. "If that's your best girl, then you ought to have her. Keep her forever along with this damn old house."

Her scream concussed like dynamite in a rain barrel. Jagged splinters tore into Johnny and his girl like half a dozen scatter guns at point blank.

Jolene didn't stick around, not this time. She needed to go find her best girl, the only friend that never did her wrong, that old mama cat. She wasn't ever going to let bad come to those kittens again.

There wasn't much left of Johnny and his girl, except for a few pieces of broken, bloody bottle and some splintered bits of guitar. Late on hot summer nights, folks claim to hear a lonely, sad song on the wind.

The Beaky Bunch

Ingrid Seymour

When her eyelashes looked like grotesque tarantula legs, Nicki winked at the mirror and blew herself a kiss. Satisfied with her work, she put down the mascara and picked up the glass from the narrow pedestal sink. Her drink – heavy on liquor, light on fruity mix – burned going down, a welcome pain. She arranged her push-up bra and gave her boobs a squeeze. "Go get 'em, tiger," she told herself, and wobbled out of the bathroom, balancing precariously on three-inch heels.

Her son sat in the hall, drooling on his bare chest and sitting in his own poop by the looks of that bulging diaper. Nicki stopped and swayed in her stilettos as she watched Little Zachary. He was facing the bedroom, staring into the dark interior, his chubby cheeks and pouty lips forming a cute profile, which would have been perfect if not for his nose. *So much like his damn father's.* His little hand went up in the air and waved bye-bye. A smile dimpled his rosy cheeks. Nicki shuddered, stumped toward the bedroom, and slammed the door shut.

"Who're you waiving at? Huh? There ain't no one there."

Little Zachary's lower lip bulged and for a second he looked as if he was going to cry. But he didn't. Instead, he crawled toward the living room, diaper drooping noticeably.

Let the witch change him. She should be here by now. Nicki glared at her Timex. Leaning against the entrance to the living room, she looked from the door she'd just slammed back to the kid. Little Zachary picked up a tiny toy truck. Nicki tapped her foot and checked her watch again.

The kid showed no interest in her. He played with his truck, watched it slide down the ramp of his Fisher Price garage set. When it reached the bottom, he picked it up and put it at the top again. He did it over and over, mechanically, with no smile, no spark in his eyes, just a fixed stare. Nicki rubbed goose bumps off her arms, looked for the cigarettes in her purse, and lit one.

The bell rang.

"'Bout time," she murmured, rushing to the door and sparing one cautious glance toward Little Zachary.

"Hello, Ilse." *Witch*, she added in her mind.

The woman offered a curt nod, barged in, and scooped up her grandson in one swift motion.

"Hi there, sweetheart," she gushed.

The kid beamed and kicked his legs in excitement. A pang of jealousy made Nicki's stomach go sour. It must have shown on her face, because the witch's expression grew smug, her beaky nose rising a whole two inches in the air. That nose, that ugly, hooked schnozzola that was the Polvani's trademark. This woman, the kid, and even Martin had had it.

Poor boy. Now that Little Zachary was young, his nose was fine, cute even. It made him look like one of those parakeets at the pet shop, but it wouldn't always be that way. One day it would look more like his father's and his grandmother's, a shiny crow's beak, perverse and ugly.

Nicki left and shoved any trace of remorse she might have felt deep in one corner. She deserved a break from her job, from the kid, from her entire wretched life, no matter if her beak-nosed mother-in-law gave her the accusing, evil eye.

Ex mother-in-law, she reminded herself. *Ex.* The woman was nothing but the boy's grandmother, his only other blood relative and Nicki's sole reprieve from it all. Martin, his father, was gone now, and that was good.

She rode to Cale's Tavern and ordered a beer, like every Friday night. A Crimson Tide football re-run droned on the overhead TV. Hell, the season was still two months away. Couldn't they give it a break?

She watched with disinterest, a cigarette snuggled comfortably between her index and middle fingers. After a drag, deep and long, loaded with nicotine, Nicki winced. The smoke tickled her eyelashes.

"Smoke it, babe," a male voice said from her right.

Before turning, Nicki looked at her empty drink and hoped for a handsome face, one without an inverted banana for a nose. She looked at the newcomer. A Roma tomato. Not pretty, but not quite unpleasant. It seemed to match his face just right, somehow. He smiled, one eyebrow cocked and insinuating.

Her eyes did a quick, assertive sweep over the rest of him. Not quite her type. Too short and starting to bald, but at least he looked fit. The number two requirement in her short list: a non-beaky nose and nice biceps.

"I like a woman who can handle a cigarette." He pointed at her glass. "And a drink. Let me buy you another one."

"Why not?" She took another drag before twisting the butt on an ashtray.

Nicki ordered a Cuba Libre. She'd be messed up tomorrow, mixing drinks like this, but at least it wasn't the white stuff. Only alcohol, nicotine and, if she was lucky, good sex. The drink went down smoothly enough, chased down her throat by Roma Tomato's wolfish stare.

"What's your name?" he asked.

"No names. Just another drink and, if you want, we can get out of here."

His eyes lit up. *Jackpot*, they said. He paid for another drink, even gave the bartender a big tip, Nicki staggered out of the bar as Roma Tomato followed close behind. They walked to his car, but before they got in, she asked the question she always asked her one-night stands.

"Are you good at it?"

He looked puzzled.

"You know." She wiggled her eyebrows. "Good in bed."

Roma Tomato's expression turned defensive.

"It should be worth my while, don't you think?" she asked.

"You ain't one of those frozen women, are you?" His tone was riddled with suspicion.

"No."

"All right, then I'll show you a good time."

They got in the car and drove a couple of blocks down to a cheap motel. Once inside, he did as promised. He showed her a *very* good time indeed, made her totally forget about those two pairs of eyes always staring accusingly at her everywhere she went, and those hook noses that might as well have been middle fingers, telling her to go to hell.

He nuzzled her neck and sucked hard. "Wanna do it again?"

"Nope, that's all folks," she said.

"You had fun, didn't ya? Showed you a good time like you wanted?" He was proud, just like they always were when they made her scream. They didn't know she was hot and easy. All she needed was for the guy to care a little, to be... vested. That's why she always asked if they were good. Men were proud creatures, especially when it came to sex.

She left him shortly after and sipped from her flask as she made her way back to the bar and her car. Nicki wanted a hit, the soaring high of the white powder she'd come to love and hate, but she had to stay clean. Martin had gotten her started on it soon after their first date, the bastard. He never mentioned that he dealt it too, or that there was always a bit left here and there – just enough to get her hooked, to make her beg.

Nicki's feet ached in her narrow shoes. She stopped at the pedestrian signal, a flashing red hand telling her not to cross. It may as well have been saying 'This is how far your life goes, darling.'

Two men appeared to the left, walking as if on padded feet. Nicki suspected that they meant to startle her, just for kicks. She gave them her Queen of the Darkness stare, accompanied by a growl. They looked spooked. *Who's scared now?* They were probably just college kids, unaware that there were scarier things in life than strangers stalking in the night: like kids that waved at their dead fathers.

A car slid to a stop.

Not my night.

The middle-aged man at the wheel asked her how much, and for a moment Nicki considered getting paid for what she loved best. The man pulled out a hundred and waved it like so many empty promises. She gave him the finger and told him to at least take off his wedding ring. She might be ready to destroy her own life, but there could still be some redemption for murder if she left others alone. Maybe when she got to hell, they'd let her shovel the coal instead of making her burn next to Martin.

She got to her apartment complex after 4:00 A.M. Holding on to the rusted metal railing, she climbed the steps. After a few tries, she managed to key the lock. The kid and the woman slept in that accursed bedroom where Martin convulsed to death. Dawn throbbed on the horizon and in her head. Bile and disappointment clogged her throat. Nicki crashed on the couch, which was now her real bed, and slept, arm and legs sprawled, mouth spewing toxic fumes.

A loud *drip* woke her up around 4:30. The sound echoed through the apartment the way a trickle might inside a catacomb. Cold crept from under the sofa, climbing from her toes to the top of her head, like a blanket being pulled over a corpse. Nicki sat up and rubbed her arms, eyes glued on the entrance to the kitchen. That damn faucet, every night.

Each drop on the metal sink pounded her temples. If sleep would have been possible with that infernal noise, Nicki would have curled up with a cushion over her head. But it wasn't. She knew she had to walk in there, had to tighten the handle to get it to stop, even if the maintenance man said he'd fixed the stupid thing three times.

Shaking from cold, anxiety, and drunkenness, Nicki stood and took two steps toward the kitchen. *Six more steps,* she told herself, quivering on the spot. *It's just the kitchen. There's nothing in there but a leaky faucet.*

Two more steps. She could see the refrigerator now, dark shapes shifting on the freezer door. She knew it was just the leaves outside, stirring in a pathetic July breeze, casting shadows through the small window above the sink. It still freaked her out, especially the way the shapes seemed to form eyes and teeth.

One more step.

Drip.

Maybe if she told maintenance that the tree had termites, they'd cut it down. Or if she got that promotion, she could afford a different place to live, one with a dishwasher, a good faucet, and no ghosts.

Gathering all her courage, Nicki ran into the kitchen, tightened the faucet handle, and ran back out. She had barely made it out of there when the shattering sound of glass burst behind her. Weak at the knees with a jolt of panic, she staggered and tripped on the shaggy rug. Nicki went down, more worried about what was behind her than the coffee table. With a *thunk*, her right temple struck wood, stabbing a terrible pain through her skull. She barely noticed. Instead, she curled up on the rug, knees to her chest, eyes glued on the kitchen threshold, as a low whine started in back of her throat. She watched, transfixed, waiting for Martin to materialize in front of her.

"I know you're there," she said between tiny sobs. Her words were but a whisper, all she could manage through her fear and the pounding in her head. "Show yourself or leave me the hell alone."

A scratchy voice grated through the room. Nicki's spine prickled as adrenaline flooded her system. Involuntarily, she scrambled toward the sofa, wondering if she could fit under it, wishing she hadn't issued a challenge. She'd backed all the way against the couch before the words she'd heard made sense. It was the old hag asking Nicki what she was doing on the floor.

Trembling, Nicki looked toward the hall that led to the bedroom. Like a specter, Ilse stood in the shadows, wrapped in a dark bathrobe, her dyed hair unusually flat.

"Hearing *things* again?" the witch asked with twisted pleasure.

"I... There's something..."

The hag claimed that the faucet didn't leak, the light bulbs didn't flicker, and the bedroom didn't still stink like Martin's Aqua Velva. She wouldn't believe that something, someone had just smashed a plate in the kitchen.

"Maybe you need another drink to clear things up a bit." Ilse inclined her head in a way that made the shadows on her face elongate, making her nose look like Captain Hook's appendage.

Nicki felt like gagging. The alcohol in her veins, the noises, the sight of that ugly schnozzola, the freaking ghost she was certain haunted her apartment, it was all too much. She wasn't crazy. The dope hadn't fried her brain like it had Martin's. Nicki knew there was something up with this place, no matter what the witch said.

Ilse made a noise in the back of her throat. Nicki pushed up onto the sofa, her gaze burning a hole in the woman's back as she shuffled in her slippers and disappeared into the kitchen. A cabinet opened and closed on squeaky hinges; water ran for a few beats. Nicki held her breath, waiting for Ilse to complain. Nothing. The hag came out carrying a glass of water, looking unaffected.

"Sweet dreams," she said, a crooked smile stretching her flat lips. Her eyes, liquid and sinister, told Nicki she knew there'd be no sleep. Had Ilse seen something and chosen not to say anything just to drive her mad? Or was Nicki really going crazy?

Exhausted with it all, she wrestled with the cushions and her chenille throw and tried to get comfortable. She tossed and turned, attempting to clear her mind. Sleep was her only reprieve. Well, that, sex, and booze. She thought of Roma Tomato, played their escapade over in her mind until the images became a soothing white noise that muddled her consciousness. Sleep caressed her, made her heart beat at a steady rhythm, made her...

Drip.

Drip.

Drip.

The sun shone brightly through sheer curtains, pushing a deadened stare out of Nicki's eyes. She blinked several times and slowly sat up. After a few minutes in deep contemplation, she pulled a pair of dirty jeans from the small basket at the foot of the sofa. Saturday was laundry day... but not today, though. She had other plans.

She smoothed her favorite college t-shirt and slipped it on. It had a ketchup stain and two small holes, but she loved how wearing it made her feel. Memories of better days always came back to her, memories of a time when she'd believed she was going places. She needed that feeling today.

Nicki picked sneakers for comfort and a pair of brand new socks. She wiggled her toes before stuffing her feet in and dared a smile. With a bounce in her step, she walked to the bathroom and brushed her teeth. Her eyebrow was swollen from hitting the table, but she ignored it. Nicki palmed the brush and toothpaste and went back to the living room. She was stuffing the toiletries in her bag when Ilse came out of the bedroom, Little Zachary in her arms. Quickly, she placed her purse inside the laundry basket under a pile of smelly onesies.

Ilse eyed her up and down. So did Little Zachary. How a one-year-old knew to do that was beyond Nicki. His creepy behavior made her feel less guilty. He and his grandmother were made for each other. They could stay here with Martin's ghost, like a big, happy family, the Beaky Freaking Bunch, thank you very much.

"Hey," Nicki said with a cheery smile.

The hag's sour face grew uglier. Nicki hadn't thought that possible. "He needs his bottle," she said, plopping on Martin's old recliner.

"No problem." Nicki might have pranced into the kitchen had she not expected to run into shards of glass. When she spotted the broken plate right in the middle of the floor, she was surprised by how little it affected her. On a different day, she would have probably shrieked and peed her pants. Today, a slight shiver was enough to get her over the shock.

Martin's influence was escalating. At first, it had only been a slight breeze, an odd scent, a dripping faucet. Last night the stakes had been raised, and she wasn't about to hang around and find out what other tricks he could pull.

Nicki popped a cup of milk in the microwave and heated it up for a few seconds. After filling a baby bottle, she brought it to Ilse, who started feeding Little Zachary. She watched her kid for a few seconds as he sucked greedily on his breakfast. There was some regret in her heart, and she acknowledged it, stared it right in the eye. After a few seconds, Nicki nodded, certain that she could live with this flimsy remorse better than with Martin's ghost. The kid would be better off with Ilse, anyway.

Nicki had lost it with Martin, had reached the limit and messed with his coke. By the time she came back to her senses, it'd been too late. The doctors called it an accident, blamed it on Martin's addiction. Admittedly, Nicki might have just sped up the process, but she'd killed him, no bones about it. She'd come close to losing it with the kid, too. Maybe the drugs and the alcohol *had* fried her brain a little, at least that motherly part women are supposed to have. She really didn't care. All she wanted was to be free.

"Well," she said, picking up the laundry basket. "I'll be back in a couple of hours."

Ilse took the bottle out of the baby's mouth and pushed to the edge of the recliner. Little Zachary didn't cry, like any normal kid would have. Instead, he looked up at Nicki with accusing eyes, a perfect replica of his grandma's.

"What about breakfast?" Ilse asked in a suspicious tone.

Nicki grew defensive and snapped, "Not hungry."

Ilse smiled, as if she knew something. But how could she?

I'm just being paranoid. "I'll grab something at McDonald's. Don't you worry about me. I'll be fine."

Ilse smirked. "I'm sure you will."

At the brink of lashing out, Nicki bit her tongue and forced a grin. She whipped around, basket perched against her hip, and left the apartment. Heat and humidity greeted her outside and she reveled in the warmth, the way it made her feel alive and full of hope.

Gulf Shores would be a good place. She imagined the beach and the ocean twinkling under the sun as if dotted with Christmas lights.

With the distinct feeling that her heart was about to burst, Nicki walked toward the stairs. She was about to take the first step when the apartment door swung open and Little Zachary came out, running in that clumsy way babies do.

"Mama," he said, arms outstretched for a hug.

Nicki stopped, gave her mother-in-law an annoyed glance.

"He wanted to say goodbye," Ilse said with a shrug.

When the boy got close, Nicki squatted and put the basket on the ground. Chubby arms wrapped around her neck. The smell of sweet baby lotion and sour milk assaulted her. Regret and guilt threatened to raise their useless heads again. She squashed them down and tried to enjoy the rare hug.

Nicki patted his bottom and pushed him away gently. "Good boy," she said. "Get back to your Maw-Maw, now."

As Little Zachary turned to leave, Nicki picked up the basket, straightened, and turned to the stairs, but before her feet were facing the right way, little hands pressed against her thigh. Nicki looked down and found Zachary staring up, a strange smile on his lips.

"Bye-bye, Mama," he said, then pushed her.

Nicki lost her balance and tumbled. The laundry basket flew upward as she tried to catch the railing. It bounced down the steps, spilling dirty clothes in every direction. Nicki followed, hit the concrete with a bone-cracking thud, then rolled head over heels and landed at the bottom of the steps in a shattered heap.

Something warm oozed from the back of her neck. Nothing felt right, yet as odd as it seemed, nothing hurt. Her eyelids grew heavy as she tried to focus on a three-headed silhouette at the top of the steps. With her last bit of consciousness, Nicki blinked to clear her vision.

Martin, Little Zachary, and Ilse looked down at her, smiling, happier than she'd ever seen them. Martin held the baby, looking as alive as ever. In unison, a cackle rose from their throats, a bird-like yapping that did their horrid beaks full credit.

Dead in Me

Teresa Howard

That crazy old witch woman inside me, I gotta get her out. It's not my fault she's dead. Well, maybe it is, but she could have changed that. If she'd just given Leroy the money, he wouldn't have had to hit her. Leroy likes to beat women, and he don't know when to stop. She kept screaming at Leroy, so he hit her until she got quiet. I was sure she was dead.

"Damn stinking bitch," Leroy said and kicked her again. He handed me a gun. "You stay here, Davy."

Leroy stomped on upstairs to look for money. There wasn't nothing worth taking downstairs. I didn't see any computer or TV. The furniture was dark and shiny, but too heavy. I went over to the body. She wouldn't need that silver necklace anymore. It wasn't worth much or Leroy would have taken it. I bent over and nudged the old woman with the gun. She didn't move. I'd never seen no dead body before. It made my hands start shaking so bad that I almost dropped the gun. I didn't know Leroy was going to beat her to death. He wouldn't have if she had just told him where the money was.

That dead woman's hand grabbed me, grabbed me hard. I about

wet my pants. The gun went off. She let out a moan and died. My head felt funny. I thought I was going to be sick all over her.

Leroy came running down the steps. "Davy, are you crazy? You done called the police."

I tried explaining how the gun went off accidentally, but he still clouted me upside the head. We had to get out of there then, without the money.

I didn't think no more about that crazy dead woman until I was in my own place washing the sweat and stink off. When I looked in the mirror, her wrinkled old face grinned back at me.

"Boy, you get on out of here. This is my body now. Go on, get!"

I shook my head. I was having one freaking bad day. "You're the one's dead. You get out, Grandma."

"That's what you think. I'm from Na'leans. Women in my family have been doing magic more than two hundred years. When you murdered me, I cast a spell and jumped right in you. It's my body now.

"Well, I ain't going to leave. This is my body. I reckon I'm going to keep it."

"Davy?" my baby's mama, Latisha, called. "Who you talking to in there?"

I looked toward the door for a minute. When I looked back, the old woman was gone from the mirror. She wasn't gone from my head, though. I could feel her in there, waiting.

Next time that old witch showed her face, I was just fixing to smoke some fine smack.

"What you doing, boy? Don't put that in my body. You stop now."

I laughed. She could scream all she wanted. The higher I flew, the smaller she got. Soon I didn't hear her at all.

I woke with a start. I wasn't in my bed. I wasn't passed out on the floor at Jobie's. I was standing at the sink at Latisha's.

"Go away" the old witch said as soon as she saw I was awake.

"What am I doing?" I asked, looking around.

"You're washing breakfast dishes, fool. Can't you see that? Latisha had to go to work this morning. She's a fine girl, you know. You should be more help around here."

I had been smoking smack on Saturday. "She don't work on Sunday and I don't do dishes."

"Well, it's Wednesday and when somebody feeds me, I help clean up."

"Wednesday!" I'd promised Leroy I would deliver some stuff on Tuesday. He was going to be so pissed. I was in deep shit.

"Don't you worry about Leroy. He isn't going to put no marks on this body, no sir. He's not going to hurt nobody else neither. Real sad about Leroy."

"What did you do to him?" That witch had been up to something while I was out.

"Me, I haven't done nothing. Bad things happen to bad people. Leroy tried to cheat the wrong folks and they shot him dead. We'd be dead too, if you had been with him."

Leroy was mean, that's true, but he'd been my friend since I was as small as my baby girl, Keisha. Covering my face with my hands, I sobbed. I just couldn't stop. You would think that old witch would have some sympathy, but you'd be as wrong as high rise pants and white socks standing on the corner. The more I cried, the madder she got. Pretty soon she was screaming and stomping in my head.

"Heartless old witch!" I splashed cold water on my face and dried off with the dishtowel.

"You and Leroy done killed me, and *I'm* heartless? Did you shed any tears over my grave? Ha!" With that, she popped out, leaving me in peace.

It went like that for weeks. Sometimes I'd be myself. I'd almost forget about that witch woman. Then there'd be times when she would take over and I couldn't remember anything, like being in a deep sleep.

Once I woke up in the biggest room I ever seen, with noise banging in my ears. Thousands of crates were stacked in long rows. A loud beeping sound jarred my head and I blinked at a pile of boxes coming right at me.

"Watch out," a deep voice that I recognized as Latisha's uncle Joe called. His big hand hauled me out of the way just in time.

I started to say thanks, but he shoved me against a stack of crates and got right in my face. "Look at me. You been doing smack?"

"No man, I'm clean. Just got a little dizzy. It's hot in here."

"Well, get some water and get back to work. These trucks don't unload themselves."

That witch done got me a job.

Damn.

When we were both awake, we'd fight over whose body it was. To make matters worse, I started having seizures. They only happened when we were both awake. I figured the old witch was causing them, but she was just as scared as I was.

"You got to let go and get on out of this body," she warned. "We can't both be in this mind or it will break."

"Get out yourself!" I yelled aloud. Baby Girl, who'd been playing with her doll, ran crying for Latisha.

"Boy, you done scared that baby again," the old witch said as if adding to my list of sins. I tried not to let on how bad that hurt. I love Baby Girl and Latisha, even if I ain't too good about showing it.

I was sure the old witch was right. One of us had to go. I just couldn't do anything until she went out again. I was afraid to even think about what I might do. If the witch found out, she'd stop me for sure.

I'm not Catholic. I don't even go to the Baptist church with Latisha, but I love scary old movies. *The Exorcist* was a good one. That's how I ended up sitting in the confessional rubbing my hands together and trying to work up enough spit so I could get the words out.

"Forgive me, Father. I done a really bad thing." I started out slow and made sure that I explained how the gun going off was an accident. It helped that the priest was on the other side of a partition. I told him all about it and how I had to get rid of the old woman or die. He didn't understand. He murmured some words about forgiveness being from God, but he didn't tell me how to get rid of the old witch. A small card slid through a slot and fell at my feet. I heard his robes rustle and the door on his side close as I bent to pick it up. It was the address of a mental health clinic I'd walked by on the way to the church.

Shit.

I wasn't getting anywhere, so I decided I had to make peace with the old witch. I told her how sorry I was about her being dead. That surprised her, and she admitted that it was Leroy's beating that had killed her. The coroner's verdict said blunt force trauma to the head.

That bullet had gone clean through her shoulder.

I was too relieved to get mad. I was a thief, and some folks would call me a junkie, but I wasn't no murderer. Sensing my relief, the old woman bristled.

"You still got to get out!" She followed this command with a sharp whack to my brain.

I bent forward and clutched my stomach, unable for a moment to speak. After catching my breath, I asked, "Couldn't we find you another body?"

"It ain't that easy. You can't grab somebody's body just like that. I have rights to your body because of what you and Leroy done. I don't have any claim on nobody else. They'd have to be awfully weak or too young to fight back."

I got off that subject right away. I waited until I was sure she was gone and then went snooping around to her neighborhood. I talked to some folks that knew her, but nobody had much to say. The old witch's name was Cassandra DeMorgan, she was born way back in 1941, moved up from New Orleans after that last hurricane, and kept mostly to herself.

"That old woman got what was her due," confided one sister as she came out of church. "We're Christians here. That voodoo don't belong in Birmingham."

I nodded agreement. "I hope there aren't any more witches around here."

She patted my arm. "She wasn't alone. I caught my niece visiting a woman over on the South Side. That one set herself up as a *Christian* psychic. I told Trisha, if she wasn't plain rubbish, she was from Satan."

I left the good sister and found the psychic. She had moved into one of the old houses off Wald Park, a large, two-story place that someone had made an attempt to fix up with a coat of green paint.

As I climbed the brick steps, I prayed that old Cassandra wouldn't wake up and catch me in the act of trying to kill her for real this time. I pushed the doorbell and a feeling of peace came over me.

Madam Bellamy was a short, round woman with dark mocha skin and piercing green eyes. She flashed me a smile.

"Come in, come in. You've come to the right place."

The lady was surprisingly light on her feet for someone almost as wide as she was tall. She seemed to glide across the hardwood floor. After settling herself on a brightly covered couch, she motioned me to a matching chair.

I took to Madam Bellamy right away. I could tell at once she wasn't going to think I was crazy or judge me for what happened to Ms. Cassandra. I told her everything. It was like a weight the size of that Vulcan statue on the mountain was lifted off my shoulders.

Her green eyes brimmed with sympathy. "Poor child, don't you worry. We'll see what we can do."

After a bit, Ms. Bellamy left the room, murmuring in some funny language. When she came back, she carried a gold chain in her hands. A small amulet dangled on the chain. She reached up, fastened it around my neck, and patted my shoulders twice.

"There, that will keep that nasty old Cassie in her place," she said with satisfaction.

"But I don't want her to stay. I want her to leave."

"Yes, yes, but I cannot make her leave. She must choose to leave. This will keep her 'out' as you say. When she realizes that she will have no control over the body, she will leave. It always works."

Hope shone like a halo, and I grabbed at it. I offered her the money in my wallet, over one hundred dollars. I didn't know where Cassandra got the cash, but I was putting it to good use. Ms Bellamy folded the money and slipped it into a pocket. Taking my arm, she escorted me down the steps. At the bottom she planted a kiss on my cheek before hurrying back up.

It had been four weeks since I visited Ms. Bellamy. That old witch, Cassandra, was locked out just like she promised. The sun was shining on a fine summer morning. The place where Latisha worked was having a company picnic and fun day at Lay Lake. I helped get Keisha ready for a day out. Latisha's Uncle Joe even gave us his car for the ride. I don't like fishing, swimming, or boats, but who's gonna pass up free barbeque and beer?

I still felt Cassandra, like a small itch. Sometimes I heard her tiny voice cursing at me. I was sure she was going to give up soon though, cause them seizures had mostly stopped.

To a boy who grew up in the city and had been nowhere near the ocean or rivers in his life, Lay Lake looked like an endless sea. The sun shimmered off its calm surface. We laughed and talked with people who worked with Latisha. Baby Girl played with their kids.

After lunch I pulled off my shirt and stretched out on a lawn chair. Shades in place, I prepared to soak up some serious sun. Baby Girl played nearby in the sandbox with her new best friend, Rachel.

Latisha gave me a playful nudge. "Don't you go to sleep. You watch Keisha now. I'm going to see the skiers."

"Baby Girl's okay. I'm right here"

That sun was warm. I must have fallen asleep for a minute. I woke up with Rachel pulling my arm and crying.

"Keshie gone! Keshie get wet."

I jumped up and looked around. It took a few minutes to spot Baby Girl on the end of the long pier. There wasn't a grown person nearby. I tried to shout, but only a low groan came out.

I raced straight for the pier. I'd almost reached it when my Baby Girl fell off the other end. I knew I had to get to her fast. My body kept running, but my mind was screaming for me to stop. I couldn't swim, and I knew if I went off that pier we would both drown. I kept running. I would rather be dead than have my baby be drowned because I fell asleep.

"Let me out!"

I almost didn't hear Cassandra's voice. She must have been really screaming to get through the block.

"Let me out!" she repeated. "I can swim! I grew up on the river."

I almost stumbled. I knew it was true and I didn't stop to think. If the cost of saving Baby Girl was letting Cassandra have this body, she was welcome to it, so I yanked off the chain and flung it away. I let go and went to sleep praying that we weren't too late. The last thing I felt was the cold as my body dove into the water.

I woke up stumbling out of the lake with Keisha in my arms. I put her little body down on the ground and begged. "Breathe, Baby Girl."

She coughed and began to cry as people gathered around. It was then I realized I was alone. Cassandra was gone.

I was happy for about a second and then I got scared. I began to shake Baby Girl. "No. Cassandra, no." I lifted Keisha's tiny face and looked into her eyes. They were red from crying, but only my sweet Baby Girl was in there. I laughed and kissed my baby all over. When Latisha came running up, I grabbed her and started kissing again.

Out in the lake, a woman rose out of the water. I almost didn't recognize her; she was so young and pretty. Cassandra must've been one hot mama in her day. She smiled and nodded at Baby Girl. Then, quicker than I could nod back, she disappeared up in the sky.

Now to tell you the truth, I know they don't let witches into heaven, but something inside me says Saint Peter gonna let Ms. Cassandra slide.

Sugar Baby

Lindsey Robinson

When Delilah met her haunted man at the movie theater, she was by herself. The film was an old black and white, from sometime after the silent movies with their wild-eyed, thin-lipped heroines and typed dialogue, but before Marilyn Monroe's round hips and cotton candy curls. It might have been something with Shirley Temple.

The movie was dubbed in French, but Delilah wasn't really watching. She just wanted to escape the oppressive August wind that held her vacation hostage. Her traveling companion, twenty-five years her senior, was stuck in a conference in the La Défense district of Paris.

The cinema was the oldest building on that block, a bygone little red breadbox bordered by a deli with hospital-style counters and a gourmet ice cream shop. In the ticket booth, an older woman with sooty black eyes took Delilah's money. She handed her a red ticket, the kind sold in rolls and distributed at fairs. Across the street, a row of red umbrellas fluttered over round café tables.

A cold thrill of air met Delilah as she entered the movie house's single cinema, and she sighed and ran her fingers through the sweat-sticky hair on her neck. The theater was nearly empty. Three old women sat in the front row – triplets with identical swirling hairdos and shapeless overcoats. Delilah wondered how they handled the diabolical heat with their heavy jackets and sculpted curls.

In the very back row sat a younger man, his head leaning against the wall and his eyes closed. He was handsome in a pale, tragic way, and as Delilah eased into a middle seat she wanted to turn around and look at him. She felt she recognized him, and trawled her memory but found no trace. When she finally did look, he was staring into the screen, his face cracked like a window. And inside the window there was a shop, filled with hundreds of beautiful crystalline figures.

Delilah slept a little through the movie, but when the lights came up she felt as if she were coming back to life. The young man had disappeared. When she met her traveling companion later that day and kissed his cheek, he said she looked younger. Like a child, he told her.

His name was Thomas Seville, and he ran the largest hairdressing supply corporation in France, although he had the big hands, tanned skin, and dramatic features of a libertine gypsy. Together the two of them maintained a relationship based on platonic contentment, financial assistance, and just the occasional sexual longing. But really, they were best friends from the day they met, when Delilah was charmed by his rugged face and lightness on the dance floor. Seville admired the sharp wit that bubbled up and surprised him underneath her shy demeanor, along with the delicate curve of her ass.

Delilah was well educated and motivated, and she never thought of herself as a kept woman. When she and Seville first met, she had tried to play into the stereotype, buying things she didn't really want and over-dramatizing her reserved mannerisms. But Seville split through that farce cleanly one afternoon when Delilah went giddy over a makeup ad in a department store.

"Oh, I've got to have her lipstick," she'd said, hoping Seville hadn't heard the forced joviality in her voice.

"Baby, you're not paying thirty dollars for a face that isn't yours," he said with some sadness, his heavy eyebrows rumpling. "You're pretty, and I like you without painting on another woman's lips."

From that moment on, Delilah stopped pretending and went back to her old ways. She read a book a week and wore her dark hair in its old style, clipped just below her chin and swinging with each of her loping steps. In a supple leather bag she carried a simple composition notebook and a cheap pen. She offered Seville conversation and manners, and he gave her security and good jokes. Neither of them felt the need to marry. There was no reason for her to work, they decided, and together they spent much of their time traveling.

The next day she came back to the theater, just as the noon heat was starting to make her skin prickle. The cool air inside reminded her of the breeze that swept through her hair the night before as Seville drove her through the countryside, just as the sun set and the world took on a warm, redeeming glow. He pulled the car over and looked into the orange sky.

"I should have met you when I was a younger man," he said. "Now I'm old and withered, like a dead tree."

"Psh, you're a horse," she told him as the sky grew dark. "And besides, when you were a young man I was just a toddler."

Seville reached over and pinched her cheek with his knuckles. "I'm a horse, right. And you're a little bird. My little bird."

As she settled into bed that night she dreamed of the movie she'd seen (and of the young man, although she wouldn't have admitted that even to herself).

She was dozing off when he sat down next to her, just as the theater went black. The couple onscreen had entered into the mouth of a cave, and Delilah was lulled into pitch dark drowsiness. When the male lead struck his match, Delilah started and saw the close-up face of the man next to her in a haunting flash.

His image lingered in her mind like an old song: his dark eyes glowed in a pale face, smooth and oddly familiar, like the sheets in Delilah's hotel room. A chic, otherworldly air settled around him. Above their heads, the movie projector crackled.

"I can see you're not very interested in antique cinema," he said in a murmuring voice. He was much younger than Seville, a little younger than Delilah, even. When he leaned toward her she detected the loamy scent of wild mushrooms, and she thought of fresh dirt and the country hills outside of town. She shifted in the deep theater seat. The pale young man leaned in to speak to her again.

"May I keep you company?" he asked into the curve of her ear. He had a rolling accent that sounded like thick honey on Sunday morning toast. Delilah nodded out of politeness – she was raised to be polite – and gave up her claim on the armrest.

She reached into her bag and pulled out a cigarette, then fumbled for her lighter. When she pulled her bag into her lap, he slipped a match out of his front shirt pocket, reaching underneath his brown tweed vest. He struck it beautifully against the curve of his thumbnail and held it up to her lips, shielding the flame with the palm of his hand. She covered the red tip as she inhaled and blew the clandestine smoke out the side of her mouth. She didn't know if it was okay to smoke in the theater, but something about the young man's presence made her want a cigarette, something to cut the air.

"Don't worry, Sugar," he whispered as he settled into the seat.

"No one is watching us."

After the credits rolled and the lights came up, he stood as she did and spoke into her ear once more. Isn't he just full of secrets, Delilah thought with a smile.

"I don't want to scare you," the young man said, "but that man of yours is dying soon."

Delilah picked up her bag slowly and held her cigarette between her thumb and forefinger. She dropped it at his feet and tamped it out with the toe of her sandal.

"I don't know who taught you how to tell jokes, sir, but..." She stopped as he held his palms up in front of her, as though he wished he could offer her better news, or some lovely trinket.

"I saw you with him yesterday. I can tell you, he's almost ready to die. I'm sorry."

Delilah didn't believe him, but something about his words made her feel a little sick to her stomach.

"You've got a real nasty sense of humor, movie boy," Delilah said, resisting the urge to spit on his shoes. He was standing by his chair as she stormed out of the theater.

"Just check the hospital," she heard the young man call. The world outside the theater was like an overexposed photograph.

Early that morning, she'd found a perfect yellow cupcake with a single flickering candle on her nightstand. Delilah's thirtieth birthday was on Sunday, and she'd almost forgotten it. Seville had been awake for several hours – he hadn't been sleeping well lately – and leaned forward, elbows on his knees.

She stretched like a cat and smiled at him. The covers slid against Delilah's hips as she reached for the cupcake, her delicate fingers crinkling the paper. As she stood and walked to the long window, the sun warmed her skin and her shadow stretched long and black against the bed. She took a thick bite of the cupcake – it tasted rich and real in the way only a French dessert can. She moaned with pleasure, and Seville laughed.

After Delilah dressed herself in a crisp white skirt and a green blouse that outlined the curve of her back, the two of them went downstairs to the hotel café for a cup of black coffee. Seville told her then that he was going to the doctor to see about a little pain in his chest, nothing serious at all, just a lingering cold mixed with a touch of heartburn.

Across the street from the theater, a young girl was wiping a table slowly, as if it were her only task in the world. Delilah fumed, but she felt a strange loosening in her belly, a need to make sure. She took a deep breath to calm herself, crossed the street, and asked the girl to point her toward the nearest hospital. There was only one nearby, the girl said, and it was within walking distance.

The doors to the emergency ward split in front of her as she strode inside, confident and shaky.

"Thomas Seville," she said to the woman at the desk. Inside her head, Delilah heard the woman tell her she must be mistaken. Was she sure it wasn't another name? No, no patient with the last name Seville. No other hospitals nearby. Yes, quite sure about that, miss.

"Room 214," the woman at the desk said.

The color drained from Delilah's face. She walked on rubbery legs up the stairs and into the antiseptic room that held her companion. He was sunken into the bed.

"I'm fine, really. This is all just a dumb formality," he told Delilah in his rough gypsy's voice. "I'll take you dancing after all this. I'll wear you out – you'll have to sit down while I dance with every other girl. I'll make you jealous."

Delilah smiled at him.

"I bet you will."

He sat up a little, leaning on his callused elbows.

"Did I ever tell you I was scrawny and pale when I was a younger man?"

"No, never," Delilah said. "I can't imagine you being scrawny, baby." She leaned towards him.

"Oh I was. I was a weak, skinny kid." He reached up and pinched her cheek between his knuckles. "I spent all my time at the movie theater, just like you. I was pretty happy, but I gave it all up when I started my business. Back then I was a real poet, can you imagine? A charmer."

"Really?" Delilah leaned back and looked at him out of the corner of her eyes. "Okay then, Shakespeare, let me hear it. Give me a poem."

Seville stretched and put his hands behind his head. He winked at Delilah and stared into the middle distance, an artistic, intellectual look on his weathered face.

"I once fell for a girl named Delilah.
I loved her greatly but I denied her
The chance to see her old man in bed
So I ushered her out of the room instead.
'Meet me at home,' I told her, 'and then,
we'll finish what we started, again,
and again,
and again.'"

Seville tapped his forehead and held out his hand, and Delilah burst into laughter as she clapped.

"Bravo, bravo," she said. "So you were a starving artist, I suppose?"

A slight, thin-boned orderly poked his head in the door just as

Seville pulled the pillow from behind his head and waved it at his girl. The orderly told Delilah in a watery voice that she needed to leave, that visiting hours were over for non-relatives and the patient needed his vital signs checked. She could return in three hours.

Delilah wiped away tears of laughter and sorrow as she kissed her closest friend on the forehead.

"I love you, old man," she said. He waved her out of the room.

"I love you, sugar baby," were the last words he said to her before she clicked the door shut.

When she returned, a doctor in a coat as crisp as new paper pulled her to the side. She didn't need to hear what he had to say. She already knew, and her face crumpled like the hotel room sheets when the maid stripped them off the bed and threw them in with the rest of the dirty laundry.

His family had been contacted, and they were on their way. The hospital was quiet as Delilah left. She hailed a taxi.

"The old cinema on Rue 14. It's nearby, but I don't feel like walking."

The same woman was selling tickets, and she looked at Delilah's tear-soaked face with pity.

"No charge, Sugar," she said.

The movie was a silent film this time, and Delilah slipped into the quiet, cool theater, into the soft music that floated behind the spectral people onscreen. The young man was in the back, just where she'd left him. She sat down next to him, and he looked at her with his heavy gypsy eyes.

"Thomas Seville," she said. He nodded.

"Tom," he said. "I'm sorry, Delilah. I did love you. You were made for better things, little bird." He handed her a stack of papers tied with a red ribbon.

"My poems," he said.

Delilah took them and looked into the screen, her tears glowing in the celluloid light. When the credits rolled, Tom Seville was gone. Delilah smelled earth and loam, that wild mushroom scent that made her think of large, open spaces.

The light outside the theater warmed her arms and stung her eyes. She crossed the street slowly and sat down at one of the outside tables, looking back at the wooden panels and heavy red doors of Seville's beloved theater. The funeral would be soon, and she would attend and kiss her companion's relatives, even though she had already said her goodbyes. Steam rose from the cup of coffee in front of her, and the air was pregnant with the smell of baking bread.

Delilah pulled out her notebook and untied the ribbon from the thick stack of poems. She began to make her plans, writing in careful script as the row of red umbrellas stretched before her like cardinals on a telephone line. The poems would be her task, the strange, beautiful locket in the box of his legacy. The hairdressing supply empire would take care of itself, or someone else would take care of it, she decided. The heat of August rose off the street in waves, like old ghosts making their way to heaven.

The Reproach

Ray Busler

Alabama on Wheels
The Quarterly Magazine of the
Association of Alabama Recreational Vehicle Dealers

Welcome back, fellow campers. Once again, Eb and I have loaded up the Winnebago for another summer tour of Alabama and our ongoing search for all those forgotten wonders this state has to offer.

Constant readers of *Alabama on Wheels* will recall our all-county tour last fall where we explained how it came to be that every county in Alabama, except Winston, ended up with exactly the same limestone statue of a glassy eyed Confederate soldier on the courthouse square. We apologize for missing the winter edition, but Eb's bout with pleurisy kept us close to home during the chilly months. The spring trip to Enterprise did Eb "a power of good," as Minnie Pearl used to say, although by the time we reached Coffee County the annual Alabama pine pollen bloom was in full swing and Eb wore out two inhalers. But you can't keep a good man down, and believe me, I've tried.

You of course remember our photos of the Monument to the Boll Weevil. In that issue we failed to mention our gratitude to the kind folks at Walker's Campground and RV Park on Hwy. 231. We are much obliged for their great hospitality, and Eb and I miss the sassafras and corn cob smoked barbeque at Walker's Wayside Restaurant and country store. We've never seen it done that way any place else. Really, nowhere.

That giant boll weevil got Eb and me to wondering if every city had a "claim to fame" even if the place was only the knitted sock capitol of America. With that theme in mind, we struck out for west Alabama, left the interstate system, and ended up in Carrolville.

The courthouse in Carrolville was burned during the War Between the States by Wilson's raiders because it was suspected of being a Confederate storehouse. Wilson, by the way, then adjourned to more important arson in Tuscaloosa where the University of Alabama harbored a dangerous corps of cadets. They spanked the boys and burned the school, but that's a story for another trip, possibly in the fall during football season.

The citizens of Carrolville recovered enough by 1889 to rebuild the courthouse into the two-story Bessemer Gray brick edifice you see today. Of course, the courthouse isn't the claim to fame we were searching for; it's the windows. Well, that one window in particular...

Sheriff Wilburn Fowler had taken about all he wanted from the citizens of Carrolville. His job was secure. He knew every voter and the name of his wife, children and dog. Every voter knew Wilburn; no one even bothered to oppose him in the last two elections. Carrolville was eight years into the 20th century, and now this thing was happening in his town.

"You'd think they'd have a little respect for me personally, if not some respect for the law. All they have to do is wait a week, two at the most, and this business will take care of itself. I ask you, Billy, why bother to get twelve men to sit through a legal trial in this kind of heat, in that suffocatin' courtroom, if you can't wait a few days for a legal hanging?"

"Oh, they'll wait, Sheriff. I figure they'll wait for about two more pulls on that jug they keep passin' around, but not much longer than that. The whole bunch is pretty worked up." Billy Preston had been deputy for the last three of Fowler's terms. Now he took off his badge and laid it on the desk. "Wilburn, I just can't stay with you on this one. I ain't scared. There ain't a man in this county I can't whip, but if we stay here tonight, me or you one will have to kill some of them ole boys before the rest will stop."

"Put your star back on, Billy. Take Toby up to the storeroom on the top floor and lock him in. The only way he could get loose from up there would be out that front window, and the fall would solve all his problems and most of mine. When you finish, we'll lock up and go home. I've known these farmers all my life and I ain't about to kill one on account of that idiot Toby. When you get him up there, tell him to set his ass still and keep his mouth shut. Maybe they'll be too drunk to look up."

Even if the store room windows had not been painted shut, the sheer drop made it an effective prison cell. By pressing his face against the pane, Toby could see the curve in Main Street. At first it looked like a swarm of lightning bugs moving slowly in the hot night toward the court house. He wiped his eyes and watched, mesmerized by the scene. Urine began to pool at his feet. He couldn't move; fear sweat kept him glued to the window glass like a squashed insect on a microscope slide.

The lights became larger and he saw they were the farmer's lanterns. Soon he heard the men's voices and smelled the stink of burning coal oil from the lamp wicks. He knew they would cut him first, cut him and geld him like a hog. His whimper turned to a whine, and then to a long, high pitched keening. He was like that when they took him. His fingernails left parallel gouges on the casements when they pried his face away from the window.

Sunday morning dawned with a promise of clear sky and more heat. Abe Sanders, the photographer from the Cooley-Byron portrait studio on State Street, loaded a tripod camera onto his buggy and drove down to the river to take advantage of the light. The studio's specialty was photograph tinting. Its display was full of pink-bottomed baby pictures and cherub-cheeked boys and girls to attract doting mothers and grandmothers as they passed the store. This picture wouldn't be tinted. This picture could only be stark black and white. Lynching was a monochrome business. Yankee newspapers and magazines wanted and expected the spectacular and ghastly. Ghouls were more profitable than angels.

After a good breakfast, Sheriff Fowler and Billy Preston followed the same track the buggy had taken into the grove of water oaks on a borrowed cotton wagon. Billy even thought to bring a tarpaulin so their returning cargo didn't offend the sensibilities of early church goers.

The strange part was that no one noticed the window for about a week. Maybe no one could hold his head up all that high, but soon enough someone saw it. Someone else said it looked repulsive, and so after a while the window came to be exactly what the people of Carrolville believed it to be.

The sheriff ordered the janitor to wash the window, but the room stank like piss and death, so the janitor refused to go in and finally quit. The mayor told Sheriff Fowler to replace the pane and the sheriff told the mayor to go to hell or replace it himself. The mayor and the sheriff are both long gone, but the pane is still there.

...so, fellow campers, every place has a claim to fame and now Eb and I have seen the famous face in the window at Carrolville. Frankly, Eb thinks it just looks like smeared glass, and I can't see the resemblance to a face. But then I don't live in Carrolville, and it isn't me the face is watching every day.

— Pearl and Eb Moody for *Alabama on Wheels*

Beachfront

Sean DeArmond

It wasn't the cool ocean breeze that lured Zelphina's eyes open; it was the vibrations of the jeep's tires slowing down.

"Good morning, starlight." Caris grinned at her from the driver's seat.

"I wasn't sleeping," Zelphina insisted.

Caris pulled the jeep in front of the lone beach house overlooking the waves. A single seagull glanced in the girls' direction, evidently not expecting to see people.

"So why are we here?" asked Zelphina.

"This is where they stayed," Caris told her. "The crew is giving us the beach house for the week."

"What about the lighthouse?"

"It's about a mile up the beach. They're setting up the equipment."

Zelphina grumbled to herself, "Well I definitely want to stay out of the way then."

"I thought you would." Caris grinned again, turning off the ignition. "Do you feel like unpacking while I give them a hand?"

"I live to serve," she muttered.

"Oh, don't be like that." Caris batted her eyelashes. "We have a week at a beach house that we're not paying for."

"How do you find these people?"

"They find me. I got us bikinis." Caris sang the last word. "They're packed in my change purse."

Zelphina's expression remained stoic. "Do they know you're a demonologist?"

"That's what it says on our website."

"Do they also know that you know nothing about ghosts?"

Caris opened her door. "People assume everything they don't understand all fits in the same box."

"So do you really think you're going to be of use to the team?"

"No, but since it's very unlikely they're going to find anything, I don't think I'll hinder the project."

Zelphina grabbed their three bags and dragged them over to the steps. Caris grabbed the lightest and hauled it up the stairs. She pointed to the charred wood on the railing as she climbed.

"This is where it started. She shot her husband with a flare gun."

"What was he wearing that was flammable?"

"I don't know. They'd had some massive commotion inside." Caris pushed the front door open and dropped her bag just into the living area. "She may have thrown any number of household fluids at him. So he burst into flames and burned to death. It's a pity he couldn't find any sand or water around here."

"When you're on fire you're not really thinking straight."

Caris looked at her colleague tenderly. "Do you just smile all at once when I'm not around?"

Zelphina ignored the question. "So after killing her husband, the wife runs a mile down the beach and dives out of the lighthouse."

"So you *were* paying attention." Caris giggled.

"Why would the team think that her ghost haunts the lighthouse?"

"As far as I know, they don't, but she was the third reported suicide in ten years from that lighthouse. The others were some businessman and a teenage girl. Apparently they were all reasonably content people."

"The married couple?"

"A little infidelity but no history of rage." A rush of cold air hit Caris so hard it blew her blonde hair back. She shook as if she was on the first drop of a roller coaster and beamed. "I love ocean breezes."

Zelphina put her weight on the first step, which creaked in discomfort beneath her. She dropped the luggage. "I'm going to take them up one at a time."

Caris scurried down the steps, skipping the bottom three by jumping to the ground. "You don't mind if I check out what kind of equipment they're using to track supernatural activity, do you?"

"I don't mind."

"Zel, you have to admit this is a beautiful beach."

"What if there's a real ghost?"

Caris nudged her playfully with her hip. "I've got you to protect me."

"Just stay out of the lighthouse until I'm there," Zelphina warned.

Caris sighed. "Do you mind me telling you what I think your central problem is?"

"You've narrowed it down to one thing?"

"See?" Caris tickled Zelphina's abdomen. "You can be funny, but you're so serious all the time. It's okay to play in the waves."

Zelphina didn't respond, and Caris chose to leave the topic alone for the moment. She swatted Zelphina's rump, informed her that she would be back by that evening, hopped in the jeep, and disappeared down the beach road.

Zelphina took in an agitated breath. "I didn't think I was being funny."

There wasn't a soul visible on the beach as Caris drove to the lighthouse, just a few gulls who took no notice of her. Once she reached a decent spot to park the car, she found the research team doing research team things on the other side of the structure. The one who looked the most professional was sitting at a group of portable tables. Two men were moving plastic tubs, and there seemed to be movement inside the lighthouse as well. Caris hopped out and scampered over to the one seated, who was fidgeting with a conglomeration of unmatched metal boxes. He stared at her coldly as she approached.

"Hi, I'm Caris." She stretched her hand out to him. "Are you Mr. Wyatt?"

"I'm Dr. Simmons," the large man replied, as if the mere act of acknowledging her was infringing on his personal time.

"Caris Roberts?" greeted a friendlier voice behind her. She twirled around to answer, eyelashes already batting before she even got a look at him. She always made it a point to flirt with the person who hired her, as it tended to make them gentler when they began dissecting her credentials.

"Speaking." She grinned. "You must be Mr. Wyatt."

"Call me Mark."

At just shy of six feet, Caris towered over him by five inches. Mark looked like he couldn't be more than thirty, and Caris wondered how he'd managed to assemble a team for a project like ghost hunting, which was frankly a hard sell to financial backers unless you had a reality television crew.

"We weren't expecting you for a few more hours."

"I'm an irresponsible driver," Caris admitted. "I wanted to go ahead and check in."

"Great!" said Mark. "Why don't we get started, then?"

Caris's heart jumped, but she knew better than to let it register on her face. She could feel the doctor at the table staring at her, and she quickly dismissed any excuse about not unpacking or needing her lucky mood lipstick as an admission of fraud.

"I'd love to," she said.

"How long have you been a medium?"

Caris tugged at her top. "Oh, I'm not. This has just been through the dryer a few times."

Mark blinked, not certain if she was telling a joke, and he glanced over her shoulder at Dr. Simmons for a cue. "No, I mean how long have you had your gift?"

Caris winked confidently, as those few seconds had bought her enough time to get her story straight. "As far as I know, I've always had it. When I was a child I felt things that I didn't realize other people couldn't feel."

"What was the most recent experience?"

"It was in April." Damn it. Why didn't she bring Zelphina? Caris got all of her performance cues from her.

"I thought your website mentioned a project from two weeks ago."

"There was no ghost." Caris wasn't lying now.

"But something happened there."

"I've been kind of sworn to secrecy for the moment."

Mark glanced over Caris's shoulder again, and it occurred to her that Dr. Simmons might be Mark's Zelphina. In dealing with mediums, there were quite a number of pretenders. As far as Caris knew, nobody really had the ability to see ghosts or talk to them. If such people existed, Caris hadn't seen evidence of it, but the charlatans brought a little magic back into the world. It was entertainment. If a target was willing to throw away their life's savings on a fortune teller, then 'good fortune teller, dumb target.'

At the same time, in Caris's experience, research teams that had nothing better to do than waste money bullying palm readers always had some ulterior motive. Sometimes it was as simple as being published for the sake of tenure. Other times, it was darker than that, and Zelphina had been keen to take them on, 'debunk the debunkers' so to speak.

Caris's role was misdirection. While she was in her trance, moaning and heaving, Zelphina would be watching the audience to figure out their subtext. Two weeks ago had been the low point, when a college professor had arranged for the intern he was sleeping with to be murdered by an apparition during a séance.

Feeling adventurous and just a little rebellious, Caris grabbed Mark's hand as if they were on a first date and pulled him away from Dr. Simmons's table. She made a beeline for the lighthouse door.

"Come on, let's see what's going to happen in there."

Dr. Simmons's glower served as a magnified surrogate for Zelphina's piercing gaze. Caris would have to try setting them up for a drink later.

She sat on the wooden crate that one of the other researchers had left. Mark latched the door shut at her request, and she took heavy breaths, her head nodding in a slow rhythm.

"Are you sure you want to do this right now?"

Caris smiled without opening her eyes. "Let's just see what happens."

She inhaled as deeply as she could and let the gentle essence sift from inside her chest.

"Do you need me to be quiet?" Mark asked.

"On the contrary, I need you to talk to me."

"Won't that mess up the research?"

"I'm not here to prove anything," Caris whispered. She took in one more deep breath and exhaled peacefully.

"Mark, do you believe in God?"

"In God?"

"Yes."

Mark hesitated. "I'm not sure what that has to do with anything."

"You're right." Caris giggled. "What could God have to do with existence after death?"

"I mean, what does it matter what I believe?"

"It matters to you, doesn't it?"

Mark was silent.

"It matters to me," Caris added.

"I guess there could be a God."

"*A* God?"

"A God."

"Not just 'God?'"

"Isn't that the same thing?"

"Telling me you believe in *a* God means you want to keep a distance from the God you think I believe in."

"Either God exists or he doesn't. What does it matter whether or not I believe?"

"Because it affects how you live your life." Caris rolled her head back like she was in a warm shower.

Mark shifted his weight. "Is this your standard topic of conversation?"

"It would be, but my partner doesn't really find the discussion all too comforting."

"I'm not really one for church myself."

"*For where two or three are gathered…*"

"Caris, are you in a trance?"

"No." She opened her eyes. "I'm faking. I've never seen a ghost in my life."

Mark eyed her up and down. "Then why are you here?"

"I'm here because it felt right to come here," explained Caris. "I don't know if I even believe in ghosts, but I believe in God, and I go where I feel God wants me to go."

"I've heard a lot of mediums use a similar explanation for why they do what they do. An invisible entity leads them somewhere."

"Maybe it's all connected," offered Caris.

"Or maybe it's all a lie."

"Mark, what do you think happens to us when we die?"

"I don't know."

"But what do you think?"

"I don't know."

"You're looking for ghosts, you must have thought about it."

"We're not exactly looking for ghosts," said Mark. "Our devices read different energy waves, and they're sophisticated enough to filter out just about anything we don't want to pick up on. Dr. Simmons thinks that a conscious thought devoid of physical form will leave a distinctive trail. It's the same principle that picks up on surges in dying patients."

"A spiritual energy?"

"Something like that. I've never really understood it all."

Caris rose from the crate and stepped into Mark's personal space. "You still haven't told me what you think happens to us when we die."

"Maybe I could tell you over lunch."

"Mmm, I love lunch."

Caris turned to head for the door, but Mark had one more question for her. "If you believe in God, why do you doubt the existence of ghosts?"

"Because it stands to reason that ghosts are lost souls, and I don't believe God leaves anyone behind."

It was midafternoon by the time Mark got back to the lighthouse. Lunch had turned into an excursion, and the excursion had turned into a dinner date.

"Have you and your girlfriend been doing research in town?" was Simmons's snide comment.

"I figured you didn't need her for the project after she confessed to not being a psychic."

"And you thought I didn't need you either?"

Mark sighed. "I assumed I wasn't needed until tonight."

Dr. Simmons scowled at him. "So she claims she's not a medium?"

"That's correct."

"Then how do you explain this?" Dr. Simmons pointed at the printout of the readings from the time Caris had spent at the lighthouse. Mark wasn't an expert, but even he could gather that the energy waves most associated with paranormal activity were elevated during the time Caris had been near the equipment.

"Do you think the lighthouse is actually haunted?"

"No, we were reading her."

"Does that mean she's actually a medium?" asked Mark.

"The evidence points that way." Dr. Simmons frowned. "Or she's recently walked through a fully conscious specter."

Whoever now owned the beach house had neglected to furnish it after the place had presumably been investigated by the police. Zelphina unrolled their sleeping bags on the living area's floor and hung up their clothes in the closet.

She had meant to check out the second floor until she noticed that the lighthouse was visible from the kitchen window. She soon discovered that by positioning one of their suitcases in the middle of the kitchen and using it as a makeshift chair, she could clearly see the spot at the top of the lighthouse from which the victims had thrown themselves. From that moment on, Zelphina was unable to take her eyes off it.

She didn't believe there was a ghost in the lighthouse. People who led reasonably tolerable lives rarely remained behind, no matter how tragic their deaths. Even if this was one of those rare circumstances where something prevented one of their spirits from moving on, they would be tied either to their unburied body, which wouldn't be the case with the lighthouse, or to a place with a powerful emotional charge – again, not the lighthouse.

But none of Zelphina's logic mattered where Caris was concerned, and she became convinced that her only friend was going to swan dive off the ledge the moment she looked away. It was pure superstition, Zelphina knew it, but it gave her an addictive combination of peace and anxiety.

Then she felt it.

It was in the beach house. It slithered toward her like an amorphous tentacle, and a single drop of chill dabbed the back of her neck. She put up a psychic wall before it crept down her spine.

"Don't even think about it," she sneered.

The slither gently recoiled and eased to the side, as if testing her perimeter. Zelphina took her eyes off the lighthouse and glared into the emptiness moving around her. It was invisible, but Zelphina locked her focus on its location. It moved to her right, then back, Zelphina's eyes following it.

"You think I don't know where you are?"

It lashed at her so hard she fell off the luggage. Zelphina regained her feet and stood at her full height, refusing to acknowledge that the impact had startled her.

"Not too subtle, are you?"

It reared back for another lash, but waited. Zelphina waited. They stared into each other. Then it struck.

Zelphina blocked the strike with her palm. The force pushed her back against the cabinets, but she stayed on her feet. She squeezed the invisible presence until it dissipated around her and reassembled in the hallway.

Zelphina spun around to face it. "Do we understand each other?" It rose again, towering over her. "You will speak to me," Zelphina demanded. A hiss of laughter crackled in her ears.

"I'm waiting."

Wait, it mocked her, still laughing.

"No, I'm serious," she said firmly.

Serious. It threw the word back at her, flipping her skirt up. Zelphina brushed it away so hard she hit her knuckles on the wall.

"Do I look like I have a sense of humor?" she snarled.

It vanished. A loud pounding echoed through the house. Dust

shook off the rafters, and from behind her Zelphina heard the sound of the clothing rack breaking, undoubtedly leaving all of her and Caris's belongings in a pile at the bottom of the closet. Zelphina pressed forward.

"What do you want? You want to show off?"

It didn't respond.

"You want to show off for me? How did you kill that couple?"

It grabbed her by her face and lifted her off the floor. Spinning her around as forcefully as it could, it showed her. It showed her what it did to make a woman so frantic she would burn her husband to death and then kill herself when she realized what she had done. And all the while, it had watched from the kitchen window, gloating at its accomplishment.

When it thought Zelphina had had enough, it held her gently in midair. She refused to show any sign of being shaken.

"And what about the girl?" she asked.

It dropped her on the floor. Her inner wall was down, and the apparition seeped over and into her body. Zelphina screamed an animalistic roar and threw it out of her. It was noticeably stunned by her resilience. Zelphina crouched on all fours and shifted her focus to see where it had gone. It recomposed itself, and she addressed its central point of cognizance.

"We're not finished."

She sprinted to the stairs leading to the second floor. It followed her, catching up before she reached the top. It flung her against the wall, pinning her inches above the floor. Zelphina spoke to it over her shoulder.

"So now what? Hold me here indefinitely? You know where I'm going."

It dropped her on the floor again and spun her around to face it.

Go, it ordered.

"Is this what you do? You entertain yourself by destroying lives?"

GO! it screeched, clearly admitting she was a match for it.

"Do you call this 'existence?' You don't belong here any more. It's time to move on."

NO! It hurled her across the room, definitely trying to kill her now. She scrambled back to her feet.

"Listen to me." Zelphina held her ground. "I don't know who you are. Or were. But this place you're in can't possibly feel like anything but a tomb. Is this how you want your eternity to feel?"

It tried to envelop her again, drowning out her vision and rushing through her ears like an undertow, but her defenses were too strong for it. After a few, futile moments, it retreated to a calmer stance.

"I don't know what waits for you, but it's where you belong now. You should go."

No!

"I don't blame you for being afraid. The things you've done in death are terrible, and you must have done something equally awful in life to be in this state. But Caris believes that God is forgiving."

Caris.

"Yes, Caris. She believes that everyone is redeemable, and I'm willing to take her word for it, but you have to sacrifice your ego."

Caris.

"Focus back to me," Zelphina snapped. "Your only way out of this house is through me. Don't you think you stand a much better chance in God's hands?"

Caris.

"That's it. I'm finding out who you are right now." Zelphina marched through the apparition, making her way directly to the attic door. Hauntings always needed an unburied anchor in a place where it wouldn't be disturbed. For lack of a basement in the beach house, the attic made the most sense.

It howled in her head so loudly that the noise disoriented her. She closed her eyes to block out the rush of energy. Zelphina hit her head on the wall and had to feel her way to the nearest doorknob.

The howling made her head pound so heavily that she thought she might lose consciousness. Sheer will compelled her forward, but the force of her opponent pushed her so strongly that her feet slid in place on the wooden floor like a mime on a park stroll. Her endurance won out, and Zelphina flung the attic door open. The howling ebbed to a silence.

Zelphina glanced back at the apparition, unwilling to accept her victory. "That can't be all you have."

It lunged at her with all its force and threw Zelphina across the attic bedroom, smashing the window. It grabbed her tightly to keep her from falling out and slammed her to the floor, striking from every direction. She felt her head twist so hard, she thought her neck might dislocate.

The front door opened downstairs, and Caris's voice called out. "Zel?"

Caris. It spoke her name with no masking of its intentions.

"Caris!" Zelphina screamed as her wall fell. She was unprotected, and the apparition knew it.

It entered her.

Zelphina sat at the top of the steps to beach house's door. It was evening now, and there were more stars out than she ever remembered seeing before. Caris innocently pulled up in the jeep and

Zelphina's eyes followed her approach.

"Zel!" Caris waved. "I came by earlier. Where were you?"

"Upstairs."

"Did you hear me call you?"

"Yes."

Caris covered her mouth in embarrassment. "Did you respond?"

"Yes."

"I am so sorry!" Caris scurried up the steps. "The waves were really loud this afternoon and I didn't think to check upstairs. I honestly thought you'd left."

Zelphina didn't answer.

"Are you mad at me?"

Zelphina shook her head.

"Are you sure?"

Zelphina stared. "You look like you haven't seen a ghost."

"We didn't. They've got some really impressive scanners and they didn't pick up anything. I think the project is going to be a bust."

Zelphina turned away.

"Zel? Please," Caris begged, "what's happened?"

"All the answers are in the attic."

Caris blinked. "What answers?"

"I don't know."

"What's in the attic?"

"I haven't been up there."

Zelphina started crying. Caris put her arms around her shoulder.

"Sweetie, talk to me."

"There was a ghost, Caris. Here. But it's gone." Zelphina shivered. "Would you be a dear? I want to know who it was."

"Okay." Caris kissed Zelphina on the forehead. "I'll go look in the attic."

Caris turned to go into the house, but Zelphina called out to her again.

"May I ask you something?"

"Of course, sweetie," Caris reassured her.

"Do you really believe anyone can be redeemed?"

"That's something I'll never stop believing."

Zelphina looked at her friend with a tear in her eye. "I'd really like to play in the waves tonight."

"So would I." Caris smiled. She ran into the beach house, leaving Zelphina alone with her feelings.

The ghost was gone. It had tried to possess her, and it had succeeded. That was its undoing. Now it was in oblivion.

Maybe Caris was right and God could rescue anyone. Maybe from hell itself, perhaps even from nothingness. Zelphina simply couldn't help but feel that no matter what terrible things the former tenant of the beach house had done, it couldn't possibly have deserved what it had gotten.

But the ghost had tried to possess a demon.

Idiot.

The Colors

Julia Jones Thompson

I reckon if it's gone get told, I best tell it. If nothing don't happen, I'll be eighty-nine come December, and I got to where some days I can't think of things like I used to. I feel pretty good today, though. The weather's cold and dry, and I believe I can get it all straight.

I woulda been about four or five when it started, or maybe it had already done started but that's the first time I come to realize they was something different about me. Anyway, I remember the first time it become real clear, and I figure it musta been nineteen and twenty-seven.

My Aunt Dot, she lived with my grandmother down in New Hope and she visited with us sometimes when the garden was coming in real big, any time somebody with a car was making the trip up to Owens Cross Roads and thought to bring her. Daddy and some of his helpers had picked corn the very day she come that summer, and we was real glad she was there to help. We sat out on the porch in the evening, hoping to feel a little breeze while we shucked the corn. Gracious, they was a pile of it.

Aunt Dot, once she got started on a job, she would of kept at it

71

all night. Long years later, the first time I saw a robot on the TV doing a job over and over with stiff arms and jerking turns, I thought he looked like Aunt Dot when she was busy shucking corn – kindly staring with her mouth helt open a little bit, shucking, silking, cutting off the top, flicking out a worm, and setting it aside in a stack before reaching for another ear and doing it over again. She never stopped to take a sup of water or wipe the sweat off her face or nothing.

I was the least one of all the children and pretty much rurned, so I mostly danced around the ones that was working and tried to get them to pay me some attention. I didn't aim to misbehave, but I know I was rotten. My brothers and sisters, they was the ones rurned me, doing my share of the work and keeping me out of trouble, all the while telling me how bad I was. I couldn't get Aunt Dot to play with me while she was working, or even to call me "Lizzie Monkey" like she done sometimes when I was acting silly. I wanted her to reach out like she was gone get me so I could squeal and twist away.

When it got too dark to see, Daddy lit the kerosene lamp and set it on the table. The big mound of corn started going down a little at a time, and the stacks of clean ears went up. Mother said we needed to finish it that night so we could start cutting it off and canning it in the morning before it got too hot.

The kerosene lamp flickered behind Aunt Dot, and what I saw next made me stop my foolishness and watch. It wasn't the first time I saw the colors. Most folks has the colors except for the littlest young'uns, but hers went real orange and began to make a shape behind her, and she set still with a half-shucked ear of corn in one hand, staring straight ahead. Her lips began to move like she was talking to somebody, but they wasn't nobody there.

"Lizzie! Stop staring!" Daddy said, and took a swing at my backside. I dodged him and danced away so I could see better. He wasn't trying real hard to whup me. "She has a spell ever now and then. It ain't nothing to stare at."

I should of listened, but I didn't. I got right up close to Aunt Dot and watched her lips. The colors got brighter and the shape got the beginnings of a face. I couldn't hardly believe it, but I began to make out some words that went along with her lips, and finally I knew what she was saying.

I'm gone have a bastard baby.

"Aunt Dot's gone have a bastard baby!" I said. Everybody always got real excited about babies, so I hopped on my dirty, bare feet and clapped, proud to be the first one to tell the news. "Aunt Dot's gone have a *bastard* baby!" I figured a bastard baby must be the very best kind.

I wish I had listened to Daddy. I wasn't paying no attention to what was going on behind me, so I didn't know he had took off his belt until I felt the first strap across the back of my legs. I hauled off and started crying real loud, because it hurt bad but partly because I knew the louder I got the faster Daddy'd give up. He wasn't through with me, though. He dragged me into the house by one arm and gave me a terrible beating, the worst and the last one I ever got.

"Don't you *ever* say that word again!" he yelled between straps. I was able to figure *bastard* was the wrong word, because I was pretty sure I had used all the others before without getting beat for it.

I tried to tell him I was just saying what she said, but he wouldn't have none of that. I tried to tell him she was just saying what the orange colors was saying to her, and goodness, that made him even madder.

"Don't you *ever* talk about them colors again. If you think *this* is a beating, just see what happens if you ever talk about them colors again!" And all the while, I couldn't help but see that his own colors was gone real red.

Mother finally got him to stop, saying, "She's just a baby, Luther, she didn't mean nothing," over and over until he let me go. She sat on the side of the bed and helt me while I cried, and talked real quiet to me. I didn't understand all of what she said, except that Aunt Dot wasn't gone have no baby, not ever, and that she heard voices and saw colors sometimes that didn't nobody else hear or see. It was real embarrassing to Daddy to have a sister who wasn't right.

I figured I best be quiet. I didn't have to get beat like that but once.

I didn't sleep much that night. I laid between my sisters under the open winder, and they patted me and whispered funnies to try to get me to laugh. I watched the curtains move with the breeze long after they was both fast asleep. Every now and then a drop of sweat would find a way to my backside and burn me where the belt had broke my skin.

Mother and Aunt Dot and my sisters was up before daylight the next morning cutting off the corn, and my brothers got the fire built in the stove, boiled water, and scalded the jars before going off to the fields. Daddy patted his hands on his legs after he got his boots on and said, "C'mon over here, Lizzie", but I turned and lifted the hem of my raggedy dress a little bit so he could see the backs of my legs, and walked away. See, I knew how to hurt people too.

Aunt Dot didn't have no more spells on that visit. Her colors wasn't bright no more, but they was there. I began to pay more attention to the colors after that, but I sure didn't say nothing about them.

Most everybody's colors is a light gray unless they're having strong feelings about something. The first time I heard this woman say she had the blues, it made me jump a little, because I already knew her colors was blue. I looked at her real hard to see if she was trying to tell me something, but she went right on complaining to everybody around her.

It's kindly funny that people's colors go yeller when they're scared and green as a gourd when they're jealous. That's how I know other people must of been seeing the colors long before me and Aunt Dot, cause somebody made up them sayings. I figure I'm not the first person got beat about it, neither.

The colors get harder to see when the weather's kindly dry and cooler. Some winters when the cold seemed to go on forever and the house wouldn't get warm no matter how big the fireplace was burning, I'd almost get to where I didn't think about them no more. But just as sure as the first warm day come around, I'd see a wrinkle in the air next to somebody, and I'd get that old feeling in the pit of my stomach.

They'd start out kindly weak, like heat rising off a tin roof, but soon the colors'd be all the way back, getting stronger ever day as the corn sprouted, grew tall, and got tassels. I don't ever remember shucking corn on the porch without seeing somebody's colors real strong, and many times they was a face. I dreaded them days. I wished they would be just one summer without corn or colors, but they never was.

Many times as a child, I'd spin around fast as I could to try to catch a sight of my own colors. I looked at the mirror and helt my eyes ever which a way to try to see them. I thought I might get real brave one day and ask Aunt Dot if they was there, but I never got a chance.

I'm ashamed to admit it, but I didn't never forgive my Daddy. I reckon it made me feel big when I learned I could hurt him by dodging away when he wanted to play with me, or turning my head and getting interested in something else when he talked to me. I remember very well how his face went sad and lost-looking. It's a real shame I was so rurned I enjoyed it. Before long, it become a habit that never did get broke.

Daddy stayed after me because I looked to the sides of folks' heads instead of their eyes. Aunt Dot done that, too. Course, I didn't see much of her after she had a real big spell and they put her in Bryce's. She got to come home once or twice after the treatments, but she had to go back pretty quick and she wasn't never the same again. Once my grandmother died, Aunt Dot didn't have nobody to come home to.

We made one or two trips down to Tuscaloosa to see her, and if a beating wasn't enough to scare me from talking about the colors, that place sure enough was. They was folks there much worse off'n Aunt Dot, walking around and doing stuff that didn't make no sense.

Daddy wouldn't let me try to talk to Aunt Dot none. He and Mother would tell her this and that, like how the cotton was coming on, and how they missed her help in the summer, and sometimes she'd try to answer, but mostly she just watched the colors around their heads with her mouth helt open a little bit and her tongue pushing against her cheek.

I was a teenager when Aunt Dot died. I was sitting at the kitchen table slicing up okrie for supper when I felt something like a strong wind knock me plumb out of my chair. Wasn't nobody else around right then. My brothers and sisters had done got married and moved off, and Mother and Daddy stood outside next to the new tractor and, I expect, talked about how they'd get it paid for.

It was a good thing Daddy wasn't in the kitchen right then, cause he'd a probably give me another beating when he seen me having a spell. Voices began to talk to me, saying crazy things. *I don't have any cheese up here. It's gettin' real hard to breathe. I always loved all a y'all. Don't touch my mules. It ain't quicksand. Take care a my young'uns.*

Men's voices, women's voices, even a child every now and then. *Mama! Mama!* Over and over. *I'm gone have a bastard baby. It ain't loaded.* And then... *Lizzie Monkey Lizzie Monkey.*

Aunt Dot died in August of nineteen and thirty-nine, and she come to me that day along with all her colors. When she first come, she still had a little strength left in her spirit.

They's ghosts, Lizzie, them colors you see. They don't mean no harm. Some of them come to me cause they loved me, and some of them come along with Aunt Mildred when she died, long before you was born. You're kindly special, like I was. Most people don't see or hear nothing outta theirs. Don't let them make you crazy. I woulda went somewhere else with them but you was the only one I could find. Plus, I loved you the best.

I talked to her, too, but I couldn't make her hear me. She began to get weak.

I stole a knife from the kitchen. I wasn't sure I could cut myself, Lizzie Monkey. I give all my cigarettes to the guard so he'd let me in, and I stole a knife. It didn't hurt real bad. I stole a knife. Soon, that was all that was left of her. *I stole a knife from the kitchen.*

Bryce's sent Daddy a real nice letter about how Aunt Dot died in her sleep, and they went ahead and buried her in the Greenwood Cemetery in Tuscaloosa. They expected she had a bad heart all along. They didn't mention nothing about a knife, and didn't nobody ask no questions.

It was real hard not to let the colors make me crazy, especially in hot weather. All them voices buzzed in my head, day and night. Now that I knew what the colors was, I had a hard time not staring at the faces when they showed up. They was hundreds of them, maybe thousands. Some was stronger'n others and I'd hear them again and again. Others I didn't hear so much, and they was new ones talking sometimes too, like they had rassled their way to the front to get heard.

I still loved my Daddy in spite of our differences, but they wasn't no way I could stay in the house with him, hearing the voices like I did. He knew something had happened when Aunt Dot died and he was forever giving me mean looks when he could see I was listening to something he didn't hear.

This boy from New Hope, Robert, took a liking to me. He didn't have nothing, course I didn't neither, and when he asked me to marry him, I did. We got married at Preacher Jenkins' house two days before Christmas. I wore the dress I was fixing to get from Santy Claus.

Robert knew I was different, and I reckon he didn't care about that. I was kindly fetching back then, and I knew how to work real hard and keep a good house, and that was enough. We started out farming alongside the families, and we done that for a good while up east of Huntsville. All of my babies was born there. I learned to sew real good making baby clothes.

Me and Robert often talked about going somewhere else, and when we started hearing about good farm land down around Alex City, we moved south. We done that 'til the children was about grown. Now, they's lots of stories I could tell about my young'uns and the different places we lived. Me and Robert tried our best to do right by the children and they all turned out strong and good. But if I get to telling all about those times, I'll be a hundred by the time I get through, and I won't finish the story I started.

None of my children ever said nothing about the colors, and I was real proud of that.

Our oldest child, Laura, got married and had me some grandbabies. It was about then we decided to do something different from farming for a while. I didn't have no trouble getting on with Russell Mills cause I could sew real good already. Robert went to work for the golf course, and the only thing he ever grew after that was grass.

I worked at Russell Mills for many years. It was hard, hunching over a sewing machine all them hours, but I was always good at doing something over and over. Must of been all them hours shucking corn and picking cotton. And they was one thing Russell Mills had that didn't nobody else have, the most wonderful thing ever was invented: air conditioning.

The thing about air conditioning is it don't just make the air cold in the summertime, it takes the wet out too. The colors can't get no strength like that. I spent all them hours every day, sewing the collars on shirt after shirt after shirt, and didn't no voices bother me. I even got to where I could make friends, because I could look at people's eyes instead of their colors, and listen to their words instead of the voices.

Laura's first two babies was girls, Susan and Sarah, and goodness, I loved them better'n anything. Nearly ever day after I got off from the mill, I'd stop by and see them and often as not take them home with me. Laura had another baby when the girls was five and six, and she had a hard time with the depression afterwards like lots of women do. She didn't talk about it, and I didn't ever ask her nothing, but I watched her colors real careful to make sure they didn't get too dark. She seemed to like it when I took the girls for a while in the afternoon.

It was on one of them afternoons when Daddy died. I was shooing the girls on in the house so I could get the air conditioning on. Robert had bought us a winder unit soon as we could afford it. I hadn't got inside the door when the force of the colors knocked me up against the frame. I slid down and set right on the floor with my legs stuck out in front of me. The girls stood and watched.

I wisht I never had beat you, Lizzie. You was my favorite one and all in the world I was trying to do was keep you from being crazy like Dot and Aunt Mildred, or jumping off a bridge like Aunt Lillie done.

I'm gone have a bastard baby I stole a knife from the kitchen it ain't loaded I don't have any cheese up here I wisht I never had beat you.

The voices swarmed around in my head like angry dirt dobbers. *I wisht I never had beat you.* Susan and Sarah didn't get upset. They just patted me and talked to each other real quiet.

"What is that orangey …?"

"I saw a face for a second. It was trying to say something."

"Go turn on the air conditioner. That'll make her feel better."

"It's getting lighter now. Are you okay, Granny? Can you get up?"

When I got my strength back, me and the girls had a long talk about it. They was so smart, even little as they was. They was worried about their mama, too, because her colors was blue. I would of never wished it for them to be able to see the colors, but if they was going to, at least I could help them not be scared, and not to talk about it to nobody but me. Their daddy was a good and gentle man, and he wouldn't of whupped them anyway, but I wanted to make sure they was careful what they said. I tried to answer any questions they asked, but the funny thing was, they seemed to understand the colors better than I did.

"They're just ghosts – they're nothing to be afraid of," one of them said to me like she was big as everything.

Susan and Sarah was able to do something I never would of thought of. They was so smart – I guess I done said that and I don't aim to brag, but they was. They learned how to use the colors in a good way.

Susan started out a teacher, then made a counselor to the little ones that had troubles. It was easy for her to read how they was really feeling and use that to get them some help in the way they needed. She kept on going to school and become a professor at Alabama. So she ended up in Tuscaloosa, but not in the same way as Aunt Dot did.

Sarah started out a teacher, too, a science teacher. She was so interested in studying on heat and energy that she kept on going to school and now she's researching on thermo-something-or-other. She ended up in Huntsville, but not farming like the family started out. She calls me on Sundays and often tells me something new she's learned about how the colors transfer energy around, and such as that.

It's kindly funny how it worked out.

I don't have Robert no more, except I hear his voice amongst the others every now and then. Most days I sit and watch the Weather Channel, the second most wonderful thing ever was invented. Sarah taught me the numbers to watch for in the heat and humidity so I always know the mornings I need to get my air conditioning on early and the days I best not even go outside to get the mail.

I know I'll be joining Susan or Sarah's colors real soon. I want it to be a good feeling that stays in my ghost, and so I don't keep no bad thoughts in my head. Mostly, I say the same words over and over, to keep them strong so the girls or whoever I find will have a good voice amongst the others.

Be yourself, I'll say. *Be yourself, cause ain't nothing wrong with you.*

Nancy's Jog

Larry Williamson

Steady breaths, easy and rhythmic, arms loose and pumping, high posture, knees churning, feet barely touching the pavement. Nancy grinned, exhilarated, enjoying her best jog in weeks. Best, that is, until she heard a child crying. She stopped, huffed a few gulps of fresh air as sweat flooded from every pore, and turned her attention to the alley from which the sobbing seemed to emanate.

She looked around with a tingle of discomfort. This happened to be the most rundown, seediest part of the city, and she wasn't totally sure of its safety, even in these early morning hours. Most of the buildings stood in need of some repair, though structured from sturdy brick over a hundred years ago. The two-story one before her was renowned locally as having served as a Civil War leather goods shop for the Confederacy, but not occupied for decades.

Nancy considered resuming her jog, but the wails of a troubled child could not be ignored. She had to investigate. She stared down the alley strewn with broken bricks and stones and trash, but saw no one. Swiping a hand across her forehead to divert sweat from her eyes, she drew a deep breath for courage and cautiously stepped into the narrow passage.

Peeking around the back corner of the building, she spied a boy sitting on a concrete block, crying. Every few seconds he paused his weeping to utter a half-scream, then resumed throes of loud sobbing. She judged him to be a teenager, maybe younger considering his smooth cheeks.

Nancy edged a few steps closer. "Are you all right?" she asked softly.

Startled, the kid lurched and scooted backward on his seat, but did not stand. He stopped crying. "Who... who're you? Don't come any closer." He sniffled and reached for the long firearm on the ground beside him and raised it toward the intruder with shaking hands and fear in his face. It appeared to be some kind of antique musket, perhaps as old as colonial times.

Nancy jumped back around the corner. "Whoa, kid," she blurted, risking a peek and raising both palms to ward against the weapon. "Don't shoot!" Then, "Does that thing even shoot?"

"Course it'll shoot." He pulled back the hammer to cock the gun. "And it's loaded and capped and it can blow a hole in you."

"Uh, please don't do that. Put the gun down. I'm not going to hurt you."

"Who are you?" he repeated. "Are you one of them?"

"One of who? Whoever you mean, I'm not them. Now, lower that bazooka, won't you?"

"Bazoonka? What's a bazoonka?" He swung the barrel aside but didn't uncock the hammer.

"Not bazoonka. Bazooka. You know, that big tube thing the army uses to blow up tanks and stuff."

"I've never seen one o' them. We only use muskets and rifles in the infantry. Tanks? What're them?"

"Never mind." She eased back to the boy's presence, switching her vision from the musket to his clothes. They were of gray wool, tattered and dirty. A pillbox cap with a short visor sat atop his head. His leather boots were worn and scuffed, and Nancy noticed a large hole in the thin sole of the one boot turned toward her. Her mind diverted back to her first question. "What's wrong with you? Are you hurt?"

Anguish twisted the boy's face. "Of course I'm hurt. I've been shot. Can't you see?"

"I'm sorry. I don't see anything. You've been shot?" she asked, her voice an octave higher. "Where?"

He snatched off his cap. "Here. Don't know how it didn't kill me." He pointed an index finger to the center of his forehead, carefully touching it to skin. His eyes widened. "Uh, here," he repeated, moving the finger around his forehead in a broad, frantic search. The eyes widened farther.

"There's no bullet wound on your forehead. You look fine, at least there. Are you hurt elsewhere?"

"Just my head," he said, looking astonished. "I was hit in the head, square over the eyes. I saw the flash of that blasted Yankee's musket and heard the ball hit my head. I blacked out right off, knowing I was dead." He explored his forehead again. "Why am I not?"

"Because, friend, you haven't been shot. That's just your imagination. A good one, I might add, with that Yankee story." She tilted her head and stared at the boy. "Were you really knocked out?"

"Yes! Yes, I'm telling you! By a musket ball. I should be dead."

"Well, you're not. If you were knocked out, it had to be from something else. A falling brick perhaps?" Nancy scanned the wall of the crumbling building, then the ground. Fragments of broken bricks and masonry lay everywhere. "You may have a concussion."

85

The puzzled boy shook his head. "I... I don't understand."

"What's your name?"

"My name's Private Augustus P.D. Elkins, of the Thirteenth Alabama Guards."

"I'm Nancy. I'm in college, but I'm home for the summer. How old are you?"

"Fifteen."

"You sure? You look younger."

"Or I was fifteen afore I was kilt."

"You haven't been 'kilt'. You're very much alive." Nancy again focused on the boy's outfit. "Why are you dressed that way?"

"Whataya mean?"

"Are you in a play or something? Or going to a costume party?"

"Costume?"

"Your clothes. Is that supposed to be a Civil War uniform?"

Augustus looked down at his frayed tunic and fingered a button. "This *is* my uniform. The only one I have."

"It's wool, isn't it? Why didn't you have it made from cotton or polyester or some other cooler material? You must be burning up."

"Don't know what pol... uh, poly... whatever you said, is. Besides, wool uniforms are warmer than cotton in wintertime."

"Wintertime? This is July, man. You aren't going to get cold in July, not in Alabama."

Augustus stared at Nancy, puzzled. "July? No, this is April."

"Uhn-uh. July, I promise. Maybe you did get a hit on the head. Where do you think you are?"

"On a picket line. We're fighting a rear guard action against that nasty Union general raiding his damn demons through the state. Wilson, I think, is his name."

"Wilson? I remember reading about a General Wilson

campaigning through Alabama at the end of the Civil War. That was 1865."

"That's who I mean. We're fighting him off here so our regiment can get reorganized and stop the varmint. He's gotta be defeated." Augustus shrugged. "Huh, at least I was helping to fight him off until I got shot."

"You haven't been shot," she reminded him again. "But I think you do have an injury. By the way, Wilson wasn't stopped. He went all the way through the state, ripping up everything."

Augustus didn't seem to hear the last. He fixated on Nancy, as if he had noticed her body for the first time.

"Where is your frock, girl?" he asked, alarmed. "Have you no shame? How can you expose your limbs such?"

"What?"

"Your bare arms and legs. Why aren't you properly clothed? Do you not disgrace yourself with such nakedness?"

"I'm not naked. What's wrong with you?" She gestured to her shorts with both open palms. "These are my running clothes." She raised a foot and pointed at the shoe. "See, running shoes. I was jogging."

"Lady, you use too many words I don't fetch. But your body should be covered. Such immodesty is frowned on by decent folk."

"Well, that's too bad. You're overdressed and I'm underdressed. A fashion standoff. Now, let's find out what's really wrong with you, concussion or otherwise. Can you stand up?"

Without answering, Augustus attempted to rise, bracing the now uncocked weapon against the ground for leverage. Halfway up, he stumbled.

Nancy grabbed Augustus by an arm to help him to his feet. She held on until he steadied himself.

"I think you should be checked out at a hospital," she said. "You definitely aren't well."

"I shan't go to a field hospital. They wouldn't trifle with me 'cause they're too busy with bloody stuff like cutting off arms and legs. Besides, all our hospitals have been captured or ruint."

"Well, I know one that isn't 'ruint.' I passed it a few blocks back." Nancy lifted Augustus's arm and draped it across her shoulders to brace her neck under his armpit. "Come on. I'll take you there."

The pair eased into the alley and slowly made for the street, the 'immodestly-dressed' jogger almost carrying the 'inappropriately-dressed' teen, who used his musket for a crutch on the off side. They reached the street and turned down the sidewalk just as a car approached from behind. Augustus turned his head at the sound and froze, wide-eyed.

"*Aaargh!*" he screamed, and broke away from Nancy to scramble back into the alley, where he cowered against a wall. He slid down into a sitting position, shaking with fear. "Wh..., wh..., what was that thing?" he stammered.

"You mean the car?" she puzzled, standing over him.

"The carriage. No horse." Augustus panted, panicky. "Can't be a locomotive. Too small, no tracks, no smoke or steam. What was it?"

"My goodness, Augustus, you've seen cars before. You've really lost it." Nancy reached to help him up again. "Come on, we have several blocks to go."

Back on the sidewalk, Nancy consciously placed herself between Augustus and the street. Still, each time an occasional car sped by from either direction, the boy stiffened and watched it with fear and suspicion.

"Uhh, is it our'n or their'n?" he asked of vehicles a couple of times.

They trudged to a major intersection, where Nancy turned the tandem toward a crosswalk.

"We need to cross here," she said. "The hospital is on the other side of the street, a block away." She guided her charge to the curb, stopped, and looked up. Augustus followed her gaze and recoiled at a new sight.

"What's that? The red lamp. How does it glow so?"

"The traffic light?"

"Oh! Now it's green. It switched! What makes it shine like that?"

"Come on, hurry. We can walk now." She hustled him into the street.

Augustus continued to stare at the light all the way across. "Why does it burn green," he persisted, "and so brightly? Ohh! It turned yellow. Now red again!" They covered the final few steps and prepared to attack the side street crossing. "How is such trickery possible?"

"You know how. Electricity. Traffic lights run on electricity. You've blanked out on everything, haven't you?"

"I know of no things of such kind. Lanterns do not burn so brightly. Not of colors, and not in daylight."

Within minutes, the couple struggled toward the front entrance of the large hospital. Augustus's eyes danced anew in wonder. "That's where we're going? I've never seen a field hospital so large. They must have lots of wounded there."

Before Nancy could comment, she had a realization and scurried the boy to the side behind a shrub to shield them from the doors.

"We can't go in there with a gun," she warned. "We'll be arrested. Here, give it to me." Augustus reluctantly surrendered the musket. "Is it still loaded?"

Augustus retrieved the weapon, cocked it, and dug the cap from the primer chamber. He lowered the hammer and reached the musket back to her. "Now it isn't. Forthwith, it won't fire."

"Forthwith? Really? Okay, we'll leave it at the front desk. Maybe that'll save us a little jail time." She grinned at her joke, but Augustus narrowed his eyes, not comprehending. She turned the musket barrel downward and grasped the stock near the butt plate. "My, this thing is heavy!" she blurted, and clutched the stock with both hands. "Let's go."

They sauntered toward the wide double doors, which suddenly sprang open. Augustus leapt backward, almost falling. His instinct was to scream, but could only manage a "Wh...!"

"It's only the automatic doors," Nancy assured. "They won't bite you." She took one hand off the musket and pulled Augustus through the door, then re-caught her two-hand grip on the gun.

The receptionist behind the huge desk had her head down as the two approached.

"Excuse me," greeted Nancy.

The woman looked up, cut her eyes to the gun, and rose halfway in her chair, mouth open and eyes wide. "What's that thing?" she managed to utter.

"It's an old musket, and I wonder if we could leave it at your desk while my friend is being looked at?"

"Uhhh, I guess so. You sure can't take it into the hospital." She continued to stare at the musket as Nancy conveyed it around the semicircular desk and placed it on the floor beside her chair. "Ooh, that thing looks dangerous."

"It's harmless," Nancy half-lied. She returned to where Augustus stood. "We need some help. At least, my friend here does. May we see a doctor?"

"Is it an emergency? What's his problem?"

"I don't know. I think he has a concussion, because he's terribly disoriented."

"I was shot," volunteered Augustus. "By a Yankee's musket ball."

"No, he wasn't shot," Nancy corrected, "but he does seem to be injured somehow. Can a doctor look at him?"

The receptionist turned and pointed to a rear door. "Go down that hall to the emergency room. A nurse will meet you there and take care of you."

They found a waiting room at the end of the hall, and within minutes a nurse entered. Nancy repeated her pseudo-diagnosis, adding more details.

"Are you a relative?" asked the nurse, jotting down each bit of information after getting Augustus's biography, but failing to glean much medical history.

"No, just a casual friend."

"Then you'll have to wait out here while we have a physician examine him." She turned to Augustus. "Come with me, Mr. Elkins. We have to get you out of those filthy clothes and clean you up."

Augustus looked at Nancy, exhibiting renewed fear and confusion.

Nancy patted his arm. "It's all right. I'll wait for you. I'll be here when they finish."

An hour later, Nancy had heard from no one and seen no one since the nurse and Augustus left. She began to get anxious when, finally, a different nurse emerged. Nancy stood to intercept her.

"Excuse me, please."

"Yes, miss?"

"I wonder if you could tell me anything about my friend? He's been here over an hour."

"I can check. What's his name?" She wrote down Augustus's name. "What doctor was he seeing?"

"I'm sorry, I wasn't told that. Also, I didn't get the receiving nurse's name."

"Okay, I'll find him. Be right back."

Five minutes later the nurse returned, a puzzled look on her face. "I'm afraid he's not here, miss. No one knows anything about him."

"That's not possible. Of course he's back there. Somewhere." Nancy peered at the door Augustus had entered over an hour ago. "Would you look again?"

"Still can't find him," the nurse reported after a second search. "I checked with the entire emergency staff and also looked through the admitting file. No one by that name has been here. Sorry."

The nurse excused herself, apologizing again, and Nancy stood stunned. For a full minute, she couldn't move. *What is going on here?* She finally seized control of her wits and walked back through the hallway to the front desk.

"Do you remember me?" she asked the same receptionist.

The lady looked up from her computer screen. "No. No, I'm sorry, I don't."

"But I was here only an hour or so ago. With a young man wearing an old, gray uniform. You directed us to the emergency room."

"I'm sorry, miss," she repeated. "I've never seen you."

"Yes, you have. I was right here. But I know you'll remember this. We left an old musket with you, a big old gun. It's behind your desk."

The receptionist scooted her chair backward and scanned under the desk. She swept her search through a second pass, then looked up and shook her head at Nancy.

"Nope," she said, "not here. And you're right; I'd remember a gun like that. Or any gun brought into a hospital."

"What! May I look?" Nancy was already circling the desk before the lady could answer. Her search also was futile. Astounded, she stood and stared at the receptionist. "What happened to it? Where is it?"

"Miss, I don't know what you're talking about. I've never seen you, and I've never seen some old gun you claim you had."

Nancy walked from the hospital in a daze and turned down the street. She ambled half a block, confused and thinking.

Where did he go? Where did he come from? How could Augustus disappear like that? Where's the musket? Nancy shook her head in bewilderment.

Though worried, she began a slow trot and evolved into a nice pace. Within a minute, she had regained the stride and elation experienced earlier before the interruption. Soon, the boy in Confederate gray had been shuffled to the back of her mind. Her jog was again on track and in rhythm.

A soldier in a dusty blue uniform peered from his perch atop one of the city's brick buildings. He surveyed in a wide arc, but saw no one. Nothing moved. He had seen not a soul all morning, not a carriage or a mounted rider or a person afoot, and certainly not the enemy. Perhaps the last of them had finally abandoned the city and retreated to the countryside.

Rotten cowardly Rebs! He spat a stream of tobacco juice to the side.

A movement three blocks up the street caught his eye. A lone man, coming toward him in the street next to the curb. *Hey, he's running! He's up to something.*

The soldier ducked low and lifted his Spencer rifle to the concrete barrier at the edge of the roof. Careful to move slowly so as not to reveal himself, he focused on the runner, potentially an enemy plotting some foolish attack. He was now two blocks distant, almost within range.

That's no Reb! That's a woman! What the hell?

As the woman closed, the man marveled at her near nakedness. He had never seen such. Had to be some kind of Reb trick, vilely using the wiles of a female.

He cocked his Spencer and raised it to his shoulder. *I don't cotton to shooting a woman, but orders are orders.* His instructions of the morning had been to allow no one under any circumstances to breach the unit's perimeter until security in that section of the city was assured. And this intruder was running straight into Union lines, intending some kind of mischief for certain.

Aiming carefully, the Yankee sniper zeroed his target, now a half-block away. His finger curled against the trigger.

The House Near the Covered Bridge

Mary Brunini McArdle

Maggie Sims and I rode the school bus together every day and became best friends in spite of our huge differences – I was an only child who lived in a really nice house on Highway 79 and Maggie and her little brothers lived in a trailer nearby.

School started early, the first week of August. It was much too hot for school that time of year. That eleven-year-old Maggie would die even before the cooler weather came never occurred to me.

Before school began, Mama took me to Miss Iris to have my blonde hair shaped in gentle waves. Mrs. Sims trimmed Maggie's bangs but left her dark hair in jagged lengths.

We had assigned seats next to each other on the bus, since "Shorkey" comes just before "Sims." Maggie had the window seat, which she loved because she noticed various things of interest along the way. I passed some of the time reading, but Maggie chattered incessantly.

"Look, Victoria, there's the cutoff to the covered bridge. I don't suppose it's very far, or the road would run right into Birmingham. There's lots of covered bridges in Alabama. I'd like to see one someday."

I nodded.

"We could walk there," Maggie went on. "Sometime before it gets dark early. Or explore that funny house."

"What funny house?"

"You can't see it because you don't have the window seat, but it's strange. Monumentally strange!"

"How?" I asked.

"Well, the grass is always cut down short, but the house is covered with green stuff, like vines or something."

"Kudzu?"

"No." Maggie rolled her eyes. "I know what kudzu looks like."

One morning she boarded the bus in a high state of excitement. "Victoria, you'll never guess!"

"Guess what?"

"Mama's getting me a new bed and bedspread from Sears. She rearranged the furniture so I don't have to sleep with my baby brothers anymore!"

"That's great, Maggie."

"Mama's working more hours at the filling station, and Papa's bought two new cows. We all have to milk them and our yard's a mess. It's not really a yard – it's a manure field. It's hard not to step on the cow patties.

"Oh!" Maggie added gleefully. "I have the best idea. Tomorrow's Wednesday – Miss Carter never gives us any homework on Wednesday. After school let's get off the bus together at my stop. Nobody'll be watching. We can walk down to that weird house."

"We'll get in trouble."

"No, we won't. We won't stay long. We can be home way before supper. Can you bring some potato chips or something? And juice? I'm not allowed." Maggie crossed her legs; she had on her mother's clunky, black suede shoes with pink socks.

"Okay. But you've got to agree we start for home at four. No later."

Wednesday morning I cut my lunch down so I could stuff my backpack with the snacks Maggie had requested. We slipped off the bus together through the back door. Since Mr. Beck, the driver, didn't turn his head, I figured we were safe.

I wiped my forehead on my sleeve. "Maggie, it's really hot. Don't you think so? I'm all sweaty."

"Just walk faster. Look, there it is!"

Maggie had been right. The house was monumentally *strange*. It wasn't far off the street, just a few yards. There was no sidewalk, no porch, so the house sat squarely down on the level lot and was covered solid with some kind of vines, still a vibrant green, not withered at all.

I frowned. "I can't see any windows, or even a door."

"They're probably covered over," Maggie replied. "Let's get closer."

We looked furtively around, then approached the house until we could actually touch the vines. "I still don't see any windows," Maggie complained.

"But there is a front door. Look." I pushed as hard as I could, and with a groan the door swung open into the house. We slipped inside and nearly jumped out of our skins when the door slammed behind us.

"Why did it do that, Maggie? There's no wind."

"Gee, I don't know."

We stood silently and looked around. The floors were bare wood

– not shiny like the floors in my living room – and there wasn't much light coming in. At first I thought there was just one room, but as my eyes adjusted I could see a tiny kitchen at one end and another door, probably to a bathroom. There were a couple of carved wooden chairs and a table, a few books on the floor, and a worn, stuffed sofa against one wall. There was a back door we could barely see, and not much else.

Every time one of us took a step, the floor creaked. I began opening kitchen drawers and found some books of matches and a couple of candles. No food, just plastic spoons. In a cupboard were a few plastic cups. The door to the bathroom opened easily.

"Maggie, do you suppose the water's turned on?"

Maggie tried the kitchen faucet and a small stream of water came out. The light in the house was getting dimmer and the room was getting hotter.

"It's got to be close to four," I said. "I think we should start for home."

"Victoria, I've got to pee."

"Well, hurry."

She came back in a minute. "It flushed, but the water's really low."

I heard a funny noise, sort of like someone whispering. I shivered, then realized there must have been enough of a breeze outside to rustle the vines. I really wanted to get out of there. I wanted to go home. I went to the front door and pushed, but it wouldn't budge.

"Maggie, this door's stuck."

"Let me help."

But even with both of us pushing as hard as we could, the door didn't move. I felt a weight in the pit of my stomach. *I'm not going to get home*, I thought. *I'm going to be here forever.*

"Let's look around," I said, "and try to find a window in the back or push on the other door."

The back door was shut more firmly than the other. In fact, part of it was nailed shut. No amount of searching, even in the bathroom, found another opening. We moved slowly, feeling every inch of wall. Nothing.

"Victoria, what are we going to do?"

"I don't know. Our parents will be worrying by now."

"But they don't know where we are. They won't know where to look."

"Let's light a candle and put it by the door. Maybe the light will shine through the cracks when it gets full dark."

"Victoria, I'm hungry."

"Then we'll have some juice and eat some chips. Just don't drink any of the water. Who knows how long it's been sitting in the boiler?"

We took our food to the sofa and sat down. "It's getting really dark," Maggie whined.

"We might have to sleep here 'til morning. By then, people will be looking for us."

"'Til morning?" Maggie shrieked. "We'll suffocate! It's getting hotter and hotter and there aren't any windows."

"Well, this was *your* idea."

We tried to sleep, we really did. We huddled together on the sofa, but we kept sweating and it was hard to breathe. A couple of hours of this and I decided we needed another snack.

"Maggie," I said, chewing thoughtfully, "I have an idea. It's damp outside. I'm going to set fire to the front door."

"*What?*"

"Don't get upset. Those vines will keep the door from really catching, but it might weaken it enough for us to kick through."

I hope, I added silently. What if we set off something we couldn't stop? What if Maggie and I burned up?

"Victoria, you're crazy."

I ignored her and took the matches over to the front door. It sizzled and smoked, but it didn't go up in flames. *Great*, I said to myself. There were no real results until I'd used two full books of matches. Then I kicked, and managed to knock out a good-sized hole. "Maggie, bring me some more matches."

She did as I asked and then huddled against the bathroom door, hands over her face.

One more big kick and – "Maggie! Come here! We can wiggle through!"

I blew out the candle and we were able to squirm through the hole. Now it was really dark and a steamy mist settled over everything.

"I don't think we should try to get to our houses alone," I said. "Let's go to the filling station where your mother works. It's closer and they'll call our parents."

We trudged north. In a few minutes we had passed the cutoff to the covered bridge.

"Victoria, I don't feel good."

"Are you going to throw up?"

"I don't think so. I'm just hot."

We finally crossed the highway to the filling station and called our folks. My frantic parents and Maggie's mother arrived at nearly the same instant. Maggie's dad must have had to stay with her mob of little brothers, all under six.

"Victoria! Where have you been? We've been worried to death

about you."

I started to explain, but before I had a chance, Maggie began to babble.

"Mrs. Shorkey, we wanted to see the covered bridge so we walked and walked but we never got there. We didn't know it was so far, and then it got dark and by the time we turned around we were lost. All mixed up." She caught her breath in a little hiccup.

My mouth dropped open. Maggie's story was nowhere near the truth, but how could I accuse my best friend of lying? It was too late to say anything. I started to cry and that got to my parents. I was almost hugged to death.

So too was Maggie, the little devil.

That night I worked on the note I would pass to her at school the next day, if we could manage to wake up in time to get there. No more suggestions, no more adventures, no more stories. Button it, Maggie.

I had nightmares about that house for two weeks. I don't know why – I was the one who got us out. During that time I was too sleepy or absent-minded to notice that Maggie was uncharacteristically quiet, which simply wasn't her nature.

Then one morning when I got on the bus, Mr. Beck told me to sit in the window seat, and a new girl with a red braid and freckles was put next to me. Her name was Judy Roche. She was cute, but –

"Mr. Beck, wait!" I called. "Where's Maggie Sims?"

"She won't be riding the bus for a while, Victoria. Miss Carter will explain things when you get to school."

Explain what?

Miss Carter had a grave expression. "Boys and girls," she began,

"I have some very sad news. Maggie Sims is seriously ill. She's in the hospital in Birmingham." She took out a handkerchief and dabbed at her eyes. "Class, let's have a moment of silence."

As the word spread, my classmates' mothers organized a baby-sitting committee so Maggie's parents could stay at the hospital. Some of the dads and older sons even milked the cows. This did not go on very long; Maggie didn't last much over a week.

The funeral was scheduled for Thursday at half past five so that we would have time to change clothes after school before going to the church service.

I didn't cry. I sat like a stone statue, sweating heavily in my good navy cotton dress. Judy Roche sat next to me, just like on the bus. Her mother had red hair too.

The graveside ceremony was private, so I waved to Judy and went on to the car with my parents. I ensconced myself on the left side of our back seat so that I could see the house near the covered bridge on the way home. I don't know why, unless it was my own special tribute to Maggie.

The funeral had been long and the parking lot full, so by the time we got to Highway 79 it was almost dark. I saw the house before we passed it, because there was a faint glow near the front door. Closer and closer, and there was the gleam of a candle just behind the hole we had made, almost unnoticeable in the September twilight. Except to me.

The shadowy form of a girl with a jagged haircut stood holding the lit candle. My breath came in short, shallow gasps. My parents were talking to each other, not paying any attention to the surroundings or to me. I turned and looked back as we passed the house and the cutoff to the covered bridge, and the glow stayed in view for a full mile more.

Wayward

Megan Ingram

Theodore shook his arm violently up and down. The hard ball in the can rattled, and an eerie metallic echo bounced among the trees. He pressed his thumb against the plastic cap and flipped it onto the ground with a resounding pop. Holding the can poised before a tree trunk, he considered his options.

"Hurry up with that paint," Norris hissed over his shoulder. He glanced nervously at the late afternoon shadows that crept toward him. The night was coming on fast, and the forest seemed darker than it should. "We need to get out of here before we can't see to leave."

A few feet away, Janice laughed, pulled a crumpled cigarette from her breast pocket, and placed it to her lips. "Scared?" she asked, flicking the wheel of a small plastic lighter thrice before it caught a flame, then holding it to the end of her cigarette. She watched the cherry flare as she inhaled deeply. A moment later, her lungs broke into a ratcheting cough and the smoke billowed out of her in violent bursts. When she recovered, she went on with a creaky voice, "We have flashlights. We're not that far from the road. Don't be such a pantywaist. There's nothing in these woods but trees and squirrels."

Norris crossed his arms and mumbled, "And the Black Widow."

"Didn't I tell you I'd kick your ass if you said anything else about that stupid ghost story?" Janice rolled her eyes and dragged on her cigarette. "Pussy."

Theodore shook the can one more time for good measure and depressed the button. A fine red mist laid a trail across the trunk of the tree as he created his design. When finished, he stood back and admired his work.

"What's that supposed to be?" asked Norris.

"I saw it online. Mystical shit."

"Sweet."

"Hey," said Janice, who had wandered away to a row of overgrown hedges. "There's a gate here. Give me that paint."

Theodore handed it off to her and tried to peer through the vines and weatherworn slats. "O-M-F-G, Norris," he said, "it's totally the Black Widow's house."

"That's not funny," Norris snapped, coming up behind him to try and see beyond the gate. "She lives around here and eats people who get lost in these woods."

Janice picked up a pebble from the ground. "Then we have nothing to worry about, because we know exactly where we are. Now back off."

She lobbed the rock at Norris's head. He yelped and jumped out of the way. Janice swung her arm in an arc, and with uneven coverage, painted a large anarchy symbol across the surface of the gate. One corner of her mouth turned up as she appreciated her graffiti. She dragged on her cigarette once more and tossed it over her shoulder. Theodore came up behind her, and she turned as he wrapped his arms around her waist.

"Nice one, baby."

She licked her lips with a flick of her tongue and then laid them across Theodore's.

"What the hell?" Norris asked.

Janice turned at the sound of his surprise and raised a brow as the dark stains of her artwork faded and vanished into the wood.

"You shouldn't be here," said a lilting female voice behind them. Janice dropped the can and the three teenagers pivoted as one. Their jaws dropped, but their screams died in their throats. Three quick slashes, and their blood splashed against the gate. The wood drank that offering as well.

David sniffed, and the scent of moist humus filled his nostrils. Shivering, he opened his eyes to find himself huddled in a fetal position among a pile of dead leaves. The wind whispered hoarsely through the trees above his head.

"Duh fuh?" He looked down at himself, dressed in pajama bottoms with no shirt, mud caked on his bare feet and streaked across his chest. A moment of despair washed over him. He thought his medication had his somnambulism in check, but perhaps his recent move had been more traumatic to his system than he had realized.

He looked around and guessed that he was somewhere in the woods behind his friend's apartment complex, but beyond that he knew nothing. Becoming aware of the ache throbbing in his head, he raised his hand to his temple. He realized then that he was clutching something in his hand that cut into the flesh of his palm, so he unwrapped his stiff, chilled fingers to reveal it.

A key. Antique and rusting, about three inches long. David had never seen it before. He enclosed it in his fist again and dropped it into his pocket.

Standing slowly, his joints creaking and popping under the strain of sore muscles, David took stock of his situation. He was filthy and freezing, somewhere in the woods of his old hometown. Lost.

He looked around for any sign of the way he had come, but he was hardly a skilled woodsman. Any direction might be right. Most of them would be wrong. He had heard stories of this forest. Satanic rituals and ghost cars chasing you down the steep, curving road to the bottom of Green Mountain. The Black Widow. A haunted place.

David took a few steps in the direction he happened to be facing. He stopped short as his foot knocked against something hard and metallic that rattled and rolled three feet away. David stooped to examine it and saw that it was just a canister of red spray paint. Flecks of reddish brown splattered the sides in a strange array.

A dark thought in the back of his mind burbled up from his throat and he spoke the word gutterally. *"Blood."* He shook his head and dismissed it as paranoia.

Still, at least the paint indicated he was not entirely outside the influence of civilization. Perhaps the pranksters had left him a trail of their art that he could follow back to a road. He spun slowly, looking for the telltale bright color against the autumn foliage. Not far off, between the branches of a massive growth of bottlebrush buckeye and kudzu, a reflection of sunlight glinted. Going to it, David pulled aside the vines and realized that what had caught his eye was a latch on a gate tucked deep in the vegetation. The wood felt old and worn, but the hardware showed almost no sign of weathering.

David tried the latch. Even if the overgrowth hadn't been holding it firmly closed, the door also seemed to be locked. His palm resting on the gentle curve of the handle, David contemplated the infinitesimal weight of the key in his pocket. He stepped back from the gate and back from the situation. For a long time he stared at the shrubbery. Then he reached into his pocket, pulled out the key, and dropped it on the ground.

Turning on his heel, he walked away.

The dawn air was damp and chilly, but as he trudged through the forest his body temperature steadily climbed. Soon his chest was streaked not just with dirt but his own sweat. The wind blew hard against his skin, and he wondered at the sensation of being simultaneously hot and cold.

He spied a few more graffiti markings as he came eventually to what amounted to a path. The path led him past a rusted fence and onto a gravel road. Following that, he soon found his bare feet slapping pavement. A small convenience store met him halfway down the mountain. David begged use of the phone from its unimpressed employee, and thirty minutes later Pasky Martinez was leaning out of his car window, leering at him mischievously.

"*A la chingada*," Pasky said as his bedraggled new roommate climbed into the passenger seat. "What did you get into last night?" More and more he gave credence to the notion that some malevolent god had it out for David.

Last week, when Pasky had taken the call from a number he didn't recognize, he was surprised by the blast of nostalgia that David's voice triggered. Back in the day, David and Pasky and five or six other upperclassmen would ditch the last period and meet in a parking lot or an abandoned playground, pass joints in a circle, and contemplate where life might take them. As David told his story over the phone, Pasky couldn't help but feel bad for the poor guy. It was straight out of a country music song: David had been fired and found out his girlfriend was cheating on him in the same day. She had taken the apartment and all of their friends.

"*Mierda. Que puta.*"

"I'm moving back to town," David had finished. "I know we haven't talked in a while, but I could use a place to stay until I get settled on my own. I was hoping you might have a couch I could ride for a couple of weeks."

Pasky ran his hand through his hair and exhaled long through his nose. Finally he said, "Yeah, man, sure. We can talk about old times and catch up."

Now, Pasky whistled a brief melody as he pulled out of the convenience store parking lot, waiting for David to fill him in on what had happened. David chuckled a little, trying to brush it off, though Pasky suspected he didn't really find it all that funny. "I guess I've started sleepwalking again."

Pasky sniffed and rolled down all the windows so that David's sour reek might dissipate a little. "Freaky. Do you do that often?"

"First time in a while."

"Do I need to chain you to the bed?"

David laughed. "You know I don't think of you that way, man."

"Ha. So where did you wake up?"

Looking out the window at the storefronts that had stood since their childhood, David said, "In the woods."

"*Dios mio.* Sounds like a dangerous habit you have there."

"No kidding."

Pasky shuddered as he listened to David recount all of the things he had done in his sleep in the past. Once, he had eaten half an industrial jar of mayonnaise and was sick for days afterwards. Another time he woke on the kitchen floor with an enormous cleaver clutched in his hand, surrounded by the diced remains of an entire bag of onions. He had even driven his car across his lawn and into a tree.

These were the things he knew he had done – but what, Pasky thought, of those things for which he had no evidence the next morning? The possibilities were terrifying. Not for the first time, Pasky wondered if his impulse to help his old friend in his time of crisis was the right one. He felt a little like he was rescuing a drowning man who would inevitably pull them both under water.

The shower felt good. Standing under the hot stream, David felt released from his muscles a tension of which he had been unaware until it was gone. The sweat and grime swirled down the drain and vanished like so many soap bubbles.

He joined Pasky in the living room. His friend had cracked his first beer shortly after they arrived home, and was now working on his fourth from the look of the collection of cans on the table. Pasky flipped through the television channels, pausing just long enough on morning talk shows and soap operas to make the dialogue seem a crazy mishmash of occult gibberish. David felt suddenly disjointed from reality.

"Want a beer?" Pasky asked, not taking his eyes from the flickering screen.

David waved his hand. "It's a bit early for me."

"What do you have going on today?"

"Go see my dad, I suppose."

Pasky looked sidelong at him. "He still lives in town?"

David sighed. "In a manner of speaking. He's in a nursing home."

"Ah," answered Pasky. "Are you two very close?"

"Not really. I'm a bit of a disappointment to him."

Pasky turned off the television. "What makes you say that?"

"Well, he's managed to tell me as much in almost every conversation I've ever had with him since I was sixteen." David lowered his voice to a growl and shook his fist feebly. "*You had so much potential, David! Thank God your mother isn't alive to see this!*"

Pasky said, "Sorry, man."

David shrugged. "It's just the way it is. I guess we never learned to appreciate each other. I don't think he has much longer to go. Hoping for change at this point is probably futile, but I can't help it."

Pasky saw a pattern in David's life, clinging to relationships that were doomed to fail. There was something noble in the effort. "So you keep trying."

"Well, yeah," said David, standing to go. "He's my dad."

Two hours later, chased by the disapproving anguish of his father's words, David hurried down the hall at the Lily Flagg Skilled Nursing Facility. The dry heat pumping into the air suffocated him until he burst through the front doors of the building. The cold hit him with a full physical impact, but he kept moving. There was nothing for him there anymore. He climbed into his car and away he drove, away, away, away.

The first beer actually cleared his head, but after five more, David was swimmingly fuzzy again. Pasky let him sit in silent appreciation of the cheap drink for a few minutes before asking him how it went.

David shook his head. "As expected." After a moment, he said, "I don't guess I'll go back for a while."

Pasky clucked his tongue but said nothing. *Fathers and sons*. No one could pick apart the intricate lines that formed that psychology. He jostled the game controller in his hands and groaned a little as his avatar died a gruesome death.

"Hey," David slurred, a thought suddenly occurring to him. "Let me ask you something."

Pasky peered blearily at him, one eye closed as if he could no longer focus with two. "Yeah, man."

"Say you wake up beside a locked door with a key in your hand. What do you do?"

Pasky wondered what parade of thoughts led to this inquiry. "That's a weird-ass question, man."

"What do you do?"

Pasky slugged down the last of his can. "Try the key in the lock."

Leaning forward, David asked incredulously, "Really? It wouldn't seem too easy? Like someone was setting you up?"

"Not necessarily. Life doesn't often hand you a mystery and the solution in one go. Seems rude to ignore it." He belched.

The heating unit in the window kicked on and clattered as it spat out a warm breeze. David leaned back, a distant look on his face.

Pasky stood, walked ten feet to the kitchenette, and opened the refrigerator door. He bent over and peered inside, then emerged with a jar of pickle spears. Prying the lid off, he dipped his fingers in the brine and pulled one out.

"Are you telling me," he asked through a mouthful of pickle, "that you wouldn't open the door?"

"Nope."

Pasky chewed. "Guess it's not surprising."

"Why do you say that?"

"That's kind of your thing, isn't it? Running away?" Pasky

replaced the jar in the fridge and grabbed a bag of potato chips before returning to his chair and the frosty glare from his house guest. He collapsed on the sofa. "Damn, boy, that look's colder than a beaner in Beantown."

"You think I'm running away." It wasn't a question.

"Aren't you?"

David bit down on the remark that nearly escaped his lips. "I think I'm ready to crash. If you don't mind."

Pasky paused, hand dug down into the bag of chips. "Yeah, alright." He reluctantly climbed back out of the couch that was David's makeshift bed and switched off the game console. He tossed the chips on the counter and then checked to make sure the front door was locked. Looking at David, and almost as an afterthought, he nudged in front of the door a heavy umbrella stand, currently housing a number of cigarette butts, a baseball bat, and a samurai sword. The latter two he had been prompted to buy from a yard sale down the street after a number of burglaries in his area. He supposed a gun might be less obtrusive, but not many people would mess with a crazy Chicano wielding a samurai sword. For now though, he removed the sword and the bat and set them in a closet. Just in case.

Then he retired to his own room and locked the door. Just in case.

The next morning, David stood before the gate in the woods again, the key in one hand and a long, curved sword in the other. In his sleep, he had hacked all of the greenery from the door.

"No!" he shouted, and threw the key as far from him as possible. He dropped the sword, not even sure from where he had gotten it, and trudged back along the same path he had taken the day before, called Pasky, and returned to the apartment.

He spent the day huddled over the 'help wanted' ads in the newspaper and studiously avoided the subject of his nocturnal activities. Pasky left well enough alone, but made a resolution to himself.

That night, after David had fallen asleep, Pasky dug around in a box in his closet and found a string of jingle bells, which he hung over the door handle. Then he sat just inside his darkened bedroom doorway and waited.

Pasky startled awake, his neck aching from the awkward position in which sleep had taken him. The bells tinkled again as David dropped them on the floor. Pasky stood up and stretched, then walked to the kitchen, never taking his eyes from his sleeping roommate. He pulled some provisions from the fridge and shoved them into the pockets of his cargo pants.

David's movements were slow and deliberate. His eyes were open but eerily glazed over, as if trained on something very far away. His lips moved slowly, minutely, but the words he spoke were too low for Pasky to hear. Carefully David unlocked the door and stepped out into the chilly night air.

Pasky, taking his coat and David's, followed his friend down a low ditch and up into the woods that lay behind his apartment complex. Somehow the sleepwalker took him to a path almost completely hidden from view. It was rough terrain at times, but Pasky had no problem keeping up.

The woods were utterly dark. The thin beam of his key chain flashlight sputtered and only served to throw menacing shadows. Pasky could hear a dog barking off in the distance, but otherwise all was silence except for the crunching of their feet against the pine straw.

After a long while, David halted for no reason Pasky could determine and fell to his hands and knees. He passed his palm over the ground, snatched at something, and crawled over to a large, impenetrable stand of bushes. Pasky leaned in as his friend's muttering grew louder and louder, the same command over and over, ending in one final guttural howl, "OPEN THE DOOR!"

Then David stood, walked a few feet, and collapsed into a pile of leaves like nothing more than a bag of bones.

When David awoke in the woods for the third morning in a row, his coat draped over his torso, he was startled by someone behind him clearing his throat. He turned, head throbbing, to see a dark shape huddled by a tree not too far off.

"*Buenos dias, mi amigo.* The good news is, you're not a werewolf. And I found my sword which you so carelessly left out here, thank you very much."

"Pasky?"

Pasky stood and crossed the wet leaves and pinestraw-covered ground. He held out a can of beer. "Thirsty? I followed you. To make sure you didn't get hurt."

David snatched at the can. "Why the hell didn't you just wake me?"

"I wanted to see what you've been doing, man. Mystery!"

"Screw mystery." David moved to open the beer and made a noise of disgust to find the key in his hand. He pulled his arm back and threw it away.

"Dude! Why did you do that?" Pasky ran over to the patch of grass where he had seen the key fall and spent a few minutes digging around, looking for it.

David ignored him and sipped his drink. Pasky returned a moment later and held the key out. David pulled a leaf from his hair and said, "I don't want it."

Pasky pocketed the key and turned. "Come on, Dave. Just open the door. How is your curiosity not killing you?" Pasky walked up and tried to peer through the keyhole. "I think there's some sort of building on the other side."

"How is that even possible?"

Pasky stood back and tried to see over the thick vegetation. The wall of kudzu and buckeye was massive, but could it really hide a house? He began to walk around, dodging over brambles and batting at bushes with the flat of his sword, and soon disappeared from view.

David sat where he was. His head ached and he couldn't wrap it around all of this. Forces he did not understand were playing with him. What loathsome lot had he chosen that this was his life now?

David realized he'd been mumbling to himself for some time and Pasky still had not returned. He looked around, spying for any sign of movement. The forest seemed unnaturally quiet.

The hairs on the back of his neck prickled. There was something he was perceiving but not quite recognizing. He closed his eyes and listened. And he heard it. Shallow breathing just behind him. He turned his head quickly...

... but no one was there.

"Hello?" he said weakly. Then more loudly, "Pasky? Pasky, where the hell are you?"

Off to his right, there was a great crashing as of a tree toppling over. David startled to his feet and spun around twice, his eyes darting everywhere. "Pasky! Answer me!"

And suddenly his friend emerged from between two trees. "Oh, man, Dave. This thing is massive. And impenetrable. It's fantastic! I can't wait to see what's inside."

"Dude, we've got to get out of here. I think I'm freaking out."

"What?" Pasky shook his head. "No way, man. I'm not going to let you run away from this."

David crossed his arms and squared his jaw.

"Fine, if you won't do it, I will." Pasky pulled the key out of his pocket and turned to the gate. He looked over his shoulder one more time to see if David would relent before fitting the key to the lock.

David was suddenly overwhelmed with the surety that this was all a very bad idea.

Pasky turned the key and depressed the latch, swinging the door wide. He looked through, blocking the view. "Whoa, *Dios mio.*" He looked back over his shoulder. "Don't be so spooked."

David took a step forward and then stopped in his tracks when a woman's voice echoed about the little clearing.

"You should not be here!"

When he was a boy, David would take short fishing excursions with his father. He'd drop the line and, when he felt a tug, pull hard on the pole and jerk the fish, flapping and flying into the air. He imagined that to his catch's little fish friends, the disappearance of one of their number must have very closely resembled how Pasky was suddenly yanked through the door. The door slammed to, and the key dropped from the hole and tinkled against the hard-packed earth.

David cried out Pasky's name, but he was gone. He ran up to the gate and began to pound on it, calling out for his friend over and over. When this elicited nothing, he backed up and stood staring at the door. The sound of the birds and the squirrels had returned to the forest. It was as if Pasky had never been there.

"Shit," David said, and then, "shit, shit." He picked up the key from where it had fallen, took a deep breath and placed it in the lock.

And then the key began to turn in the lock on its own. The door swung forward, and an icy blast met him. David stepped through the entrance.

There was no sign of his friend or anyone else, but David took note of a splatter of fresh blood on the paving stones that led a path away from the door. The vine barrier through which the gate passed was about six feet thick. On the other side, scraggly trees and barren shrubbery spotted the vast circle of enclosed space. A fine layer of frost coated the rocky ground. And then there was the house.

The structure was three stories tall and loomed precariously over the entire garden. Flaking yellow paint coated its walls, and what windows that were not broken were soot-coated and opaque. The shutters hung at odd angles and a webbing of dead wisteria vines choked the entire structure.

David realized as he looked upon the house that he was clenching his jaw. He forced himself to take a deep breath and stepped into the winter garden.

"Pasky!" he shouted again, and his voice echoed back to him, slicing through the silence. Something off to his left glinted in the stark light of dawn. David spotted Pasky's sword in the grass and stooped to pick it up.

The door behind him slammed shut with a resounding clatter. David closed his eyes against the rising panic, but refused to turn his head. He resumed his even pace down the path, calling out for his friend twice more, and still nothing answered.

He stopped at the foot of the stairs that led up to the front porch. The lumber looked rotten, as though his foot would go right through should he step on it. A broken porch swing creaked and wobbled back and forth in the chill breeze. David tested his weight against the first step, and then the second and third. The fourth board cracked and he took a giant leap up over it onto the top step. He was standing just a few feet from the front door.

He stared at it for a moment. Someone within laughed a merry trill. David suddenly understood. The house was hungry for him.

So be it. It would have him, but he could be sure he'd stick in its throat as it swallowed.

Inside, the air shifted slightly and shimmered. There was a subtle change in the motes of dust filtering through the thin light from the broken skylight. The world stood on a precipice...

David put his hand to the knob, but as he did, it was pulled away from him and the double doors were thrown wide with a flourish. Standing there, framed in the doorway, was a young woman in a flowing white gown. Her raven hair cascaded around her shoulders and her slight frame cast a silhouette within her dress against the light from the space beyond. On her face she wore a full harlequin mask.

"Welcome," she said. Though he couldn't see a smile, David sensed an intense aura of happiness around this woman, one that was inspired by his presence and made him feel distinctly uncomfortable.

He looked her in the eyes, but found he could not hold the gaze. "Where is my friend?" he demanded, shifting to look past her into the house.

She tilted her head to the side, as if she did not understand his question. "Come inside the house," she said.

David knit his brows and took a step back. "Who are you? Who do you think I am?"

"Come inside the house."

"Where is my friend?" He raised Pasky's sword, the point angled to her throat.

Her body seemed to sway in the breeze for a moment. He could see her deep blue eyes through the holes in the mask and they pierced him, tugged at him. The swirling designs on her mask wavered. Then suddenly she stepped aside and gestured widely. "Your friend is inside the house."

David gritted his teeth, balled his fist around the hilt of the sword, and stepped across the threshold.

And the world transformed.

What he had seen of the house beyond his hostess had been gray and rotting. Spider webs, dust covers, dry rot. Nothing about it had spoken of a living inhabitant. It was a dead space.

But now, bewildered, David looked all around him. The room was a stately foyer, decked in pristine antiques and in carmine and ivory. Music played, a string quartet, beyond a door to his left, and the muffled sound of happy celebrants filtered through as well. Turning his head and looking out behind him, David viewed a lush garden in full summer bloom. Through it, couples strolled in ball gowns and finery, their faces each covered with masks and feathers. On the newly whitewashed porch, a gentleman in a half mask raised his glass in David's direction, and a lady batted her eyelashes at him from behind the fluttering of her fan.

For a moment, a noise filled his ears, drowning out all other sound. *Scritch...scritch... scritch...*

David turned slowly back to the woman, who dipped her head at a slightly unnatural angle, and something in his mind broke. Terror crept up his spine and his every impulse screamed at him to *run run*

RUN! but his body was frozen, sword clutched in his hand. The music in the other room came to a rest, and in the few seconds of silence a single thought surfaced in David's mind. *Pasky.* And suddenly everything was very easy.

"Show me to my friend," he said, dropping the sword to his side. "Please." He offered his arm to the woman, and she looked at him curiously for a moment before her entire figure was transformed by her grace and her graciousness. She swept over to him and hooked her arm through his.

She was cold. Even through the sleeve of his coat, he could tell.

She led him across the foyer and through a set of double doors leading down into a grand salon. Party guests sat talking, listening to music, all dressed in clothing from an indeterminate but antique period. And each guest was masked.

A servant with a drawn, pale face and blank stare appeared, a tray of *hors d'oeuvres* in hand. The man's eye twitched with a nervous tic. The woman on David's arm gestured for him to partake, and he reluctantly took a toast point with some unidentifiable gray paste spread upon it. The servant disappeared as easily as he had come, and the woman watched David with an eager, catlike gaze.

David sniffed the toast and took a bite. He swallowed hard, and the dry, earthy paste was like a peach pit traveling down his gullet. Goose bumps chased their way across his arms, and he had the feeling that he had just made a terrible mistake.

They sauntered through the room, and each of the guests followed his movements. Their gazes prickled at his neck. Above the fireplace hung an enormous portrait of a seated man in a Confederate uniform holding a sword across his lap. When David glimpsed it, he did a double-take.

"Is... is that me?" he stuttered.

She shook her head slowly. "That is Jesse. My husband, long passed." The sibilance of the final word stretched out into a long hiss. "He doesn't look a thing like you."

David eyed the portrait again and she was right. Had it changed? A trick of the light? He didn't know why he had thought the man in the portrait was himself. The woman assumed a slightly predatory posture, took his wrist, and lead him into a ballroom where guests paraded across the dance floor like clouds bustled about by gusts of wind. Onto the floor she took him, her talon grasp still tight about his wrist.

David was never much of a dancer. He had allowed his girlfriend one slow dance at weddings only, no more than that. But here in this place, with this woman in his arms, the music seeped into his skin, crept into his brain, *one two three one two three,* and his muscles flowed. The sword clattered to the ground. He waltzed.

As the freedom of the dance washed over him, he felt his tongue loosen as well. "Who are you?" he asked again. "What is this place?"

She chose to answer the second question. "It is a home for the lost. The runaways. Like you."

"I'm not lost."

"No?"

The strings sung. *One two three one two three* and then suddenly, with a violent *twang,* the violinist broke a string. David's step faltered. "What happened to my friend?"

She looked off over his shoulder and sniffed. "He doesn't belong here."

"Where is he?"

"David," she cooed. "This world can be a beautiful one. The house has many wonders. Do you wish to see another?"

She led him to an anteroom. Upon a table stood a perfect

miniature replica of the house, decked in summer splendor. David bent and peered through one of the tiny windows. Through it, he saw a small room with a male figurine dressed in pajamas, bent over an even smaller dollhouse. David blinked and wobbled, overwhelmed for a moment with vertigo. He spied the doll dancing with a woman in mask and ball gown through another window. Through yet another they made love on a four-poster bed.

"What is this?" he gasped.

"The house has dreams too."

David clenched his fists, realized he had dropped the sword, and stared the woman down with the last weapon he had: his own determination. "Take me to him."

The mask on her face slipped a little, and David's vision staggered. The glorious mansion around him vanished for an instant, replaced with an environment dark and cruel, and he felt cold chains around his wrists. There was that noise again: *scritch... scritch... scritch...*

But the next moment, she was standing before him in the light, airy space, her cold fingers tracking feathery paths down his cheek. "Be happy, my dear. You have been welcomed into the house. You needn't worry about anything ever again. Death will never touch you, not so long as you are here. Every comfort and luxury is yours. Every day is a grand affair." Standing on her toes, she tilted her head and spoke, the lips of her mask just inches from his, "Isn't that what you want?"

"No," he whispered.

She clucked her tongue, then closed the gap between them and pressed the hard, painted lips of her mask against his. A tear streaked down David's cheek, though he did not know why. His whole body trembled.

"And Pasky?" he asked, but he looked into her eyes and found his answer. Pasky was dead.

"This is where you belong. You are such a delicacy, my boy."

His eyes snapped open. The phrase echoed in his head in his father's voice: *You are such a disappointment, my boy.* A spark of resistance flared in his mind. He pushed her away and dashed back through the door, back into the ball room. Ducking and weaving through the dancers, he made his way quickly up the staircase to the exit.

She stood on the top stair, arms crossed, watching him.

He reversed, scurried away, and found another exit into a small library where men stood around in half-masks, smoking cigars and sipping brandy. Their conversation ceased as David flew into the room, and their eyes followed him. David stood for a moment in indecision between two doors. The men lifted their masks to get a better look at him, and David gasped, choking, as he saw that each of them wore his face.

Everywhere, reflections.

He grabbed at a doorknob and snatched open the door, but behind it stood the terrible woman, laughing as he stumbled backwards and fell.

"Are you finished, my boy? There is nowhere to go."

The world shifted again. The bright tiles and paint, the shining marble and gold, all of it crumbled, tarnished, and chipped away.

David was chained naked to a wall. His arms ached, hung above his head. To his right, not far off, he spied the servant who had brought him that desiccated morsel. He worked over a table with his back to David, and when he turned, a strange smile played across the man's lips.

"Another taste?" the man asked, holding out a knife dripping in blood, a hunk of flesh speared upon it.

David's mouth opened in speechless horror and he turned his head away. A few feet in front of him hovered a being, vaporous and light, and David knew it to be her.

"What do you want with me?" he cried.

It chittered at him, *scritch...scritch... scritch...* and he heard her voice in his head. *To feast. Come back where you belong.* Her hands shot out and grabbed at his jaw, plunging her fingers into his mouth and spreading his lips. He shook his head violently, and the metal rattled at his wrists. There was no more running away.

And as she leaned in, he felt her cold breath upon his skin. The smell of fresh cut grass and summer campfires filled his nostrils. Somewhere a string quartet played. One place left to run. Into the maw, the gaping maw.

The Haunted House

Larry Hensley

The
house was
haunted, of that there
could be no doubt. The sign
said so, the one in the front yard that
read "Haunted House." (And if you can't believe everything
you read, what *can* you believe?) Of course,
even if you couldn't read, or didn't believe
everything you read, you'd still know the
house was haunted. Just one glance at the
door was proof of that.

The front door,
hanging on its hinges,
banged open and shut with every passing breeze.

Creeeeeeeeeak. Bang! *Creeeeeeeeeeeak.* Bang!

The hinges were rusty, and no wonder.
The air was hot and muggy, as only the Deep
South can offer, all filled with the scent of honeysuckle and magnolia blossoms. Hardly the kind of smells
for a haunted house, but there you are. Fiction is stranger than truth,
unless you live in the South. Here, our haunted houses
smell like a perfume factory. Up north, where them
Yankees live, their haunted houses probably smell like
skunks, dead people, or whatsoever. But
down here in the land of Dixie, we do our
ghosts proud – Estee Lauder proud.
Then there were the windows: broken. The
shutters: dangling. The roof was caved
in, the gables sagged, and the chimney, for
its part, had long since tumbled down. Even
the confederate flag was ripped, torn, and
dangled by a thread like maybe it had
been there for a hundred years and plum forgot the
civil war was over. But back to the house.
It was covered in vines.
What kind of haunted house doesn't have vines?
The leafy tendrils crawled all over the place,
crept in through the windows,
and fell round the chimney,
which was on the ground anyway,
so the vines didn't have far to fall.
Lucky vines.
Yep! This house was haunted.
Of this there can be no doubt.
Except for one problem.

Now every story has to have at least
one problem, and this story is no exception.
Mind, some problems are easier to see than others,
and when it comes to ghosts – them being invisible and all,
the problems can sometimes be hard to see indeed. This particular problem, however, was about as hard to spy as a Republican Govn'r. But we're talkin' ghosts, not politics, so try and stay with me. And when it comes to ghosts, the ghosts that infested   this particular haunted house were not only   invisible, they weren't even there! Yep. The Haunted House was quite entirely hauntless! Can you   imagine? A haunted house that isn't haunted?   Neither can I. Neither could any of the other houses! Bad enough that she was an eyesore, a run-down shack in the middle of an upscale community. One could forgive the confederate flag, all torn and stained and tattered and mildewed. The vines weren't so bad neither, since they covered the peeling paint. And that "George Wallace for President" sign?

So faded you couldn't read the letters.

No, all the other houses of the neighborhood
       could have forgiven the ruined pile of rotting
             lumber if she had just had herself an honest ghost
                  for a bit of character. Can do wonders for
           property values, ghosts can! Drag in visitors
      from far and wide. Windows what got faces
infused in the glass, or a mess of rotted planks
       stained the color of dried blood – now them
             things can raise property values all around
                  right better'n a bank full of loan officers.
             But what the heck is an Unhaunted House good for?
      You can't boast about being next to a run-down shack.
Faded signs and shredded flags don't impress
       folks what gots BMWs and Rolex watches.
             So none of the other houses in the neighbor-
                hood talked to our Unhaunted House. Truth
           to tell, they never even looked at her. Pretended
      she wasn't there. They turned their chimneys up
so high at that poor house, I don't think even the
       clouds managed to scuttle their ways round all
             them stuck up affairs. As for the sidewalks, those
                spotless paths that lined the streets and
           sidled past flowerbeds and perfect "Green
      Guard" lawns, they stopped right where the
creepy vines began and didn't begin again until
       well past the broken down fence.

Poor house.
Poor lonely house.
How would you feel
if all the other houses in
your neighborhood called you
"The Spectorless Spectacle?"
Or worse yet,
"The Hauntless House!"

Well, you're not a house, so you probably wouldn't mind.
But it bothered our house.
It bothered her a lot!

You see, she was a nice little house.
She really was, and very kind.
She was probably the kindest, nicest,
friendliest house you ever did see.
Now this might surprise you a bit, what with the George Wallace
sign and Confederate flag and all, but you can't always judge a house
by the company it keeps, especially since a house can't just up and
walk away if the company gets offensive.
So anyway, where were we?

Oh yeah.

The friendly friendless house.
Our Unhaunted Haunted House.

That was her problem, of course. The reason she had no ghostly friends and couldn't get none to move in was that she was nice. She was kind. And while she maybe couldn't up and walk away when the company got offensive, she most surely could up and "Shoo!" any ghosts that got scary! Don't ask me how, I'm not a house. It's not my job to know how to scare ghosts away. My job is to tell you a story, and the story is that this house scared away any and all ghosts that weren't nice.

Now, have you ever heard of nice ghosts?
Think about it.

Why would a haunt haunt a haunted house
if the house didn't want to be haunting?
And since our house only wanted
unhaunting haunts...

Well... you see the problem.

And there really is no solution to a problem like this. It's called a conomdrom, or conundram, or condumdrim, or something like that. But anyway, it's one of them type problems what's got no solution. So I'd be kind of stuck, and this story wouldn't have no happy ending, if'n this story were just about a house.

Which it isn't.
Nope.

Our story is about a ghost.

And our ghost had a problem.

You already know the problem. Have

guessed it   well and   truly.

Our ghost   was   friendly.

Yep.

That was our ghost's   problem.   And quite a

problem it was, too. Would explain why he didn't

have any friends. I mean, have you ever heard of

a friendly ghost that wouldn't scare no one?

That never said "Boo!" That hadn't

even once snuck up on some poor

lost soul wandering in the dark

and shrieked in his ear?

Neither have I.

Neither had

any of the

other

ghosts.

Truth to tell, they were so
ashamed of having a friendly ghost
in their midst that they wouldn't talk to him.
Pretended he wasn't even there. In fact, they stuck their cold
invisible noses so high in the air that I think maybe even the clouds
shivered when they floated right through 'em. Know I would have.
Ghost noses are cold. Maybe even as cold as a politician's comfort,
but we're talking ghosts here, not politics, so try and stay with me.

Our friendly ghost
- and I'd call him Casper
except that would be a copyright
infringement, so let's call him
Joe instead   - our Joe
the friendly   ghost was
all alone, and   really very lonely.
He just flew from place to place and from
there to here. He had nowhere to go. No
graveyard wanted him. What kind of a graveyard
wants a ghost that isn't scary?
None of the haunted houses would
have anything to do with him. Empty   churches and
burned out hollows, run down shacks and   fallen down shanties
– one and all turned cold shoulders, or roofs, or whatever it is that
they turn, when our friendly ghost Joe showed up. He couldn't even
land in a junk yard! The rusted out cars rolled up their windows
and slammed their doors. So Joe just flew, and floated,
drifted and wandered. Maybe you don't know this.
Maybe you've never heard it before. But when you
think about it, you'll know I'm telling the truth.
Even lost souls need somewhere to stay,
some place to call home. I mean, what's
a haunt without a haunt to haunt?
So perhaps you'll believe me
when I tell you that Joe was
disappearing.

You   might imagine that since
ghosts   are already dead and invisible,
they don't   have much disappearing left to do.
But that just shows what you know about being a ghost. No, this was
no laughing matter. Joe, the friendly ghost, was disappearing almost
as fast as yellow dog Democrats! In fact, Joe was almost entirely
gone. But then something happened, and I think you know what.

Joe spied a house. It was covered in vines, with a tumbled
down chimney and a sign out in front. The sign said
"Haunted House". Joe knew he wouldn't be welcome.

Knew he didn't have a chance. Knew there wasn't no point
in even trying. But he couldn't help it. It's not that he flew down.
Not really. He sort of just fell. Drifted down with wisps of vapor
trailing away as he disappeared. Joe the friendly ghost was giving
up the ghost. A sad ending, but there you have it. Couldn't be
otherwise. After all, we had ourselves a bit of a
conomdrom, or conundram, or condumdrim,
or something like that, but anyway, it's
one of them type problems what's got
no solution. A haunt that won't haunt
can only make for a haunting ending.
Fortunately, our story is not just about
a ghost.
Nope.

Our story is about a bulldozer.

133

There were lots of them.

They came with the other machines:

back hoes and wrecking balls, dump trucks and haul-aways. What's worse was what came behind them: asphalt trucks, paving machines, and lots and lots of men with maps and plans and diagrams. Worst of all were the street signs, the ones that said "Highway 20." Crooked politicians! Where were they when you needed them? All those federal grants, and they decided to actually build a highway rather than pocket the money? What was the world coming to? Whatever would the houses do? The whole community of Happy Houseville trembled. One and all they

were to be

torn down,

replaced

with a

highway!

"Whatever

shall we

do? Who

can save

us now?"

They cried.

And wept.

And trembled.

Especially the Haunted House!

"I'll die!" she wailed. "All these years I've never had a ghost because I was too kind, and now I have no one to protect me!"

And *that*, my friends, *that* was when it happened.

That was when our friendly ghost
> who was too nice to say "Boo!"
>> discovered his place, and knew his mission.

That was when our ghost stopped falling and started flying.

> Down, fast, fast as the wind and maybe even faster!

Closer the bulldozers came, tearing up sidewalk and ripping out vines. A tree fell. Another toppled. The front steps started to crumble. The Unhaunted House was about to fall.

"Help!" she cried.   Joe swept down!

But what could Joe do? Cry "Boo?" Friendly, nice little Joe who hadn't scared anyone in his entire lifeless life? How could he scare anyone now? Practice makes perfect, they say, and practice in saying "Boo!" was exactly what Joe didn't have.

But then again, they also say something else: "There's an exception to every rule." And this was an exceptional day!

Because this was the day that a certain ghost who had saved up a hundred years of "Boos" and maybe even a thousand, this was the day that a ghost who had wandered far and wide and very nearly disappeared, this was the day that Joe, the friendly ghost, grabbed himself a lifetime of silence, and...

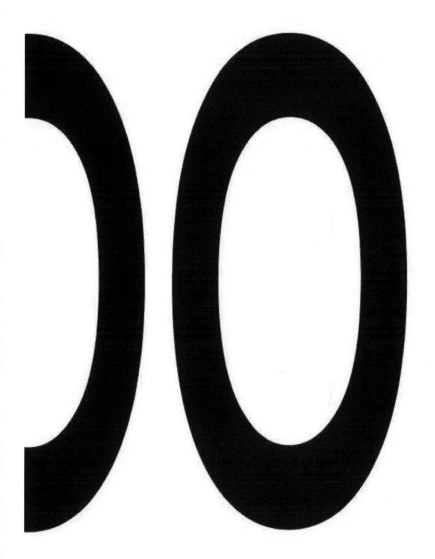

You know what those bulldozers and back
hoes, wrecking balls and dump trucks,
asphalt trucks, and paving machines said?

YEEK!

They all turned and fled just as fast as their wheels would carry
them, rolling all the way to Georgia and maybe even the Atlantic.
For all I know, they got themselves a boat and sailed for Europe!
That's a part of the story I'll guess we'll never know. But what I can
tell you is this:

> Everything I've told
> you is the truth. And if'n y'all
> don't believe me, just grab yourself a
> four pack of wheels and head down south to
> Highway 20. Take it Mississippi
> way and you'll run into Happy
> Houseville. Can't miss it! When
> the highway makes a sudden right,
> *just go straight*. First house you'll
> come to has a sign in the front yard.
>
> It reads – "Haunted House."

The Apparition

Bret Williams

"Hey, Mom! We're home!" Backpacks went flying, shoes popped off, butts hit the couch, and the TV clicked on.

"Hey, don't you dare turn that TV on," Mom shouted from upstairs. "I'll be down in a minute."

The twins let out a synchronized sigh and Scott let his disgust out. "It's Friday, Mom! Ya know, the weekend?" His half-hearted argument went unheard and Marie turned the TV off, picked up her backpack, and headed to the kitchen for the daily 'interrogation.' Scott used every ounce of his teenager attitude to keep his butt on the couch, but his respect for his mother won out and he followed Marie to the kitchen.

Shara came downstairs carrying an arm-load of laundry. "Spill it. How was school? How'd you do on your tests? Any projects for the weekend?"

She plopped the dirty clothes on the floor and swept her hair from in front of her eyes. It was obvious to the kids that, even though it was Friday, she was not in any mood for play. Since her husband's death in a car accident a year and a half ago, her extra chores and parenting responsibilities had been an escape from the sadness and anger, but they kept her from ever relaxing.

"Well, I got the Student of the Month Award," Marie said with a deceptive, deadpan look, which she couldn't hold long as it crept into a full-on smile set off by her gleaming blue eyes.

"Really? That's great," Shara said without even noticing her daughter's pride as she turned toward the washing machine. "Scott, what's up?"

Scott tried to make good news out of nothing. "Well, I got five goals in P.E. and I found the sweatshirt that I lost in January."

"Great." Mom sighed and her words oozed with sarcasm. "It's March. You don't need it anymore. And, you've been going without one all winter? Geez... Sometimes I wonder about your brain. I've told you this so many times, I want you to try harder to be a responsible person. I have a lot to think about around here, I can't think for you too."

"It's 'teen-brain,' Mom. We learned about it in science last week. Our brains have an excuse not to think. It's a condition."

"Uh-huh. A condition. Don't give me that. What else? How about tests and projects?"

"Umm, I've got to write an app for computer class," Scott said. "Ms. Shell said it can be for a phone or computer. And we have eight weeks to finish it. So no hurry."

"I'm glad I'm not in computer class," Marie said. "My year-end photography project is a dessert cookbook, ten recipes and the pictures to go with 'em."

"That sounds fun, Marie. Why don't we start tonight. Could you start on dinner please? Spaghetti," Mom said. "Let's get back to this app. Did you get any examples or anything?"

"No, she really didn't give us any examples besides a calculator or grocery list or drawing app or... Mom, I've got eight weeks. Can't we wait to talk about this?"

Mom interrupted, "No, we talk about it *now*! No examples, huh? That sounds like more than *none*. So, have you given it any thought?"

"Not really," Scott said. "I wish Dad was here. He'd know what to do."

Shara stopped doing laundry for a split second as her shoulders slumped. She knew he was right, but she was also getting tired of hearing it. Their father was the epitome of a computer geek, a programmer who would go on and on about things like object-oriented programming and multi-platform compatibility for days. His help with things like this was invaluable and missed every day.

"You can look at his stuff," Shara suggested. "It's still on his computer downstairs."

"True, but I still need an idea," Scott said.

Mom sighed impatiently, looked around the house, and said, "Then do something for me. I need a phone number list, or a grocery list, or..." she paused and looked around a little more.

"Or how about a smoke detector?" she said with the first sign of enthusiasm for the day.

"Nah, too easy, too boring, and too impossible," Scott said as he shoved a handful of Doritos in his mouth.

"That's what you're going to do," Shara insisted. "Think about it, you can somehow make a smoke detector for my iPhone. That would be cool, and even if it didn't work you'd get a good grade. Here's my phone. See if somebody's already made one."

Marie grabbed the phone and started tapping on the screen. Mom continued with the laundry while Scott looked on with Marie.

"No, go to the App Store," Scott urged, and moved his hand toward the phone.

"Duh, I know that!" Marie spouted back and jerked the phone away from her brother's reach.

"You two, quit it and just look up the app," Shara growled as she aggressively shoved laundry into the washing machine.

"He started it!" Marie rebutted and tapped the words 'smoke detector' into the iPhone screen. The search results narrowed to 'No results found.' "Nope. Nothing," she said.

"See, I told you. It must be impossible," Scott said. He shrugged his shoulders and started to walk away.

"Don't you walk away," Mom said as she stopped with the laundry and turned to Scott. She grabbed him by the chin, gave it a little shake, and said, "You remember this. *Nothing is impossible*. It just may be that no one has done it yet."

"Or that it's impossible," Scott's attitude spoke up again.

"I think it *is* possible, but maybe not in the normal way. Obviously there's no smoke sniffer, or whatever, on the phone but maybe you can use the camera. Think about it and get it started real soon. I know your dad used to spend days on a project, sometimes weeks, before there was anything even half-way useable." She paused to let her orders sink in to his teen-brain. "And, Marie, I am very proud of you for your Student of the Month Award." She grabbed her daughter and pulled her close for a hug.

"Thanks, Mom. Let go."

As the conversation settled into normal banter, a scratch came from behind the basement door with a little whine to back it up.

"Oops, I must've locked Smokey downstairs," Shara said. Marie opened the door and in bounded their bear-like chow.

"Hey boy!" The twins greeted him together as he jumped up and almost knocked Scott over. "Ha ha! Calm down boy."

After a few days of consideration, contemplation, and procrastination, Scott made a decision: He would try his best to make it look like he was trying his best. His classmates were doing what was expected of them, making a grocery list or a calendar, or something mundane. Scott's mom wouldn't allow that type of mediocre behavior. So, with that in mind, he decided to attempt to build the 'smoke detector' for his mom's iPhone.

School was in its final quarter and this was Scott's last computer project of the year. His teacher, Ms. Shell, was a bit skeptical of the idea, but knowing Scott's potential when he was excited about a topic, she was very supportive. Her classroom mantra was "Sure, try it. What could it hurt?" As long as her students put forth an honest effort and did their own work, she was happy to give them full credit.

Everything Scott needed was available on his dad's laptop, which was collecting dust in the basement. Even though their dad was obsessive about computing, he had never wanted to force it on the kids for fear that they would push it away. Scott didn't get much instruction from Dad, but he was blessed with his problem-solving ability and enthusiasm.

Scott pulled the dusty laptop from the shelf where it had sat since the car wreck and booted it up. Ms. Shell had taught him the basic steps of software development – requirement gathering, designing, implementing, and testing – but he had not learned any particular programming language or techniques. She gave the class a list of some websites to reference, but didn't show them how to use any programming tools. He was on his own to learn.

As the computer came to life, Scott looked around the basement at all of the books his dad had collected. Many of the topics Ms. Shell had touched on were seen on the spines. He noticed one titled

Build Your Own: Mobile Apps.

"Ah-hah, that's the one I want," he said to himself and pulled it from the shelf. He opened the book to the table of contents and noticed the title of chapter one: *Hello World!* "What the heck does that mean?"

The computer finally booted up and Scott was faced with the login screen. The cursor sat in the empty password field, blinking at him.

"Mom, do you know what Dad's password is?" he yelled in no particular direction.

"Umm…" She thought for a second and yelled from upstairs, "Try 36-24-36. That was his favorite number."

"Okay." Scott typed in the number but thought to himself, "That can't be it. That's dumb. What does that even mean?"

The computer beeped and denied access. He tried again by typing 'S-M-O-K-E-Y.' The login box faded away, chimes rang from the speakers, and a familiar voice, Scott's dad's, said, "Welcome, your last login was May 7th 2010." Scott smiled a little and blinked back some tears.

Two hours passed. Frustration brewed with every click of the mouse. He found the application to build an iPhone app, but he had no clue where to start.

"There's got to be a better way to do this," he mumbled to himself. Just then, Smokey strolled in followed by Shara carrying the vacuum cleaner.

"How's it going?" she asked.

"Not good," Scott replied, and she could tell he was having a little trouble. "I don't know what the heck I'm doing. I've been sitting here clicking on everything. I just don't know where to start." He put his hands over his eyes and let out a long sigh.

"Well did you look at these books? They should help you… maybe."

"Yeah, I found this one," he said, and held up the book he had pulled from the shelf.

"Did you open it?" Shara asked, with just as much sarcasm as she could without seeming unhelpful.

"A little," Scott replied.

Shara let out a sigh that was twice as long as Scott's. She changed her tone as if she was talking to a four-year-old and said, "I'm pretty sure you'll find some answers there. So, open the book and look at chapter one. It's usually a great starting point. And quit giving me extra work. Do some things for yourself."

She left the room to finish her chores and Scott opened the book to the first chapter. After reading and following the instructions line-by-line, he finally made some progress. His program was ready to be tested. He pressed the 'Run' button and the words "Hello World!" popped up in an iPhone simulator window.

He jumped up, startling Smokey, who had been laying at his feet, and yelled "Hello World!" At that minute, Scott noticed in front of him, on the book shelf, an old baby picture of him in his dad's arms. In the picture, Scott was wearing a t-shirt with the exact words printed across his chest.

"Oh, Dad," Scott said aloud, "you were such a geek."

As if someone was blowing out a candle, a puff of cool air hit the back of his neck. He turned to see who was blowing on him, but all he noticed was Smokey staring off in the same direction. A little spooked, Scott reached down to get some comfort from his dog.

"Hey boy, I get it now!" he said in an excited whisper. "I get it." The example was the perfect starting point. Now it was time for a Coke and Cheetos break and to show off his achievement.

"Mom! Sis!" he yelled as he ran up the stairs with the laptop and Smokey wagging right behind him. "Look at what I did."

They were both sitting at the kitchen table staring at Marie's laptop and pictures of desserts for her photography project. They both looked up with great expectation, but as soon as Scott flipped the laptop around so they could see it, their eyes and grins fell flat. They were definitely not impressed.

"You typed *hello world*?" his mom asked. "Ummmm... Good work?"

"No, I... Oh, nevermind," Scott said as his shoulders slumped and he headed back to the basement.

He had no idea what his app was going to look like or what it was really supposed to do. He tried bouncing ideas off of Smokey, but that didn't work. He'd get the same answer every time, a cocked head and a look that said, "Hmm? Did you say *bacon*?" Eventually Marie asked him how it was going.

"Not fast," he responded. "I don't even know what I want it to do."

"Don't you just want to point the camera somewhere and detect smoke?" she asked.

"Yeah, I guess so. That sounds easy."

"Then after giving it a camera, you should add a 'start' and 'stop' button. And maybe a 'Call the fire department' button. And then, add a 'Notify insurance company' button and give it a 'Fire extinguisher' add-on..."

"Whoa! Easy Sis," Scott interrupted. "One little thing at a time. A fire extinguisher, really?" He stared out the kitchen window pensively, "I wish Dad was here to help."

"Yeah, me too. But I can help you when you need it," she offered in a conciliatory tone.

"You have helped," he assured her. "Now I know where I need to start. The hard part will be trying to figure out how to *see* the smoke. Maybe you can help me there too, since you do photography. I better get started, though. I've got to show Ms. Shell some progress on Monday. I wish Dad was here."

Scott's whole weekend was filled with the puzzle of his project. It had engulfed his brain; every thought Scott had was somehow related. By Sunday evening he had figured out how to use the iPhone's camera in his app. He was able to use the video program too, and save the pictures on the phone. He decided to show off his progress to Mom while she was mopping the kitchen.

"Whoa! Stop! The floor's wet. Don't come in here," she shouted as she put the mop down. "What is it? I'm a little busy here." Scott turned the laptop around and showed her the screen. "Neat, Scott. That's really cool," Shara said. That was the kind of response he had expected with the 'Hello World!' step. "Can it detect smoke?"

"No, not yet. I've got a while to go before I can do that. Marie said she has some ideas for taking pictures of smoke. I still need to make the thing beep or turn red or explode." He smiled. "Or something to let you know there's smoke. Some kind of alarm. I think I'll make it vibrate and beep as loud as it can. Or play a really annoying Justin Bieber song, which is *every* song." Scott was starting to feel more relaxed and comfortable with his progress.

Monday in class, Ms. Shell was also quite impressed. The other students were looking on as if he had invented fire or the wheel. The more achievement-oriented of them decided to go back to the design phase and add a camera to their own apps.

Finally, Friday came around again and he was able to dedicate some more critical thinking time to his project. Marie had had a week to think through how she'd help and found some neat camera filters.

She tried a few of them on her project. She discovered that the sepia filter gave a great contrast and, with the flash, was able to pick up the steam rising from her freshly baked cookies. After seeing the pictures she'd taken, Scott was convinced that it was possible to 'detect' smoke. The weekend programming task had taken shape.

He began early Saturday morning, 6:00 AM, trying to use the different filters. Weekend mornings in the house were the quietest. The basement was cool, almost cold, and Smokey would lie at Scott's feet. By lunch, Scott had finished his whole weekend's workload and started working on his next task – making the phone issue an alert.

Everything came together, and after another week of nightly programming sessions, the app was ready to be installed on an actual iPhone. Although she had said it was okay to load it on hers, Shara was still very worried that it might permanently mess it up. There really was nothing she could do, though, except pray for the best. It was her idea after all.

Scott loaded it on the phone, started it up, and began to hoot and holler with a few over-dramatic fist pumps thrown in for good measure.

"Let's light something on fire!" he screamed.

Smokey stood up from his napping position and added a loud bark to the Scott's hollering. The two of them were so loud that the walls vibrated and knocked three hanging pictures to the floor.

"Oops. Calm down boy," Scott said to Smokey. As if nothing strange happened, he started rehanging the pictures. The last was of his dad blowing out the candles on his birthday cake with his cheeks puffed out like Louis Armstrong on a trumpet.

"Oh yeah," Scott said to himself, "Dad's birthday is next week." He hung the picture in its place and headed toward the stairs, but before he could leave the room, the picture had fallen to the floor again. Scott stared at it, shrugged his shoulders, then continued out of the basement.

"Hey Mom, did you hear me? What can I set on fire?" he yelled as he ran up the stairs. He burst into the kitchen, but there was no one there. Closing the basement door behind him, he accidentally locked out Smokey, who was following as fast as he could. Marie's dessert project was scattered on the kitchen table, but she was nowhere to be seen.

"Hmm..." Scott said as he looked around. He was determined to test his smoke detector, regardless if anyone was around. After his 'teen brain' decided that a small fire would work fine, he found a piece of newspaper and rummaged through the junk drawer for some matches. He grabbed a plate from the cabinet, placed it on the kitchen table, and proceeded to light his small pile of paper ablaze. It caught fire quickly and sent smoke billowing into the kitchen air.

"All right," he said as he smiled at his fire. He grabbed the iPhone and started his app, but before he could start his testing, the real smoke alarm in the hallway began howling at a high pitch. "Oh crap," he said to himself. "Maybe this wasn't a good idea." He ignored the beeping fire alarm and continued testing.

In seconds, yells of distress from upstairs started. "Mom, fire! Something's burning!" Both Shara and Marie came barreling down the stairs and into the kitchen to find Scott facing the other direction with an eerie glow and billowing smoke coming from the other side.

"What are you doing?!" Shara yelled at Scott.

"Testing my app. Why?"

"You started a fire in my kitchen!" Shara yelled, as if Scott didn't already know.

"Yeah, Mom. How else am I gonna test my app?" he yelled back as he pressed the "Detect" button on the iPhone screen. The phone immediately began to vibrate and sound a fire truck siren. "It works! It works!" Scott yelled in celebration. Even Smokey showed his excitement by letting loose a howl from the other side of the basement door. Marie opened it and in bounded their chow with full force.

"It's okay boy! It's just your idiot master setting fire to the house. It's okay."

Just as Smokey plowed into the kitchen, the iPhone stopped howling and vibrating. Shara, now armed with a water-filled spray bottle, began dowsing the fire and sending more smoke into the air. The iPhone still remained silent.

"Hey? That's weird," Scott said. "It just stopped. It was working. You saw it, right?" He looked at them as they exhaled sighs of relief. "It was working," he reiterated with a sense of wonder. "There was even more smoke after you put it out. It shouldn't have stopped." He was disappointed, but at the same time impressed that it had worked at all. "I guess there's a bug. Can I try it again?"

"No!" both Marie and Mom shouted.

"Are you dumb? You can do it outside," Mom continued. "I like my house and don't want it burned down."

"Okay, fine." Scott gathered his fire material to try it outside.

They all marched to the back yard, and Smokey followed. He sat by Scott as he tried to detect the fire again. This time there was no success, not even a peep of siren or a hint of vibration. Turning to Mom, Scott pleaded, "Can I *please* try it inside again?"

"No," Shara replied without hesitation.

"How about in the garage? Or the storage shed?"

"No. No. And whatever the next idea is – No!" she said as she, Marie, and Smokey began walking back toward the house. "I've got stuff to do. I guess this really wasn't that great of an idea after all."

"Wait! It's working! It's vibrating! Oh, never mind. Here." He handed the phone to his mom. "It's Nana calling."

Marie and Smokey continued into the house. Shara stayed with Scott and talked to her mom on the phone. "Hey Mom," she said, "Can I call you back? Scott's trying to detect if our back yard is burning down."

She quickly finished the conversation and handed him the phone. Scott pessimistically turned on the app, pointed it at what remained of the fire, and pressed the 'Detect' button. Immediately it started vibrating and howling.

"See?!" he yelled to his mom. "It works! See?"

She turned toward him, smiled, and said, "Make sure that fire is completely out before you come in, okay?"

"Yes ma'am," he responded sheepishly.

Taking a closer look at the image on the screen, Scott noticed a stray spark hovering above the ashes. He closed the app and focused on the real fire with the expectation of seeing more sparks, but the fire was out. Only a pile of ashes remained, but like a good kid he finished it off by stomping on it.

He only had two weeks until his project was due. It kind of worked, but 'kind of' wasn't good enough for Scott. The problem was, though, that he didn't have much of a way to test it again.

Monday, Tuesday, Wednesday passed, and Thursday was a special day at the house. Thursday was a day of remembrance and celebration. The family had vowed never to forget Dad, to always remember how he left his mark. So, on his birthday, they would celebrate as if he were still with them.

Being only the second birthday since the accident, it seemed that maybe it would be easier to just forget. Mom wouldn't let that happen. The Chinese takeout was warm and ready to serve, the picture of Dad blowing the candles was sitting at the table, and the pineapple upside-down cake with forty candles poking into the air waited to be lit.

After the sweet-n-sour chicken was gone and everyone had their fill of fried rice, Shara picked up the cake and carried it to the kitchen to light all forty candles, which took a few minutes.

"Ready?" she asked the kids in the dining room.

"Wait, I need my smoke detector!" Scott said as he quickly got up from the table. "I want to see how much smoke forty years of candles puts off."

"Hurry!" Shara said. "The candles are about to melt all over the cake. Maybe next year we should just do one big one."

Scott rushed to get Shara's iPhone. Smokey, who was banished from the dining room during dinner, lay on the kitchen floor but looked up to see the commotion. Noticing nothing of interest, he continued with his hangdog expression. Scott rushed back into the dining room, turned off the lights and sat down.

"Okay, ready…" he said.

A glow began to grow from the kitchen as the family commenced to sing, "Happy Birthday to you… cha cha cha… Happy birthday to yooooooou!"

Scott held the phone in front of the candles. Through it, the view of the cake was beautiful; the sepia filter added an antiquity to the image. But something was different. The flames in the view finder were surrounded by sparks, as if Shara had used sparkling trick candles.

"Whoa, look at that," Scott said as he showed the phone to Marie.

"Wow, that's cool. What color filter did you use?" she asked.

Just as Shara put the cake down and came around to see the view, the phone began to vibrate and the siren began to sound, causing a stir. Startled by the noise, Smokey let loose a loud bark from the kitchen, "WOOOF!"

The three of them, staring at the phone's screen, were then amazed even more. As if Smokey had been in the room, blowing on the candles with his bark, the sparks dispersed and disappeared, leaving behind the burning candles. A few pictures on the wall rattled and, at that exact second, the detector became silent and still.

Smokey couldn't resist anymore and came to the dining room threshold to inspect the activities. He cocked his head and whimpered his concern.

"What was that about?" Shara asked. "We've got to blow these out quick." The candles were now leaving puddles of wax on the brown sugar and pineapple rings. All three took deep breaths and let loose a mini hurricane, which immediately extinguished them.

Shara, still confused about what they had seen, began cutting the cake and doling it out to her kids. She was a little speechless, but managed to say, "Scott, I think your app is ready to be turned in." He nodded in agreement and put the phone away. They sat in silence while eating the cake.

The due date for his assignment came quickly. Scott had to take his mom's phone, his dad's laptop, and any material he used during his project to school. The 'Smoke Detector' was a highly anticipated project, but Scott couldn't get it to work. Ms. Shell allowed him to light a candle, which did put off smoke, but the app did not detect the fumes. Even when Scott blew out the candle, causing it to double the amount of smoke, nothing happened. He tried to explain what had happened during testing, but it came out sounding like excuses. Even with a failure of execution, Ms. Shell was impressed with the amount of work he'd accomplished and awarded him an A-, which was just fine with Scott.

The kids had made it through one more year of school. Summer break had arrived, and the kids settled into a more relaxed routine. Shara, however, was as busy as always. As a way to relax this summer, she decided to take the kids to the July Fourth fireworks display in downtown. It thrilled the kids to relax on their blanket among the other spectators, listen to patriotic songs over the sound system, even if it was Lee Greenwood, and take in the beauty of the fireworks display.

"Hey, Scott, get out your smoke detector app," Marie suggested as she pointed up toward the fireworks. "See if it can pick up those clouds of smoke." Scott nodded and gave an 'okay' look of agreement.

Shara handed him the phone and he turned on the app just as the deluge of fireworks began to light up the sky for the finale. As he aimed the phone toward the fireworks, it began to vibrate and sound the siren. He turned the volume down so the sirens wouldn't disturb anyone.

"Hey, it's working again," he said with a little laugh, as if it really didn't matter. "Look, Marie. It's kind of cool – look at all these little extra sparks it makes."

Marie looked on with Scott. Together they noticed the extra

sparks moving in unpredictable ways. In some spots, they seemed to close in together, and separate in others. The sparks weren't following the flow of the fireworks at all. Marie started to notice that a pattern was being formed.

"It's like those sparks are getting together or something. What's going on?" she wondered aloud. "O-M-G! O-M-G, Mom! Look at this!"

"Quit saying O-M-G, Marie. That's dumb," Shara said as she squeezed in to be able to see the view. "What is that?"

"It's the same sparks we saw at home," Scott said. "It's what's been happening every time I'd get it to work."

The sparks started to move in a more organized manner. They started to become a recognizable form, taking the shape of letters. The family looked on while silently mouthing the forms as they appeared. "H-e-l-l-o W-o-r-l-d-!"

"Holy smoke! Hello World!" Scott exclaimed. "It's Dad! Dad is here! It *has* to be him. There's no other explaining it!"

Shara grabbed Scott by his face and covered his mouth. "Shh!" she said, "People will think you're crazy."

The words remained there, floating on the screen for a few seconds. Then all but one spark fled from the screen. That one stayed and seemed to fly around in the iPhone viewfinder for ten seconds more.

Shara covered her mouth and blinked her eyes to hold back the tears. "I think you're right, Scott. It is him," she said with laughter. "And I think he's made a few friends over there, too."

The three of them smiled at the phone and at each other as the 'ghost detector' continued vibrating in Scott's hand until Dad vanished from sight.

Fourth of July

Margaret Fenton

Lauren eased down the ladder into the warmth of Smith Lake. She pushed off with her feet, splashing very little, and floated on her back. Her ears filled with water, drowning the sound of the fireworks being launched from the house on the other shore. She looked at the stars – so many of them – and wondered if he would show up tonight. He had to, she thought, on the tenth anniversary...

She rolled onto her side and swam back toward the dock. Up the ladder. She grabbed a towel and dried her body and her hair. The girls had stayed up at the cabin. She heard Lisa laugh. Loud Lisa. Louder if she was drinking, and the margarita maker had been fired up for a few hours now. Someone had cut the radio on and found the classic rock station. Aerosmith echoed faintly down the hill.

It would be quieter without Lisa and Rachel here, but she didn't trust herself. It would be too easy to swallow the bottle of antidepressants with a few cups of booze if her best friends weren't here. She'd had the pills for what, two years now? Why hadn't she done it last summer? She couldn't remember.

She sat down on the dock and dunked her feet. The boys across the lake were shooting roman candles now; flashes of green and red reflected on the smooth surface of the water. She heard the screen door slam behind her, and someone began to stumble down the sloping path.

"Hey!"

Lisa. And the whole lake could hear her. The margaritas must be strong. She made it to the pier and plopped down next to Lauren. "Whoop!" Lauren caught her arm to keep her from pitching forward into the lake. "I'm okay, I'm okay. You're missin' all the fun up at the house."

"I see that."

Lisa's arm slipped around her shoulders. "You okay?"

"Yeah."

"You sure?"

"I just wanted a moment alone."

"Sorry."

"It's okay."

"I don't know why you want to come up here, this weekend of all weekends."

"It makes me feel closer to him." She hadn't told anyone about the ghost, not even her best friends. Or her parents. They dealt with Jonathan's death differently.

They'd stopped coming up here after that summer. Lauren half expected them to sell the cabin, but they hadn't. They just didn't use it anymore. It was like it didn't exist. Lauren tried, the first few years, to be with her parents on this day. Her father would spend the day out in his woodshop, sawing and drilling whatever project he had going on. Her mother, God, her mother just sat on the couch, television on, the vacant stare on her face indicative of the fact that she wasn't processing any of it.

"There's no wrong way," the grief counselor had said.

"Everybody does it differently, and you have to let them." Finally, her father suggested that maybe a visit on this day wasn't the best thing.

She wondered when Jonathan would show up. He'd appeared four years ago when there had been a crowd of people with her on the dock, and no one had reacted. That was the year she learned that she was the only one who could see him.

"Why don't you come up to the house? We wanna go watch the big fireworks show at Wilson Bend in about a half hour."

"Yeah, I'm going to take one more dip, then I'll be up."

"Okey dokey. I'll keep a 'rita cold for you." She stumbled up the path.

Lauren slid off the dock, back into the warm embrace of the water. She floated on her back again. Her mind wandered back to that day, ten years ago.

They'd come up to the cabin as they had every other year. She was twelve. Jonathan had been eighteen that year, had graduated from high school in Birmingham, and would be off to the University of Alabama in the fall. He'd brought Jerry and some girls with him that weekend.

Tall, lean, tan, blond Jerry. Lord, she'd had a crush on him, following her brother and his best friend around all summer like a lovesick puppy. Jonathan had suggested the boat ride and she eagerly joined them, anxious for any attention from Jerry.

She remembered the day in snapshots now, like a collection of photographs burned into her memory. It had been a beautiful day. She'd skied first, jumping the wake and slaloming, showing off. Jerry said she skied well and she beamed. The girls, lying on the bow of the boat in their bikinis. Jonathan. Tall, strong Jonathan, in his board shorts and a life jacket. He jumped overboard and Jerry pulled him up on one ski.

Jerry looked at her, uttered that fateful sentence. "You wanna drive?"

She'd been so eager to impress him. She nodded and stood in front of the wheel with him behind her watching Jonathan. She'd gone too fast and she knew it. She was driving recklessly. Too close to the rocks. Again, showing off.

Snapshots. Jerry screaming, "Stop!"

Turning and seeing Jonathan face down in the lake. That girl – what was her name? – Tina, screaming a high pitched scream. "Oh, my God! Oh, my God!"

The marine police. How had they gotten there? She couldn't remember. Her brother's body being pulled out of the lake. The ride with the police back to the cabin. They told her parents the news. A pervasive, hollow feeling in her stomach.

The funeral.

Jerry totally covered for her, telling her parents and the police that he was driving. She hadn't corrected him. Not once. She often wondered where he was today. He'd be twenty-eight. He was probably married with kids by now. She'd thought of contacting him this Fourth of July, too. Decided it was better to let the past stay in the past.

She treaded water. Reminded herself that Jonathan's death was instantaneous. He hadn't suffered. One blow to the head on the rocks had done it.

She floated on her back again. He was starting to appear, just as he did every year. It started with a thin, silver fog, like a haze over the water that congealed into a shape. His head, distinct and defined. And his torso, less defined, white. It didn't look like he was wearing a shirt, exactly. It looked kind of... ruffled, really. Or maybe furry.

She never saw his legs. His mouth was always moving, trying to tell her something, but she could never hear the message. This was her punishment, she decided, her torture for killing her brother.

He hovered ten feet or so over the water. She swam out to him, floating directly underneath him on her back. She'd never dared to get this close before.

She could see every detail of his face and it was just as she remembered. He'd been so handsome. What was he trying to say? She treaded water again, clearing her ears.

"What?" she asked aloud.

She heard his voice, in her head, clear as could be.

I forgive you.

She smiled. Tears pricked the back of her eyes and she sobbed, once. Her eyes filled and the tears spilled over, adding to the warmth of the lake.

I forgive you.

He smiled back at her, holding one of his white arms down toward her. She felt warm air brush her cheek, lightly.

She heard the door to the cabin slam again and Lisa shouted down, "Lauren? You all right? We're about ready to go!"

"Yeah, I'm all right!" she shouted back.

Jonathan's ghost nodded and smiled. He was fading, his face becoming more difficult to see, becoming a silver mist again. Then he was gone.

She sobbed a couple of times. Then she felt a strange peace within her that hadn't been there before. She stopped crying and splashed some water over her face to wash away the tears. He forgave her. It was time to forgive herself.

She made her way to the dock and dried off. Slipped a t-shirt and running shorts over her bathing suit. The key to the boat was in her pocket. She lowered the boat lift and her friends climbed aboard.

"You okay?" Rachel asked. "You look different."

"I'm great. Let's go see some fireworks."

Shades of History

Lin Nielsen

The smoky August night cried out for ghosts, and so did the Historic Huntsville Association. His boss had wanted him to lead a ghost tour, but Tommy Blevins didn't believe in spirits.

He felt a flutter of excitement as he looked over the heads of his little flock. "Welcome to the first ever Twickenham Evening Stroll. I'll be your guide tonight for a walk through the past."

Tommy stood on the weathered limestone mounting block in front of the Weeden House Museum. Half a dozen people had gathered for the tour. It was a small assembly but an enthusiastic one. They had all arrived in period costume.

A pair of young men wore buckskins and homespun shirts with powder horns slung over their shoulders. A man in a black frock coat and top hat squired a lady in a voluminous green hoop skirt. A more modestly dressed young woman wore a white bonnet trimmed extravagantly with lace. And there was the inevitable gentleman in the gray uniform of a Confederate officer. Huntsville had its share of serious re-enactors.

Of course there was always the possibility that his worthless cousin Daniel had put them up to it. Today was Tommy's birthday, and it was the kind of complicated joke Daniel loved.

"Let's get started." Tommy hopped down from the block and stooped to retrieve the old kerosene lantern supplied by the museum for atmosphere. "I'm sure you all know this is the Historic District. Twickenham was the name that Leroy Pope first gave the city, naming it for a town in England. Anti-British sentiment after the War of 1812 caused the change to Huntsville in honor of pioneer John Hunt."

Tommy led his group south. "Tonight we'll walk to McClung Street, up Echols Hill and down to Maple Hill Cemetery. That's about a half mile each way." He glanced doubtfully at the shoes of the ladies, which were more like slippers. "If you don't feel up to hiking that far, feel free to turn back at any time."

A contractor by profession, Tommy enjoyed volunteering at the Weeden House. The Blevins family were early settlers in the area. In fact, half of his ancestors were buried in Maple Hill. He'd been interested in local history since studying the Civil War in school. He'd given so many of the regular Saturday morning tours that he could have led a group in his sleep. Indeed, this August night had a dream-like quality with his group all in costume.

Tommy talked about the Weeden House, built in 1819, and about Maria Howard Weeden, famous local artist and poet whose books provided a colorful record of life after the Civil War. As they walked to the corner, the woman in green said, "I knew her, you know. Maria. Such fine person, so concerned with those below her station in life."

Tommy nodded and smiled, going along with her story. He knew re-enactors adopted a historical persona and tried to stay in character. At the end of Green Street, they crossed McClung. No traffic on this Saturday night. Tommy shepherded his group across the road to pause in front of a white-painted brick house.

"This is the Mastin House, built in 1823 and purchased by Captain Francis Mastin for his wife and four sons." A stone statue of a warrior clutching a shield regarded them sternly from the garden. "You can still see the bachelor's wing where the boys had their rooms."

The two young men in buckskins had been playfully bumping into each other as they crossed the road. Now the pair broke away from the group and strode up the walkway toward the house.

"Hey!" said Tommy. "Uh, they aren't expecting visitors. This is just a walking tour."

The larger boy waved over his shoulder. "Never you mind. We live here, that's all." They both sniggered like it was a joke. Two antique gaslights, flickering with period charm, lit the small front porch. For a moment the young men seemed to flicker too, passing into the house so quickly there hardly seemed time to open and close the door.

Tommy blinked. Odd. But he'd had stranger things happen on his tours, like the time a young woman did the Saturday stroll leading her llama.

He paused at the corner of McClung and Adams to point out the Leroy Pope house, huge white columns shining through the trees as the house tried to look over downtown. Tried, but didn't entirely succeed due to the Spite House on Lincoln Street, which had been built with 16-foot ceilings on every floor to spoil Pope's view of the city.

At the top of Echols Hill, the fashionably dressed couple bid the group good night and turned up the drive of the Patton House. That left Tommy with the Confederate officer and the young lady. But not for long. The gentleman said, "If you will excuse me, sir, ma'am,

I'm expected at the McClung House for dinner. It has been a most informative and pleasurable evening."

As Tommy shook the officer's proffered hand, he felt a coin pressed against his palm. "This isn't necessary. We aren't supposed to accept gratuities."

But the man merely tipped his hat to the lady and walked away.

Tommy felt suddenly awkward. His tour group had abandoned him, except for his one remaining charge. He smiled tentatively. "We can finish the tour by walking down to the cemetery, or we can go back to the Weeden House. Whatever you'd like to do."

The white bonnet obscured her face; only her mouth and chin were visible. A shy smile answered his. "If you please, I would like you to accompany me to Maple Hill."

Tommy held up the lantern and they strolled side by side. Nervous at having so intimate an audience, he chattered a steady stream of names, dates, and bits of local trivia. He talked about the famous people buried in Maple Hill Cemetery, including five Alabama governors and Mollie Teal, who had operated the town bordello but was well known for her philanthropy, donating her house of ill repute to be the city's first hospital.

They crossed Andrew Jackson Way at the stoplight. The cemetery sprawled to their left, tucked under a quilt of darkness. Here and there, a wink of lantern light bounced back from a polished tombstone. Flattered by the attention, Tommy could have talked all night to his pretty audience, but she reached to touch his elbow with a white gloved hand. Her bonnet brim tipped up, and he lifted the lantern so he could see her sweet face.

She said, "I've enjoyed the evening so much, Tommy. But my companions have all gone to their rest, and now it's time for me to seek mine."

"Don't you want me to take you back to your car?"

She shook her head. "That's not necessary. But I did want to wish you a happy birthday."

"How did you know it was my birthday?" he asked in surprise. Maybe Daniel was behind this after all.

"Your mother told me."

Tommy felt a shock like he'd burned himself on the lantern. "That's not funny. My mother's dead."

The young woman looked at him with sympathy. "We say 'passed on.' It doesn't sound so permanent that way."

"But how did you know it was my birthday? Did Daniel put you up to this?"

She smiled. "Cousin Daniel is a scamp, but this wasn't his doing. Your mother asked me to check on you. I am your great-grandmother after all." With those parting words she turned to walk through a break in the low stone wall around the cemetery and up the path into the dusk beneath the trees.

All he could think to say was, "Wait, you can't go in there. The cemetery closes at sundown."

She didn't answer. In fact, he didn't know where she'd gone. He might not have heard her footsteps because of her slippers, but the white bonnet should have been visible even in the heavy shadows draped between the old trees. He raised the lantern high to peer after her but found only darkness, silence, and peace.

Tommy set the lantern down carefully on the field stone wall and sat beside it. He would wait a few minutes to be sure the strange young woman didn't change her mind and return. He wondered who she really was. He wouldn't mind seeing her again.

Reaching into his pocket, he retrieved the coin the re-enactor had given him. Curious to know his own worth, he held it toward the light. A seated Lady Liberty shone crisp and bright on the face of the small silver coin. The date was 1858.

The lantern flame shivered in the night breeze.

Family Ties

Joan Kennedy

"*Keep her safe.*"

The words were spoken so softly Crystal Phillips wondered if she'd imagined them. She turned toward the other end of the hall, fanning the beam of her flashlight over the walls and floor.

"*She will die.*"

Crystal shivered as a chill crossed her cheek. This was all wrong. Her heart raced.

"Did you hear that?" she whispered.

"Hear what?" Rory Kelly's response wasn't a whisper. She lifted the flashlight to her shoulder and turned abruptly, smacking her petite friend on the head.

"Yow, Rory. Give us a warning here." As Crystal rubbed the spot, her short, black hair stood on end.

"Oops, sorry. What did you hear?"

"A voice. It said something like, 'Keep her safe.' Then something about dying."

"Keep who safe?"

"I don't know. It didn't say."

"Was it the ghost you saw in the bedroom?" Rory asked.

"No. That spirit is residual. It doesn't speak."

"How do you know that?"

"I've been seeing ghosts since I was three. Trust me." Crystal moved to the end of the hall where the voice originated. "Nothing. There's no one here."

"Did that ever happen before?"

"Yes, but it's different this time."

"Why?"

"I can't explain. Just different." She aimed her flashlight beam at Rory, whose blonde curls made it appear she was wearing a halo.

"Turn that off." Rory held up a hand to block the light. "Do we have to do this in the dark? I thought you could see ghosts during the day, too." She started toward the other end of the hall.

"Don't let her go."

Again Crystal played the beam of light over the walls behind her. "Tell me you heard that."

"Sorry. I didn't hear a thing."

"And there's nothing behind me?"

"I'm not the one who sees ghosts." Rory tried to hide her grin.

Crystal left the spirit at the other end of the hall and caught up with Rory. "Let's check the other bedrooms before the Stewarts get home. This invisible ghost is starting to creep me out."

Twenty minutes later they were downstairs turning on the lights as Trace Stewart pulled into the driveway. Winston Stewart, his wife, played the gracious Southern host by making sure everyone was comfortable in the family room before asking her youngest daughter, sixteen-year-old Connor, to help with refreshments.

"I hope sweet tea is fine," Winnie said as Connor set a tray of pecan mini-tarts on the coffee table. "I can make something stronger if you girls would like."

"Mama, sit," said seventeen-year-old Mallie. "I want to hear if we truly have ghosts living here with us."

Winnie gave Mallie's arm a gentle slap as she sat next to her. "Don't go spoiling your mama's fun, darlin'."

Both girls resembled their mother, tall and slim with long, blonde hair. They seemed to shift closer to her on the sofa at the mention of ghosts.

"The tea is delicious," Crystal said. "Tell me something about the history of your house. Do you know when it was built?" She popped a mini-tart into her mouth and closed her eyes a moment to savor the sweet, crunchy goodness.

Trace answered. "Around nineteen-twenty. For a banker. Forest Park was developed after the wealthy neighborhoods directly south of Birmingham. We've been here eight years. The house stood empty for a number of years after the previous owner's death. Some type of family dispute over a will."

Crystal gave Rory a long look.

"It took us a while to repair the damage before moving in. About a year, wasn't it?" he asked Winnie, who nodded.

"Did the construction involve a lot of work?" Crystal asked. "Tearing down walls and such?"

"Yes, it did."

"And when did you start to wonder if you had ghosts?"

"Not right away." Winnie looked at Trace. "Maybe three years or so after we moved in. But they've never been malicious or anything. We weren't even certain they were here or if we were imagining the whole thing. The girls had been watching a slew of paranormal shows with their friends at the time."

"The ghosts are here," Crystal said, "and you're right, they're not malicious. I've found three so far, what we call residual ghosts. They're spirits of people who once occupied this space, kind of semi-material forms who don't realize they're dead and don't realize you exist. They simply go through the motions they did while alive. If you can't see them, you might be able to feel their energy, but they do absolutely no harm." She offered a smile to show how safe everyone was, then prepared to tell another white lie to reinforce their comfort. "I saw all three in the upstairs bedrooms, which makes sense since it's the time they would have been getting ready for bed." The lie. They never got ready for bed. "If you feel uncomfortable having the ghosts here, I can get someone to perform a simple ritual to help them move on."

"What kind of ritual?" Trace asked.

"If you're religious, we can get a priest or pastor from your church. I've found that most are willing to help. If you're not, there are other ways to deal with the problem."

"If they're not dangerous," Connor said, "I don't mind having the ghosts here. I mean, now that we know they won't hurt us. They never really bothered me. Mallie? How about you?"

It appeared Mallie wasn't as comfortable with the idea as her younger sister, and took a long moment to answer. "I guess so." The look she gave Winnie seemed unsettled.

"Mallie's the one who suggested we get someone to check the house," Winnie said. "She felt a bit uneasy with the idea of ghosts."

"Have you had any experiences with them?" Rory asked.

Mallie squeezed her hands together until the fingers were almost white. "I kind of felt like someone was here, but they never did anything, you know, bad."

Crystal patted her arm, then said to the others, "How about this.

Let me see if we can bring in a paranormal investigator who uses special equipment. It might put your minds at ease. If you still feel uncomfortable, Mallie, we can try to get the ghosts to leave."

They agreed to the plan.

"Has anyone else had encounters?" Crystal asked.

"Just a feeling we were sharing the house with someone we couldn't see." Trace said. "When could you come back?"

"It'll take several days to find someone in the area." Crystal deferred to Rory.

"As I explained earlier, Crystal came here from Connecticut at my invitation. I'm familiar with her reputation for finding ghosts because we grew up together. She doesn't use technology, you know, cameras and recorders. So I'll either get in touch with someone local who does paranormal investigations, or we can call in someone she's worked with before."

"One more question," Crystal said. "Are any of you planning to go out of town anytime soon? So we can schedule a return visit," she added.

"No vacations, if that's what you mean," Winnie said. "School's starting soon. Mallie's going camping in North Carolina next week with some friends, but that's it for travel in our immediate future."

As they were leaving, Crystal noticed a framed family portrait on a side table. She picked it up. "Do you have three girls?" she asked Winnie.

"Yes. Our oldest, Jameison, is in college. She's studying abroad this summer, but will be home in a few weeks. She'll be a junior at Sewanee this fall."

Crystal set the photo on the table. A chill slipped down her back.

On the way to the car, she whispered to Rory, "I don't know how you can live down here. It's nine-thirty at night and has got to be over eighty-five degrees."

Rory chuckled. "And the humidity is probably the same. Don't worry, you get used to it."

"I'm not planning to stay long enough. Turn up the air," Crystal whined.

She clipped on her seat belt and studied the house as Rory backed out. It was a large two-story in the arts and crafts style, tucked on a slope at the foot of Red Mountain. A wide porch faced in river rock ran the length of the facade. It overlooked the street with a partial view of the residential neighborhood below.

"It's a wonderful house," she said to Rory. "I had no idea Birmingham was so beautiful."

Rory's apartment was on Southside, the neighborhood adjacent to Forest Park. As they drove, Crystal said, "Do you know any paranormal investigators?"

"I thought maybe we should call Brian McKenzie."

Crystal huffed. "Not Brian. He's in Connecticut. We need someone fast."

"You told me he's really good. Has all that fancy equipment, plus experience in forensics."

"Rory, we work together. I don't want to be the topic of conversation around the water cooler. Besides, he's just a kid."

"Five years younger doesn't make him a kid." The grin disappeared when she glanced at Crystal. "Okay, I'll ask around tomorrow, see if I can find someone local."

Crystal laced her hands together and squeezed tight. She realized the action mirrored Mallie's and forced herself to relax. Rory hadn't missed it.

"I'm guessing you didn't ask the Stewarts about their vacation plans just to set up another visit." Rory studied her a moment.

"You're really upset about that voice, aren't you? What makes it different from the other times this happened?"

"That's why I'm worried. I can't figure out why."

"Do you think whoever it is could hurt us or the family?"

Crystal knew that many people considered her crazy because she claimed to see ghosts. Probably a majority, if hands were counted. She decided not to treat the question as lightly as she normally would.

"In all the years I've seen ghosts, I've never been able to verify a single instance where they actually harmed anyone. I know a lot of people claim this happens, but there's never any real scientific proof. I'm not saying those people are lying, just that I've never seen a spirit attack a person."

"So why are you worried?"

"The voice sounded desperate. It was a warning. I'm worried about who's in danger, and even more, what that danger is. We have to find out, or I think something terrible will happen."

Rory worked at an art gallery, and Saturday morning Crystal dropped her off and took the car. With Rory's directions and the GPS, she went downtown to the library to research the Stewart house. The Archives were in the old library, across the street from the new, modern building. She was soon seated at a table studying the history department's wonderful old murals, while a reference librarian first checked the computer for details, then searched the shelves for old records.

As he set the ledgers down, Crystal took out a pen and paper. "How does it feel to be named after a president?"

Zach Taylor smiled. "I'm named after my Granddad. The rest is just coincidence."

He opened the first book to a section marked with a small piece of notepaper. "We have most of this on computer, but I thought you might like to see the original records." He ran his finger down the page. "Here we are. For the year 1924, we see the property was owned by Mr. Phillip Wheaton. His occupation is listed as banker."

He set the deed records aside. "I then went to the census for 1930 to find the family. Oddly, it listed Wheaton and two grown sons at this address. I wondered why he would have such a large house for three men, especially when two would probably be on their own soon." Zach opened the book listing the census records. "So I went back to 1920 to find Wheaton, and discovered there were twice as many family members. He also had a wife and two younger daughters."

"This doesn't sound like it has a happy ending," Crystal said.

"I'm afraid not." He set aside the census records and opened the last book on the table. "This lists births and deaths for that period, and shows that in 1928 Mary Wheaton and her two daughters, Elizabeth and Dorothy, all died within a short period of time. Several days. The cause was said to be food poisoning." Zach moved the book closer so Crystal could see the entry. "I'm afraid it happened more often than people realize. There was an obituary. It's on microfilm if you'd like to see the story. Or I can print out a copy, if you'd like."

"I'd appreciate that."

Crystal paid the nominal fee, thanked Zach for his help, and picked Rory up at six.

"I found out who the ghosts are," she said, then explained about the deaths. "I have the obituary. The father was at a business dinner that night. The sons were at University in Tuscaloosa. I can't

175

imagine how awful it must have been for them."

When Rory finished reading the article, Crystal said, "Did you find someone to help with the investigation?"

"Yes, but not anyone close to Birmingham. They're flying in tomorrow afternoon. And I talked to Trace, so we're all set for tomorrow night."

The art gallery was closed Sundays and Mondays, so after a late Sunday lunch, Rory and Crystal headed to the airport. Rory pulled to the curb on the lower level of the terminal.

Crystal shot up in the seat, her eyes on a tall, wiry figure. He spotted the car and waved.

"How could you do this, Rory?" Crystal said. "I told you I didn't want Brian involved."

"I tried to find someone local. Honest. No one was available. We needed someone fast. Brian was happy to come."

Crystal narrowed her eyes. "I just bet he was. Everyone at work is going to hear about this, and no one will believe he came just to hunt ghosts. You owe me, Rory. You owe me big time."

She jumped out and ran over to grab Brian's duffle, figuring it was the lightest of the three bags. The cases full of camera equipment had to be heavier. Before she could pick it up, Brian reached down from his six-foot-four height, wrapped his arms around her waist, and swung Crystal off her feet and in a circle.

"You are the best. I don't know how to thank you for bringing me to Alabama for this investigation. It's my first time here. Yow, it's hot."

He set her down, but not before she spotted Rory, her cell held high as she snapped a final photo of Crystal flying through the air in

Brian's arms. Rory grinned and waved, then jumped back in the car. Crystal dumped the duffle into the open trunk, followed by Brian with his cases. He reached for the back door.

"My seat." Crystal slid in before he could. "You sit in front. I am not having another argument about this, Brian. Get in, or get left behind." She slammed the door shut.

Rory gave him a quick hug before putting the car in gear.

"We'll drop your things off at Rory's place, then grab something to eat," Crystal said. "We can fill you in on the case over dinner."

Brian must have noticed the edge in her voice. He said to Rory, "If it's too much trouble, I can stay at a motel."

"It's not a problem," Crystal cut in.

"Is he allowed to decide what to eat for dinner?" Rory asked through a crooked grin.

Crystal's wasn't nearly as friendly. "You are on thin ice, girlfriend," she whispered.

Rory agreed to help with the cameras. She'd taken photography in college, and Brian felt she could easily adjust to the differences in the paranormal equipment. During the discussion, they went over the historical material and the disembodied voice.

"You've heard those before," Brian said. "What's the big deal?"

"I can't explain. I'm just worried. I hope you can catch some images."

The Stewarts had made plans for dinner and Trace left a number where they could be reached when the investigation was over. As the family was leaving, Crystal spotted a portrait of them hanging in the front hall. She hadn't noticed it before, and stopped Trace and Winnie at the door.

"I'm sorry to bother you about this, but why are there four girls in this picture?"

The Stewarts glanced briefly at one another before Trace answered. "It was taken a number of years ago. Over six, at least. The fourth child was our oldest daughter, Ashleigh. She was killed in an accident just before graduating from high school." Trace put his arm around Winnie's shoulder and squeezed. It was clear how deeply they still felt the loss.

After the door closed, Crystal scrutinized the photograph. Rory came up behind her.

"She takes after Trace," Rory said. "The other girls all have blonde hair like their mother, but Ashleigh's is dark brown. How awful it must be to lose a child."

Crystal's smile was warm. "Or a mother. At least we know your mom is at peace."

"I just hope we can do the same for the Stewarts." Rory stood silently as she studied the family, then turned and said, "Brian's busy setting up his equipment. I have to say, I'm impressed. He knows what to do with it, doesn't he?"

"Oh, he does, I guarantee. He keeps trying to teach me."

"And I can tell from that look of disgust just how much you want to learn." Rory's grin was huge. She slipped her arm through Crystal's and started toward the stairs.

Crystal leaned close and whispered, "If one, just one, of those pictures you took at the airport shows up on any cell phone within a hundred miles of Newtown, Connecticut, I'm calling up every ghost I've ever met to haunt you for eternity."

They took Brian on a quick walk-through of the house before going 'lights out.' Crystal saw a ghost of one of the Wheaton children in an upstairs bedroom and asked Brian to keep a special watch for any others on his equipment. This time she held one of Brian's night vision scopes so she could see where they were going in the dark without a flashlight. Rory had a recorder to pick up any voices, both those they heard and those they didn't, a full-spectrum camcorder, and a night vision camera.

Brian looked like a display at a paranormal technology store. His equipment included several meters that recorded changes in temperature and electrical energy, and the camera Rory coveted: a thermal imaging recorder that showed temperature fluctuations in a rainbow of colors. The heat signatures often disclosed spirits that were invisible to the naked eye.

"This is so cool," Rory said for the umpeenth time.

Crystal was already exhausted from listening to the comments. She backhanded Rory's arm. "Shut it or you're out of here."

Fifteen minutes into the investigation, Crystal suddenly stopped in the dining room. "Shhh. I heard something." She looked at Rory. "Make sure your EVP is on."

"The voice recorder thing?"

Brian looked over her shoulder to check the equipment, then gave Crystal a thumbs up. He focused the thermal imaging camera on Crystal, scanned the area around her, then the room. He shook his head.

Crystal listened intently. "It was the same voice, same message. 'Keep her safe.' Make sure all the equipment is running, including the K-2. Brian, set that on the table so we can catch any energy, and let's do an EVP session."

"Whoever is with us, please make yourself known," Brian said. "Crystal can hear you, but we need to see you too. You can make the lights on this meter turn on if you're with us. Can you do that now?"

All three stood perfectly still, their eyes on the K-2. Rory gasped as the lights flickered in an arc at the top of the meter.

"Are you a woman?" Brian asked. "If you are, make the lights blink once. If not, make them blink twice."

Again they waited, not breathing. Again the lights blinked, just once.

"Are you Ashleigh Stewart?" Crystal asked. "Once if you are, twice if not."

The wait this time seemed interminable. The meter blinked twice.

"Shoot," Crystal whispered, then said, "Are you one of the spirits from the Wheaton family?"

The lights stayed dark.

"If you are Mrs. Wheaton or one of her children, make the lights blink once," Brian said. "If not, blink twice."

Again the meter stayed dark.

"Whoever it was is gone," Crystal said. "I can feel it. The air is different."

"How can you do that?" Rory asked. "Teach me how to do that."

"Just hang around," Brian said. "It'll happen."

"This is so cool," Rory whispered, then yelped as Crystal stepped on her foot.

"Let's go upstairs," Crystal said. She grabbed the K-2. "Our chances might be better up there."

They took twenty minutes to go through the four bedrooms. Crystal spotted the residual ghosts as she had before, and asked Brian and Rory to scan and record everything.

"Okay, I'm still not hearing the voice," she finally said. "Let's stay in the hall for a while. That's where I heard it the last time."

It was a center hallway that ran from one side of the house to the other. The stairs were near the middle, and Crystal stationed herself there. She directed Rory to the far end near the Stewarts' master bedroom, and Brian to the other end. She wanted him in the same place she was standing when she'd first heard the voice.

"I'm not sure this will work," she said, "or how long it will take. But based on what Trace told us, we still have two hours. You up for this?"

Both agreed they were.

"Let's try another EVP session, but make sure all the cameras are running." She sat cross-legged on the floor, with a view to either end of the hall.

"I want to talk to the person who spoke to me Friday. I have to know who's in danger and what that danger is. Please use all the energy you can to communicate with us. If you're still here, please speak or light up the meter on the floor next to me."

They waited in vain for several minutes. Crystal knew it often took time for a ghost to generate enough energy to respond, and she was patient.

"Please let me help. You sounded so desperate. Who's in danger? Are you with us? We will not harm you."

"How–"

"Shh." Crystal held up her hand to silence Rory.

The lights on the K-2 blinked.

"Who is in danger?" Crystal said. "Is it Jamie? Light the meter once for yes, twice for no."

"Who's Jamie?" Brian whispered from the end of the hall.

Crystal waved her hand frantically to keep him quiet. The meter had gone off and she was waiting to see if it would go off again. It did.

"Jamie is the oldest daughter. The one studying in Europe. She's due back home in a week or so. You remember the others, right?"

"Connor's the youngest," Brian said. "Mallie's the one who's afraid of ghosts."

"Good. Any more questions?" Crystal asked. "Okay. Please hold further questions until we're done." She adjusted the placement of the K-2.

"So Jamie's not in danger," she said. "Is it Connor? Once for yes, twice for no."

It took a bit longer this time, but again the meter lit up twice.

"Is it Mallie?"

A sense of unease enveloped Crystal. The meter went off once.

"Oh, my God," Rory whispered.

"Now we know why she's afraid of ghosts," Brian said quietly.

"Y'all are going to have to be quiet," Crystal said.

"Wow, Crystal. Y'all? You've been in Alabama too long."

"Brian, shut up."

Crystal waited until everyone was still before going on. "Are you Ashleigh?"

The meter stayed dark.

"See what you did, Brian," Rory whispered. "Now she's gone."

"If you two don't stop talking, I'm turning on the lights." Crystal closed her eyes. "I heard your voice when we were here before. Can you speak to me like you did the last time?"

"I feel something," Brian whispered, then grew silent.

"Is Mallie in danger?" Crystal asked again. "Either tell me or light the meter."

"*Yes.*"

Brian moved the focus on the thermal, aiming it directly at Crystal.

"Is it the camping trip? Will she be in danger on the camping trip to North Carolina?"

182

Crystal's heart raced. She took a deep breath to calm her nerves. There was no response.

"We can wait. We're here to help Mallie. Take the time you need. Is it the camping trip?"

The meter started going crazy, the entire row of lights flashing.

"Help her. No trip."

"The EMF is going nuts," Brian said softly. "Readings went from point-oh-one up to five. Holding steady."

"I'm getting some variations on the full-spectrum camera," Rory said from her end of the hall. "I don't understand them, but I'm recording."

"I'm freezing," Brian said. He checked the temperature. "I'm down to sixty degrees."

"We have two other spirits with us," Crystal said. "They may have been disturbed by the activity out here. It's the two Wheaton children."

The three ghost hunters remained calm, waiting to see what would happen. After a minute, Brian reported that the temperature was rising.

"Ashleigh? Are you still with us?" Crystal waited for a response. "Can you light the meter? Speak to me?"

She heard a giggle. "Is that Elizabeth? I hear you laughing. Can you speak to us?"

"One of the Wheaton kids?" Rory whispered.

Crystal nodded, a finger to her lips. "Ashleigh, please talk to me. Can you tell us any more about Mallie?"

"Temp is back to normal," Brian whispered.

Everything was quiet.

"The children are gone," Crystal said.

She waited another minute before saying, "Is anyone else in the family in danger?" then held up her hand to keep the others from speaking. "Once for yes, twice for no."

Again it was over a minute before the meter lit up. Twice.

"Am I talking to Ashleigh?"

They waited patiently to no avail.

"Please let me know so your family won't worry."

After three minutes, Crystal asked once more.

Brian waited two more minutes before saying, "She's gone."

"How do you know?" Rory asked. "We still have time. The Stewarts will wait another hour."

"Brian's right. She's gone. I say we wrap." Crystal stood and reached for the light switch.

"Darn, I'm not ready to quit," Rory said. She shielded her eyes against the light. "That was awesome."

Crystal grinned. "I can't believe you said awesome."

Rory gave Crystal's shoulders a squeeze. "Thanks for including me. I might have to start my own paranormal group. Brain, you can teach me how to do this."

"I have to go over all the evidence tomorrow. You can help me do that."

"Better you than me," Crystal said under her breath.

Rory called Trace to let them know the investigation was over. They could have their house back. Before leaving, Crystal told the Stewarts they had to review the evidence, but would stop by Monday evening with the findings. She wanted to add that there were no concerns, but after the encounter with Ashleigh, she wasn't so sure.

At the door, Mallie stopped Crystal and glanced around to make sure her parents weren't listening. "I didn't want to say anything before, but it's like I can feel someone near, hear a voice. Only I can't make out the words."

Crystal took Mallie's hand. "Don't worry. We'll figure this out. You'll be okay."

Rory was eager to go over all the evidence on Monday. Right after breakfast, Brian set up the equipment on the dining room table and closed the drapes. Crystal wanted no part in it, and was told if she wanted to watch TV, she'd have to do it in Rory's room with the doors shut.

The investigation had lasted only two hours, but they had to review material on three cameras and the voice recorder. The fact that it was Rory's first time meant the job took most of the day. After a late lunch, Brian collected the information they would show the Stewarts, including several images of the residual spirits that were brief and hazy, but Brian felt the Stewarts would find them interesting. Most of the encounters with the ghost who spoke had taken place in the hallway and held more detail. All the evidence could be condensed into a fifteen-minute presentation. At four, Crystal sat down with the others to double-check the material and edit anything she thought would be unnecessary. That's when she spotted the anomaly.

"Brian, look at the images Rory recorded on the full-spectrum camera."

He scooted his chair next to hers. "What am I looking for?"

"Remember when we had the highest activity? When I heard the voice? Look right here." She pointed to the left side of the monitor. "Can you see a figure?"

"Yes, I marked that specifically so we could show it to the Stewarts."

"I don't think we want to show the Stewarts this. Take a good look and tell me why."

He played a loop highlighting the image. It was faint, but clearly depicted a contemporary young woman, not one of the Wheaton spirits.

"I don't get what's wrong. We all think this is Ashleigh, the daughter who was killed in that car accident."

"Look again. Tell me why you two think this is Ashleigh."

Rory came over to peek at the screen from behind Crystal's chair. "What are you talking about? It looks just like that portrait we saw last night."

"Brian, what color is Ashleigh's hair?" Crystal asked.

"Blonde. They're all blondes."

"No they're not. Look right there." Rory pointed at the figure. "See the blonde hair? I know it looks pale on the computer, but that's because it's like a black and white negative. Her hair looks light on the screen because it's a reverse of her dark brown hair in real life."

"Oh, my mother's bloomers," Brian said softly.

Both women rolled their eyes.

"Tell Rory what's wrong, Brian," Crystal said.

"Cloth changes color, which is why your black shirt looks white, but hair color doesn't change on these cameras. Not that much. This woman had pale blonde hair when she was alive, just like we see here. Which means, if Ashleigh had dark brown hair, it couldn't have been her. Then who else could it be?"

"I have no idea," Crystal said. "But I don't want to show this to the Stewarts. Winnie said the girls love to watch those paranormal investigation shows. They could easily spot this. We don't want that to happen until we know exactly who this person is. Did you get anything on the EVP?"

"Sure did. It's not real clear, like we can recognize the voice or anything, but might be clear enough for them to believe there's a warning for Mallie. Let me edit everything down so I can make them a copy of the voices and images without the one in question."

The meeting with the family went better than Crystal anticipated. At first the Stewarts questioned the warning that Mallie could be in danger, but when she took the words to heart, especially after hearing the voice recorder, they agreed it would be best for her to rethink the trip.

Crystal and Rory did some discreet questioning about other friends and family who might have passed away over the last ten years, but the Stewarts had no answers. None of the women in their extended family, including aunts, cousins, and grandmothers, had died recently, only a friend of Ashleigh's who had been in the same car accident. Crystal let it drop.

The Stewarts were comfortable with the results and were happy to have a copy of the prominent events of the investigation. Mallie seemed to take the news best, and was the first to say she would not be going camping with her friends. The three ghost hunters decided there was nothing more they could do to identify the elusive spirit.

A week later, after Crystal had returned home, she got a call from Rory.

"I didn't believe in ghosts before you came to Birmingham to investigate the Stewart house. Now I'm a firm believer. I'm just sorry it had to happen this way. Those friends of Mallie's who went camping? There was a rafting accident. Two of them were killed."

Crystal felt as though the air had been punched from her lungs. She fell into a nearby chair. "How awful. I can't believe that. We were right. She was in danger."

"That's not all."

Rory was quiet for so long, Crystal asked if she was still there.

"Did you hear about the plane crash in France yesterday?"

"No. Don't tell me that, Rory. Don't tell me."

"Jamie was on that plane. It wasn't Ashleigh who was trying to warn us about Mallie. It was Jamie. Crystal, I don't understand. She was still alive when we were at the house. It couldn't have been her."

Crystal used her fingertips to squeeze the tears away. "I should have seen it. Especially after reviewing the images on the computer."

"Why didn't she just call to warn Mallie?" Rory said, her voice husky. "Why did she get on the plane?"

"Don't you see? Jamie didn't know. It was her spirit. Her spirit warned them."

"How can that happen? Have you ever seen live ghosts?"

"No, not before that day. The phenomenon has to do with energy and intense emotions. You know why she had to do it?"

Crystal heard the sorrow in Rory's voice. "So they wouldn't lose three children."

"She's the one we saw at the Stewart house, Rory. Anything's possible when strong family ties are involved. Family ties and the power of love."

The Exorcism of Mary's House

Jessica Penot

It was just one of those ordinary houses, nothing but brown bricks stacked up with a couple of pink flamingos stuck in the azalea bushes. The yard was neat, but not special. I didn't think much of it. I don't think anyone would. It was my sister who really brought it to life. I mean, I knew it was haunted. I saw the ghost in the bathtub clear as day, but I knew that the ghost didn't care about me. I knew that there was nothing to be afraid of.

I was sitting out in the woods that day, on a rock, smoking. I didn't really like to smoke; I just liked the idea of fire in my lungs. I felt like I could become something mythical by exhaling it. I had pulled my sleeves up, temporarily letting down my guard to reveal the rows of shallow cuts that went up and down my arms.

My mom always asked me why I cut myself, but I didn't really know. I liked the feel of the metal. I liked to feel awake. Most of the time I felt like a ghost drifting through life, half awake, but when the blood bubbled up I felt like I was human, not just a shadow.

I had to hide the cuts most of the time, but in the woods I was free to be myself. My mom had been calling me home for at least an hour, but I had a good lie so I lingered. I embraced the moment and the peace it brought, surrounded by the soft summer flowers and green grass.

When I walked into my house, I was accosted by the warm smell of food and the melodic sound of my older sister's voice. My sister was beautiful, but broken. She was nothing but a little bit of flesh stretched over bone. After every meal, she would retire to the bathroom to vomit. We ignored this, not because we didn't care, but because Mom had already fought the battle for Alia and lost. She had already sent her to every psych hospital there was, and Alia had made it through them all, unaltered and eternally rebellious. Her eyes were large, glowing orbs in the thin mix of bony angles that was her face. She grabbed my shoulder and pulled me downstairs.

"So, spill it. You went to a haunted house?"

I had to stop and think. The house hadn't really made much of an impression, but I liked my sister paying attention to me. My sister was cool. It made my mom mad that I thought so, that I cared more about what Alia thought than what she did. Long before my mom had found Jesus, she'd named Alia after a witch from some sci-fi novel I would never read. Alia was proud of it. She loved her name.

Alia was a writer. She wandered the country gathering up stories and selling them to whoever would have them. She especially liked murder and ghost stories. Alia never brought boyfriends home, but the one man she did bring home talked to me for a long time. He asked personal questions about her and asked me how he could keep her. I shrugged. What the hell did I know? I will always remember what he said about her. He said she was a devil, a god, the queen. I had smiled longingly. That is what I always think of her as. She is the devil, a god, the queen.

"Oh, you're talking about Mary's house, right?" I answered

"So what did you see? Did you spend the night there?"

"Yeah," I said eagerly. "That place is filled with ghosts. Mary doesn't like us to pay attention to them because she says that makes them mad, but you have to look because they're everywhere."

Alia smiled. Her angular face lit up with shadow and light. She was excited in a way that I had rarely seen. Usually there was a coolness about Alia. She hid her emotion in layers of sarcasm and ambivalence.

"They throw stuff at Mary, like spoons and crap, and if you take a camera in the house and take a picture of anything in there, they are always there. Every single time. I have pictures of them."

Alia put her hand on my shoulder. Her smile faded a little, but the light was still there. "Can I see them?"

I nodded and we walked down the hall.

When Alia left home, I'd taken over her room. There were some of Alia's old paintings from art class on the wall. I could stare at them for hours. They were images of nude women melting into the ground or fading into the fog of starlit nights. The women seemed happy. They leaned into their own destruction. Old books on demons and monsters cluttered the bookshelves, and scarves and bits of saris hung from every blank section of wall. There was a huge Mayan rug on the floor that Alia had picked up at some flea market. She made candle holders out of plastic skulls and red wax dripped down, giving them a morbid fascination. The room spoke to me of everything I found wonderful and mysterious about Alia. It spoke to me about a world I would never know.

"You haven't changed anything," Alia said when she followed me in.

"I like it the way it is," I answered.

Alia looked around for a while as I dug through my underwear drawer, trying to find the photographs Alia wanted. My mother's voice drifted down the stairs, crescendoing in a kind of desperate plea. Dinner was ready. Alia didn't even move. She had always been immune to any kind of desire to please our mother. Most of the time, it seemed like Alia was in another world altogether.

"Here they are," I said, handing Alia the photographs. Alia looked through the stack slowly, taking her time with each one. There were tears in her eyes by the time she reached the end.

"All these years," she whispered. "I've looked for them and they were right next door."

"Who?"

Alia ignored me. The evening light filtered in through the drapes, painting Alia's face in a soft purple light. She was so beautiful it left me breathless. She was almost too beautiful. There was something unnatural in her loveliness.

"Tell me about them?" Alia asked.

"I saw a girl and an old man," I said. "Mary says that the girl always used to sit just on the third stair, but after her aunt performed an exorcism the girl is everyplace and the ghosts hate it when you take their pictures. Mary says that they just sit and stare at her all night when she does that, and then she can't sleep."

Alia was enraptured. Our mother called for us again, but Alia continued to ignore her.

"Where have you been?" I asked.

"Europe," Alia answered. I noticed her back. It was covered in black tattoos I hadn't seen on her last visit. I struggled to understand them, but they were written in a language I had never seen.

"What do the ghosts look like? Do they look like these photos? They just look like dark fog in the photos. Is that all they are?"

"No. They don't look like ghosts," I said. "You know how in the movies they're all wispy and, like, torn up and hard to see? In the

192

photographs they're just black, but these ghosts are just like us. They're like people that walk around the house."

"Why doesn't Mary's family move?"

"Because Mary's dad is a complete jerk. He yells at the ghosts and tells them to go away and Mary's mom pretends they aren't there."

"Did someone die in the house?"

"No," I said. "I knew the guy that lived there before and there was nothing in the house before Mary lived there. This guy never saw the ghosts and the house that Mary lived in before was haunted too."

"Can we go there?" Alia asked.

"Mom doesn't like me going over there anymore. She says Mary is a bad influence."

Alia put her hand on my shoulder. Her eyes were so green I felt like I was still in the woods looking at the grass.

"Don't you know that Mom is nothing but an obstacle?" Alia said. "There is an entire world out there that she has spent her life hiding from. She wants us to hide from it too, because she is afraid. Don't hide. There is too much wonder in the world and it will all be lost if you hide."

"I've never seen any wonder," I answered.

"Not yet," Alia said. "But I can show you wonder if you come with me. Forget Mom. Forget the rules."

"Do you mean just tonight?" I asked. "Or can I go with you when you leave?" I was suddenly a little afraid of both options, even though I wanted them both desperately. I wanted to go to Europe and Mexico and chase ghosts and old stories riddled with darkness. I wanted to find wonder.

I could hear Mom stomping down the stairs. Alia got up and

locked the door. She pushed her back against it, shutting my mother from the room.

"Take me to Mary's house and I'll take you with me back to France when I leave."

"I don't have any money," I said.

"Money isn't a problem,"

"Do your stories really make that much?"

"I don't get my money from stories."

"Where do you get it?"

A shadow passed over Alia's face. "Do you want to come with me? Do you want to get away from this place? I'll show you the world, but you can't ask me questions. Will you take me to Mary's house?"

"OK," I said. "Let's go."

We had to sneak out. We waited until Tuesday when we knew Mary's parents were gone, and we got Mary to let us in by asking her for the clothes I had lent her. She let us in sullenly. Mary always looked sulky. She was fat, orca fat, and she always wore black. Her hair was short and her skin was sallow. Mostly, I felt sorry for her.

Alia pushed her way past Mary without as much as a 'hello' and walked into the house like it was hers. She went right up into the living room and took out an old Milton Bradley Ouija board. She told me to come over and we sat down and began our work.

Mary yelled at us in dismay. She told us that the ghosts would get angry, and she put on some elaborate dance that involved shrieking and cursing. I started talking over her, trying to convince her that it would be really cool if Alia published a story about her house. I used everything I had over Mary's head to get her to shut up, and finally she did and sat down next to us. Alia continued setting up her board as if Mary wasn't there.

I wasn't afraid when the little girl walked in. Alia smiled. The girl was young, maybe five or six, wearing a pink t-shirt and dirty old jeans. Her hair was blonde and tied back neatly in a pony tail. She sat down next to us and watched what we were doing. The old man came in too. He sat on the couch, lit his pipe, and smiled at me, showing his yellowed teeth. Mary shuddered and drew her knees up under her chin.

"Why are you here?" Alia asked the girl.

The lights began to flicker and finally went off. The oddest clicking noise filled the room. Mary rustled around in her little brother's toy box and yanked out a cow-shaped flashlight that let out a distinct "MOO" as illumination splashed from its mouth.

I laughed, but the laughter was supplanted by muffled gasps. The room was filled with little girls in pink shirts and blue jeans. They surrounded us and filled the gaps between us. If they had been tangible, I would have felt their tiny feet on mine. Alia stood in the light and turned around in wonder. She smiled and put her hand over her mouth in genuine delight. The flashlight mooed again in some preprogrammed echo.

Alia tried to touch one of the girls' cheeks, but her hand passed through it. "What are you?" she whispered. There was no answer, only an increase in the resonant clicking that now began to fill the house.

I pretended I wasn't afraid. I laughed again, but the little girls were staring at me with their sublime blue eyes. I could feel them burning through me, like the cigarette smoke had before, or like the tip of a knife. I caught my breath as the cow flashlight mooed again.

Alia moved through the crowd of girls and finally knelt at the old man's feet. She looked into his smoky eyes and tried one last time. "What are you?"

"We are gods, the devil, the emperors," he answered.

"I knew it," she whispered. "I've been looking for you."

She leaned over and placed her hand on his leg. He smiled and she crept up towards him, placing her lips gently on his. He placed his hand on her cheek, in the gentlest gesture imaginable, and ran his fingers through her raven hair.

Her kiss transformed him. Time melted away and his skin became young and smooth. The pock marks of age disappeared, leaving the most brilliant man I had ever seen up close. The lovers embraced and we sat in an ocean of pink clad girls, listening to the ever mooing cow, while the two collapsed into each other. It seemed like forever before they stopped.

She smiled as he transformed again. She held the beast that devoured her warmly as he killed her. He ripped her apart, until my sister was nothing but a shred of fabric and a piece of hair on the floor.

The two of us stood petrified. We were rooted to the ground. I could hear only the pounding of my heart. It was Mary who whispered, "Run. If we don't run, they will kill us."

We ran out onto the front yard, collapsed in the soft, summer grass, and screamed. We sat there for a long time staring at my sister's car, wondering what had happened.

No one believed us, of course. When Alia's mutilated body was found days later in a dumpster, everyone assumed she was killed by some drug dealer. They thought we had probably seen it and made up this weird story to protect her or us or some combination of the two. My family mourned Alia. My mother wept and wondered why she could never save her. My father said very little.

It's funny to me that the ghosts no longer haunt Mary's house. It's quiet now and Mary can finally sleep in peace. She's lost weight, and her skin has a deep tan that always makes me think of summer.

I feel better too. I sleep well. The smoke has left my lungs and I don't need to cut my arms. I know that I am human. I know that I can feel.

The Ghost of Bear Creek Swamp

Tracy Williams

It was late August in 1983, the summer before my second year of college. I, along with several of my friends, had planned a final weekend at the lake before settling into the long school year ahead. The others had gone earlier in the day, but since my boyfriend Steve had to work, I stayed behind to keep him company on the drive. He arrived around six on Friday evening and informed me that he wanted to make a quick stop first.

"I have to get this assignment done before Monday." Steve was the only one of us who had decided to take a summer college course, and since he was working at Wolfe Camera, he'd chosen a basic photography class. "If I take the pictures today, we can enjoy the rest of the weekend."

"Okay," I said, looking at my watch, "but let's hurry. I'd like to get up to the lake in time to eat dinner with the others."

He nodded. "It shouldn't take too long."

Fifteen minutes later we turned off the highway and stopped. Ahead of us, the red dirt road disappeared between rows of huge, old oaks covered with Spanish moss and kudzu.

"Where are we?" I asked, glancing around.

"Bear Creek Swamp," he replied.

I turned to look at him with an arched brow. "You're taking pictures here?"

The swamp was a well known local attraction for paranormal events, something that most people either found intriguing or frightening. Since I wasn't prone to believe in the supernatural, I found it neither – at least not for that particular reason. The swamp was also known to have an unusually high number of snakes, lizards, and various other scary creatures. It was the thought of the reptiles that made me shiver.

"Why in the world would you pick this place?" I asked as I stared nervously out the windshield. At seven o'clock in the evening there was still plenty of sunlight, but even so, the road beyond the trees was foreboding.

Steve chuckled. "Don't worry. I think the ghosts only come out after dark."

I rolled my eyes and turned to look at him. "It's not ghosts that scare me. It's the creepy crawlies with fangs. Please tell me we're not here to take up close and personal shots of snakes or alligators."

He laughed again. "No. The assignment was to capture images of the natural beauty of our environment. But then again..." His lips curved into a mischievous grin as he regarded me out of the corner of his eye. "Snakes and alligators *are* part of the environment."

I shivered again. Grinning, he wrapped an arm around my shoulders.

"Don't worry," he said. "I'll protect you."

"With what? Your camera?" This time we both laughed. "Seriously, why would you pick such a vile, infested area like this one? Why not a nice pasture with trees and cows?"

He removed his arm and shook his head. "Too common. This

place has character and great natural light. I think I can get the best images as the sun is setting. And of course, mornings and evenings are the best time to catch the gas coming off the swamp."

I looked back at the road and heaved a sigh of resignation. "Well, let's get on with it, then. The sooner we get in, the sooner we'll be out."

Slowly he inched the car towards the entrance to the swamp. We weren't going to be able to go any faster than five miles per hour, since the road was full of pot holes and ruts formed by heavy rainfalls.

The first few minutes of the ride seemed pleasant enough. Huge kudzu-covered branches of oak trees hung over the road, blocking out most of the hot summer sun. Underneath the trees was a collage of greenery dotted here and there with colorful flowers of red, yellow, and purple. We both glanced around as we putted down the road, but nothing seemed extraordinary. About a mile into the swamp Steve slowed the car.

"Look," he said, and pointed to our right.

My eyes followed his finger to see a concrete structure about waist high, barely visible from the overgrowth of kudzu around it. The stone was dark from dampness and aging. A one-inch round metal pipe jutted out from the top, spilling water freely into the bowl.

"A fountain!" I was surprised to see such a thing out in the middle of nowhere.

"It's an artesian well," he said. "There are supposed to be several underground springs around here that feed into it."

"I wonder who built it."

He shrugged. "Don't know, but it looks like it's been here a while. The Indians that settled here centuries ago believed the springs had healing powers." He arched a questioning brow. "What do you think? Wanna try some?"

Curious but still a little apprehensive, I glanced around before answering. There was nothing – no other cars, no people, and most of all no snakes. I shrugged and smiled.

"I guess everyone could use a little healing water."

The humid air hit me instantly as I opened the door, and my skin went damp with perspiration. I could smell the rich, damp earth around the well combined with the slight tang of metal. The gurgling of the water as it flowed from the pipe was almost hypnotic. All around us, I could hear the loud, high pitched trilling of cicadas singing in tandem. As one's song diminished, another's would begin.

The water was ice cold and tasted pure and clean, unlike anything out of a faucet. Although the air around the well seemed cooler than anywhere else, it was still very hot. I patted some of the water on my wrists and neck. Completely forgetting about the reptiles, I wondered why so many people found this place daunting. To me, it seemed tranquil and picturesque.

We drove for maybe another mile or so before we reached the swamp. Once again Steve pulled to the side of the road, but this time he turned off the engine. As he fumbled around in the back seat for his camera, I walked around to examine our surroundings, keeping an eye out for anything with fangs. The swamp was smaller than I'd expected, but from the overgrowth of vegetation it was hard to tell exactly where it started and where it stopped.

From where I stood, I could easily see across to the bank on the other side. The water was stagnant and murky with green sludge, but even so, it rippled with movement. All around, I could see the fish jumping to snap at the assortment of bugs skimming across the surface. A musty, fishy odor wafted up from the bog, making me wrinkle my nose. There was a light breeze, and the sour smell suddenly mixed with the sweet scent of honeysuckle. Absently I slapped at a mosquito on my forearm.

I was brought out of my reverie by the rapid click of Steve's Nikon echoing loudly through the woods. I turned, and the camera was pointed straight at me.

He looked up and grinned. "Wanna be my model?"

I laughed. "I thought the photos were supposed to be of natural scenery."

"The natural beauty of the environment," he corrected. "And what's more natural and beautiful than the female form?"

I rolled my eyes and chuckled, but put my hands on my hips and flashed him a brilliant smile.

All of sudden, an intense burning shot thru my left foot. I let out a shriek and jumped up and down. Steve jerked his head back from the camera and looked at me wide-eyed.

"What? What happened?"

After all the worry over snakes, it had been the fire ants that bit me. "Damn, damn, damn," I said as I leaned over to brush them away.

He gave me a quick look of sympathy before returning to his task. I rubbed my burning ankle for a minute and then walked over behind him. The sun was beginning to set and the swamp was rapidly growing darker. I felt safer staying close to him.

As if called out by the darkness, the crickets began to chirp and the deep croaks of bull frogs drifted up from the water to join them with their melancholy song. Just as Steve had expected, a fog of swamp gas started to form over the marsh. Intrigued, I watched over his shoulder as he continued to take pictures.

The night air was still very hot and I could feel perspiration accumulating around my hairline, on my upper lip, and trickling down my spine. Joining the darkness, along with the crickets and frogs, were the mosquitoes who had decided to dine on my arms and legs. I slapped at them again.

"Okay," I said irritably. "I'm ready to go now." The swamp wasn't so interesting any more. My ankle was still burning, and as I headed towards the car, I continued to slap at the insects attacking every exposed part of my body. Steve continued to snap pictures for several more minutes before joining me. He seemed unperturbed by the pests of the night.

"I think I got some really good shots," he said as he carefully deposited his camera before settling into the driver's seat.

"Cool." I scratched at a mosquito bite. "Can we go now?" I was antsy to leave, hungry and uncomfortable.

"Why are you in such a hurry? Are you sure you're not afraid the ghosties are going to come out and get us?"

"No." I snorted. "I'm just ready to get up to the lake."

He started the engine and moved slowly down the road. "Well, it's going to be a little while longer before we get there."

I looked at him curiously. "Why?"

"We have to turn around and go back through the swamp the way we came before we can head towards the lake."

Because of the road conditions, it would take us a good thirty minutes to get back to the highway from where we were. We were already about halfway to the lake. It made no sense.

"Why in the world would you do that?"

He looked astounded. "Apparently, you haven't heard the legend of the woman in white."

"Apparently not," I replied dryly. "Wanna fill me in?"

"Well," he said, "I think there are a couple of versions, but this is the way I heard it. Years ago – back in the Sixties I think – there was a coven of witches that used to come out into the swamp and have some sort of ritual. Some say they were devil worshipers."

"Well, which was it?" I asked.

"Which was what?"

"Was it a coven of witches or was it devil worshipers?"

He narrowed his eyes. "What difference does it make?"

I grinned at him. "Just wanted to get the story straight."

He frowned, but continued. "The people who lived near the swamp said they could hear chanting coming from deep in the woods, but none of them were brave enough to go out and see what was going on. I guess no one really knew for sure who they were.

"Anyway, one day a local sixteen year old girl came up missing. She just disappeared from her home one night and no one ever saw her again. The police looked for her for a while, but finally came to the conclusion that, since she was somewhat of a 'wild child,' she'd probably run off with a boy and was living somewhere in California in one of those flower child compounds or something."

"So they never found her?"

"No, but her parents kept insisting that she would never run away and cut off all contact with them. They said she didn't even take any clothes with her. The last time they saw her, she was dressed in a night gown, ready for bed. Even so, the police gave up looking, and that's when the rumors began. People started saying that the coven of witches kidnapped her, took her into the swamp, and sacrificed her to the devil."

"What? Was she supposed to be like a virgin sacrifice or something?"

"Something like that," he said. "After that, anyone who went into the swamp would come out scared to death."

"Did they see the witches – or demon worshipers?"

"No," he said, shaking his head. "After the girl disappeared and the townsfolk kept reporting the strange happenings, the police went in and drove all the vagrants away. They found burned areas where someone had been building bonfires, but nothing to indicate a murder – no blood, no bones, nothing that would suspect anyone of foul play."

"Well, what scared everyone, then?"

"They said that as they drove through the swamp, they could sense an evil presence, and by the time they got to the end of the road it felt as if something had followed them out. Most people would just head home, trying to get away from that eerie feeling, only they couldn't shake it. Several people reported all sorts of weird things happening to them afterwards. They all said that the only way to get rid of whatever had followed them out was to take it back in."

"So you're saying we have to turn around and drive back through the swamp in order to keep this entity from following us out?" I asked skeptically.

He nodded. "Yep. The key is that you have to go back the opposite way to get rid of it."

I laughed. "Please tell me you don't really believe this!"

His face blushed slightly and I could tell that he did.

"Nah. Not really. But it doesn't hurt to be on the safe side, does it?"

"It's just a silly ghost story," I said. "It was probably made up by someone's parents who wanted to keep their kids from going into the swamp. I'm sure there's nothing to it."

By this time, we were at the end of the road and I suddenly felt a chill run up my spine. I shuddered slightly and secretly blamed it on the air conditioning and my sweat-dampened clothes.

"Let's just go." Even as I said it, I felt goose bumps rise on my arms.

He hesitated, and for a moment I thought he was going to disagree. With a sigh of resignation, he said, "Okay, but if some girl shows up in our tent tonight, you can deal with her." He turned out onto the highway and headed towards the lake.

It was well into the night when we arrived at the campground where the others had already pitched their tents and built a small fire. We joined them with hot dogs and marshmallows, telling them about our adventure.

"I've heard about the woman in white," said Carrie, "but I've never known anyone to actually *see* her."

"There must be something to it," said Jenny. "Aren't all legends based on some sort of truth?"

"I guess some of the story could be true," I said. "There very well could have been some crazy people out there making sacrifices to the devil. And they might even have killed that girl. But I don't believe her ghost is roaming the swamp waiting for someone to come get her out."

The rest of the night was spent debating over which ghost stories we thought might be true and how much could be explained.

"What about the Red Lady that haunts Huntington College?" asked Jenny.

"Or the face in the courthouse window?" said Mark.

"Yeah, there are several stories like those in that book, *13 Alabama Ghosts*," said Carrie.

"Thirteen, to be exact," chuckled Brad as he pushed another hot dog into his mouth. We all broke into laughter.

"I'm sure there's an explanation for all of those as well," I retorted.

It was the wee hours of the morning before we finally headed off to bed. The night was still hot and the fire, regardless of its small size, hadn't helped. My clothes were soaked with sweat and my bug bites itched like crazy. I changed into a tank top and a pair of light cotton shorts to sleep. Steve and I were both exhausted, but while he dozed off quickly, I was restless. I all wanted to do was scratch! I tossed and turned for a long time before finally settling down.

Outside our tent, I could hear crickets chirping and smell the damp, muddy scent of the ground around the lake. The waves lapped at the banks, lulling me deeper into slumber. I was on the edge of sleep, that last moment when you're still aware of your surroundings, when suddenly I felt that someone was watching me.

My eyes fluttered open and I caught sight of a white figure standing at the entrance to our tent. I bolted straight up and the image vanished. I crawled quickly out of the sleeping bag and rushed into the night.

It was still very dark, but the moon lit a good portion of our campground. Out of the corner of my eye, near the water's edge, I saw a flash of white. Stupidly, I ran towards it, more curious than frightened. For all I knew, it could have been a serial killer. But when I got there, it was gone.

I looked up and down the banks and behind me. There was no way anyone could have gotten past. The site we'd chosen was a small peninsula where no other people would be near us. No one could have come through our camp without circling the tents or coming through the water. There had been no noise or movement, nothing that would reveal the presence of a human being.

I shook my head and snorted, feeling stupid. It was all those silly ghost stories. I went back to bed and the rest of the night was uneventful. Even so, I found it very hard to sleep.

After breakfast the next morning, we headed straight into the water to spend the rest of the day sunning and soaking. In front of us was a cliff about twenty feet high that boasted a large, sturdy tree with a rope swing. While I might not be afraid of ghosts, I was definitely afraid of heights. Therefore, my job was to remain in the water below and judge the dives of the others from the swing above.

I positioned myself on a plastic floating recliner, donned my sunglasses, and looked up at my friends. I smiled as I watched them argue over who was going to go first and who was going to do the most amazing jump. As I relaxed on my float, I let my hands wave gently back and forth in the water, enjoying the cool feel of it on my skin.

All of a sudden, the hair on my neck rose up and I felt an icy chill on my shoulder, as if someone had splashed me, but I wasn't wet. I whirled around to see what could have caused it, but there was nothing there.

A loud splat behind me made me turn to face the cliff once more. Brad had apparently done a somersault and I'd missed it. His face popped up from beneath the rippling water with a wide grin and an expectant look. I quickly gave him a return smile and a "thumbs up," even though I hadn't seen a thing.

"Eight!" I said, knowing it would be enough to please him but would also give me room to let one of the others take the lead if necessary. I glanced around once again as the next person prepared for their jump. But still, I saw nothing.

As the sun set on our tired, sunburned bodies, we took down the tents, packed everything away, and headed for home. It was after dark when we pulled into my driveway.

"I'll call you tomorrow," said Steve as he gave me a light peck on the cheek.

"Not too early," I said with a yawn. "I'm going to sleep late."

He nodded and yawned in return. His eyes were as bloodshot as mine, a result of too much sun and lake water. "Me too. But I have to work from noon until six, so it will probably be tomorrow evening before I get a chance to call."

"Ok, talk to you then." I kissed him and went inside.

The house was dark and quiet. Since my dad had passed away, it was just me and my mom. She hated to be alone and had gone to spend the weekend at my grandmother's, so it didn't surprise me that she wasn't there.

I dropped my bags and headed straight to the shower. Even in the hottest of Southern summers, nothing feels better than a scalding hot bath before bed. I emerged with squeaky clean hair, bright red skin, and a satisfied smile. After slipping on a light cotton gown, I pulled the covers back and climbed in bed. The sheets were cool and I sighed with relief. The air conditioner's hum was quickly lulling me to sleep. I rolled onto my side, closed my eyes, and was out like a light.

I'm not sure how long I slept before I became aware of the presence. It felt as if someone had sat on the foot of my bed.

"Mom?" I said groggily as I rolled to look, but there was no response. I blinked several times to pry my tired eyes open. When I succeeded, I saw, less than two feet away, a dark haired woman dressed in white. Her head was cocked to the side as she regarded me with dark, vacant eyes.

I let out a shriek and was instantly on my feet, scrambling to turn on the bedside lamp. My whole body shook as the adrenaline rushed through me. I stared at the end of the bed and gasped as the mattress slowly rose back to its original form.

I spent the rest of the night in the living room with my back against the sofa, every light blazing and the television blaring. For the second night in a row, I wouldn't sleep.

The next day Steve didn't call, he just showed up around seven with a stack of photos. Even though it had happened several times now, I still didn't want to mention the apparition. In the light of day, it sounded ridiculous and I just knew that it had to have been my imagination. At least that's what I kept telling myself.

"Look at this one," he said proudly as he handed a photo of me standing next to the swamp. I abruptly pulled my hand back, letting the photo fall and making a small, strangled sound. Steve looked questioningly at me and I pointed at the picture.

When he'd handed me the photo, I had been looking at it upside down. From that angle, in the swamp water behind me was a clear image of a young woman with long dark hair, dressed in white. There was no one on the opposite shore, so it couldn't have been a reflection. The woman's arms were stretched above her head as if he was reaching out for something. My eyes followed the length of her arms and saw that they extended up the swamp bank to where I'd been standing. I looked down and gasped when I noticed the pattern of round, red ant bites curved around my ankle in four perfect semi-circles like clutching fingers.

"We need to go back through the swamp," I said in a low monotone, still not believing what I was seeing. "Now."

Although it was already getting dark, I couldn't stand the thought of spending one more night with that translucent specter. As we made our way down the highway, I told Steve of all the encounters I'd had since our first expedition through the swamp. He listened intently, keeping his eyes on the road but not speaking until I had finished.

"What if this doesn't work?" he asked.

"What do you mean? You said taking her back was the only way to get rid of her." My voice rose an octave higher than normal and I cleared my throat.

We turned onto the dirt road and stopped. He looked at me and I could see the uncertainty in his eyes.

"Just because part of the legend turned out to be true, doesn't mean the rest will. How do we know that once an entity has latched on to someone, they can get rid of it again?"

I held my breath for a moment before answering. "I guess we don't, but we have to try. I can't spend the rest of my life with this ghost following me around." The pitch in my voice went up again. He smiled and took my hand.

"Don't worry. If this doesn't work, we'll figure something out." He kissed my cheek before turning his attention back to the road.

Looming in front of us were those now-menacing oak trees hunched over the entrance. Spanish moss swayed in the breeze as if daring us to enter. The headlight beams extended only about twenty feet, and beyond that was nothing but darkness.

Slowly we drove into the swamp. Even with the windows shut, I could hear the night creatures outside. The sounds had once been like a beautiful melody; this time they sounded ominous. I kept looking behind me as if the spirit would be in the back seat, but I saw nothing. It seemed like hours passed, but it couldn't have been more than thirty minutes when we reached the middle of the swamp where Steve had taken the pictures.

So far nothing had happened and I was beginning to relax. I frantically sorted through various explanations in an attempt to debunk everything I'd been through, when we saw what appeared to be the headlights of another car coming towards us. They were moving fast. *Too* fast.

"Wow," Steve said as he pulled over to get out of the way. "How in the world are they going that fast on this bumpy road?"

"Maybe it's someone else trying to dump off an unwanted ghost." I laughed nervously.

The moment the lights reached us, they immediately swerved straight up and disappeared. There was no car in sight.

We both leaned over to look out the driver's side window and up into the darkness, but the lights were gone. Not even the moon or stars were visible. A canopy of limbs, Spanish moss, and kudzu had the night sky completed blocked. We looked at one another, our eyes wide, but neither of us had a clue as to what had just happened.

Suddenly Steve jerked and let out a yell. "JESUS!"

I whirled around and there she was – the dark haired girl – standing in the road about five feet in front of the car. Once again she cocked her head to the side as if contemplating something. Without averting her gaze, she lifted an arm and pointed out into the water. I could hardly tear my eyes away to look where she was pointing.

Then I heard the sound of drums and chanting. Out over the swamp, tiny balls of light about the size of softballs where hovering over the water. They moved slowly towards us, bouncing in rhythm with the beat of the drums. The swamp gas made them look like lamps in a fog. The chanting was indistinguishable, but it was becoming louder. As the music grew, so did the balls of light, coming closer and closer.

As they drew nearer, coming out of the fog, I could make out images of faces illuminated behind them. They were horrible, angry, contorted, with dark, sunken holes where eyes should have been. Every hair on my body stood on end and I heard a scream that made me jump out of my seat. It took me a moment to realize the scream had come from me.

Apparently the sound of it brought Steve out of his stupor and he punched down hard on the gas pedal. The car roared straight through the transparent girl, fishtailing and throwing gravel in every direction. We'd only gone a few yards when a scaly creature ran out in front of us. Steve swerved to miss it and almost ran us off into the ditch. He slammed on the brakes just in time and the engine stalled.

Behind us I could still hear the steady beat of drums and the distorted voices. The noises of the night seemed to sing along, taunting us with their eerie melody. I glanced around wildly and saw the lights slowly making their way towards us. There were even more of them now.

"Hurry! Hurry! Hurry!" I squealed, yanking furiously at Steve's arm as if that could some way help the situation. My heart pounded like a jack hammer, keeping time with the drums.

I was just getting ready to jump from the car and make a run for it when the engine roared to life and we backed up. Steve hammered the gas, throwing me back against the seat. Once again, gravel went everywhere as we flew down the dark bumpy road. Every time we hit a rut, the car would leap into the air and then crash back down, throwing us around like rag dolls in a clothes dryer. Maybe it was my imagination spurred on by fear, but it appeared as if the limbs of the trees lining the road reached out to grab us as we sped by.

Finally, seeing light in the distance, I let out a sigh. That relief was quickly quashed when a huge object hit the windshield with a thump and a crack. I screamed and Steve shouted before slamming on the brakes again. There was a snake the size of an anaconda only inches from my face, staring at me through the now-broken windshield. I was still screaming when we went into a tail spin.

The momentum caused the snake to fly off the hood and into the woods. When we finally stopped spinning, we were facing the opposite direction, and as the dust began to settle I could see the balls of light bouncing towards us again.

This time I didn't have time to respond before Steve threw the car into reverse and punched down on the pedal. We flew out of the swamp backwards and at full speed. The tires squealed as we hit the paved highway and Steve shifted into forward without slowing. He didn't stop again until we reached my driveway.

We sat in silence, both of us trembling as we tried to comprehend what had just happened. There was nothing to say. We'd both seen, heard, and experienced the same thing.

The next day I still couldn't get the night's events out of my head, so I went to the library. It took several hours of scanning through the microfilm of old newspapers before I found what I was looking for. The article revealed almost the exact same story Steve had told me about the missing girl. A chill ran up my spine when I finally ran across her picture. Undoubtedly it was the same girl I'd encountered. She had long dark hair, dark brown eyes and fair skin.

Letting the events of the evening run over in my mind, I came to the conclusion that the girl herself had meant us no harm. In fact, I wondered if she'd been trying to help by warning about the others – those evil entities that had taken her and were coming after us. She smiled pleasantly back at me from the photo and my heart went out to her. I felt as if I knew her. And I was certain she'd saved our lives.

A few years after graduation, Steve and I married and had our first child, a daughter named Chloe. She was a happy, friendly, and inquisitive, but she also enjoyed spending time alone.

One day, when Chloe was about three years old, I left her to play in her room while I cleaned. I could hear her chattering like a magpie to her stuffed animals – a small collection of cats I had started getting for her right after she'd begun to speak. Unlike most children, whose first words were "mama" or "dada," Chloe's had been "cat." I checked on her frequently as I worked, smiling at how animated she was when playing.

Steve, who was still very much into photography, had recently purchased a new video camera for us to record all of Chloe's accomplishments. Needing the practice and knowing this would be something Steve would enjoy seeing, I pulled out the camera and quietly nudged the door open just enough to get a clear view without disturbing her.

Later that evening, after dinner, I put Chloe to bed and popped the video into the VCR before snuggling up on the sofa next to Steve. I smiled as the image of my daughter came to the screen. At first I didn't notice anything unusual, but it was the sound of Steve's gasp that alerted me to something askew. My mouth fell open when I spotted the semi-transparent image of a dark haired girl dressed in white sitting in front of Chloe as she prattled on.

Steve immediately leapt to his feet and ran into Chloe's room. Oddly, I wasn't alarmed and leaned forward to watch the interaction on the screen. Nothing the ghost did seemed malevolent. In fact, it was quite the opposite. She appeared to be watching over Chloe. Call it mother's intuition, but I came to the conclusion that her only desire had been to go home. And since she could no longer be with her own family, she'd chosen to be with ours.

Steve returned from Chloe's bedroom shaking his head as he focused once more on the television. "She's sound asleep and there's nothing I can see in there with her." Still, he seemed slightly disturbed. I smiled up at him reassuringly.

"I don't think we need to worry." I patted the sofa and Steve, taking the cue, settled in next to me. I wrapped my arms around him. "Did I ever tell you I researched the missing girl after our encounter? I found out that her name was Catherine. But her friends called her Cat."

Feral

C. M. Koenig

Kassandra Rodriguez had known two rules for a long time.

First, deny the fact that she had known her Mexican-American father, lest her friend count drop like flies (not that it could get much worse – basically a party of one) and her family sneer at her as if she were filth. Don't mention him in front of her reformed mother, who was now happily back in the graces of her racist family with a new, blue-eyed, blond husband and two perfect children who didn't smell of her past mistakes.

Second, she wasn't to mention her mother's grandmother, who had been insane and another, albeit older, disgrace on the family.

Kassandra, Kessie to her singular friend, had already bucked rule one by going back to her true father's surname.

She feared she'd soon break the second rule.

She sat anxiously on the cement porch steps, wringing her hands where they rested on her thighs. The air hummed with bug noises, and pollen constantly scratched at her nose, seemingly even indoors. It was hot and she smelt – an acid scent that came in waves. She figured she smelled like a wet dog, but both the A/C and water pipes were dead and in need of repair. No amount of deodorant seemed to fix the fact that her whole body felt greased.

Yet she disliked the outside even more. *It* had first come to her there. But with her inability to stay safely indoors –

She sighed and flicked at a dragonfly, then got up and padded across the crunchy lawn to the Confederate Rose bush that sat a few yards from the side of her house. She sat herself down in the shrub's shade and tilted her head back, looking up into the burning green leaves. She wished for two things: one, for Ezekiel to come quickly, and two, for the shattered and welded wrong things in her mind to heal before anyone caught on to the fact that she had changed.

They couldn't know about *it*. She pictured its yellow eyes and shivered despite the heat.

She heard the rattling purr of Ezekiel's car's engine and hoped that was a sign.

The pool was a welcome relief. Admittedly, it was filled with leaves, random clumps of hair, and smelled strongly of chlorine. There was also the fact it was ringed in a rusty chain-link fence and sat next to a big intersection. She'd once found a dead baby bat in it and, another time, a live snake. She'd learned to make do, however. It was free and an excellent place to cool off if she ignored how ill-kept it was.

Ezekiel, after hauling himself out of the pool and finding his land legs, ran up panting. He was lean with no muscle to his name, and his swim trunks almost slipped right off his hips. He was sopping wet, with his longish, dark brown hair slicked instead of crazy, and he hopped around on the hot cement, clearly excited about something. His nut brown eyes were lit up with amber flame, and between them (and down the bridge of his nose) a smudge of white sunscreen was sadly quite obvious.

"What's up?" she asked, following script.

"I found some money on the bottom of the pool." His lips drew up too far when he grinned, making him look like one of the snarling wolves atop the totem poles at the Boy Scout Camp down the road.

Obviously he was happy, but Kessie still felt a flash of cold at his manic behavior. She could see why he was generally left alone: for the same reason fireworks were left alone except on the Fourth of July, even if they *were* brilliant.

"I assume it was a good amount?" She looked warily at the murky greenish water of the pool, wondering what had caused him to go diving in there. There was never any surety there wouldn't be an old bandage or rusty nail, which was why she stayed in the shallows when she wasn't sunbathing.

He merely smirked and laid a wet, wrinkled bill on her leg. She almost flicked it off out of reflex, but her eyes widened and her hand froze.

"Is that fifty dollars?" she whispered.

"Yeah," Ezekiel agreed, back to his crazy smile. "I'm lucky."

"I'll say.*" Much luckier than me.* "Make sure and hide it good. I know there are plenty of chumps around here who'd take that in a flash."

"They wouldn't be chumps. They'd be smart. Everyone wants money." Ezekiel shrugged and then put it under his cap on the lounger beside hers. "I'll take that to heart, though. Wouldn't want my dad taking it."

"No," she agreed, and he frowned. She felt bad for what she had to say next. She should probably stay and make sure he was all right. He did have mood swings like a menopausal lady. "Um, hey, Ez?"

"Mm-hm?"

"Restroom break?"

"Go ahead."

Kessie had to laugh. "Two minutes," she said, and ran off.

There was no one to blow a whistle at her.

While washing her hands, Kessie avoided looking at the mirror. In a previous time, she'd have looked and noticed how horrid she was. Some people seemed to think that biracial children would always end up beautiful. She had the feeling they were thinking Asian and white. She, on the other hand, was just an ugly duckling with no hope of swan-redemption because she'd long passed puberty. At least she was glad her acne was gone. She still felt like she'd gotten the worst from both sides and, according to her former bullies, was fat and weasel-faced. Now she didn't dare look at herself because what looked back was worse.

The thing that looked back wasn't her.

Unfortunately, she still responded normally to stimuli.

"Hey, Kass!" It was Shelly's voice, nasal and high-pitched, and Kessie looked up.

She just *had* to look up.

She saw Shelly, traditional female bully, with her pretty, heart-shaped face and glittery, glass green eyes. She saw her not-smudged, painted, pale burgundy mouth and black eyeliner. She noticed everything, even the wisp of hair that had escaped Shelly's uptight ponytail.

She would've been pleased that there was a small sign Shelly was human, but the thing in the mirror made her wonder what *she* was, so she couldn't take the time to enjoy the slip.

In the mirror, a brown dog – some sort of mutt, maybe a

Rottwiler mix, with muscles rippling under its skin and ferocious yellow eyes – looked back at her. There was no sign of her own reflection, only a dog trapped behind the glass staring lightning-daggers at her.

She wanted to scream, as per usual, but she wasn't ready for a straitjacket yet, so she forced herself to croak out, "Shelly."

Shelly slunk over to the mirrors and smiled at her. "Hey," she said. "So my girl Molly has the hots for that guy you hang around." She rolled her eyes. "Think you can get him to talk to her? I mean, he's *safe* right? I'm pretty sure he's on drugs, personally, but she thinks he's cute or some – wait, where are you going?"

"*Away*," Kessie barked. She felt like slapping a hand over her mouth a second later.

The dog growled as she left.

Kessie stalked back to the side of the pool, eyes frosted with watery tears that begged to be shed. She didn't want to cry, but at the moment it seemed unstoppable.

Ezekiel, sitting on the edge of his lounger, looked up at her muffled sniffles and his eyes blew wide. He jumped to his feet and was at her side in seconds.

"Hey, are you okay?" He put a hand on her arm.

She narrowly avoided jerking away as he stroked her skin, clearing the goose bumps that seeing what mirrors seemed to think she looked like had raised. He noticed the aborted movement but said nothing.

"Not really." She wiped at her face. "I need to go home."

"Okay," Ezekiel said. Concern sunk into his eyes, toning down their colors. He picked a towel up, put it around her, and rubbed her shoulders gently, his mouth in a thin line. He seemed to be holding back.

Kessie was grateful for that. He was a natural confidant – the right amount of caring, nonjudgmental, and nosy. If he truly tried to ferret out why she was so upset recently, he'd get it. She'd never been able to resist him when his irises turned honey-colored and his ability to broadcast a sense of comfort came into play.

"So you want me to drive you home, yeah? No stops or anything?" His tone was almost awkward, words stilted. She had to wonder why.

"No, I'm fine." She looked up at him, uncertain. He'd taken to wringing his hands.

"Okay then." He nodded and seemed to shift into his man-on-a-mission persona. "Let's go."

She offered him a weak smile. "I really am okay."

He let out some sort of mutant huff-snort at that.

Ezekiel's ancient car pulled into the driveway, tires making noises of complaint as they rolled into the two dusty ruts of earth. He had a peculiar expression, Kessie noticed. He didn't normally look so focused. He switched off the engine and settled back in his seat, then let out a long sigh and scrubbed at his face.

Kessie heard the soft sound of his calloused hands against stubble and the muted noise of a mockingbird in one of the baby trees nearby. Otherwise, everything was dead silent. She shifted in her seat, looked at her porch, and then back to Ezekiel.

He was certainly troubled.

"Kessie," he said. There was a trembling note to his voice, and he was hesitant when he reached out and let his hand lay over hers on the divide between driver's seat and passenger's. She flinched. His eyes frowned, and his mouth did too. He rubbed his thumb over her soft skin. "Hey, look at me."

She looked up, back to his face. His eyes were golden, honey-colored. She winced.

"Is someone hurting you?" he asked, voice soft.

She blinked. She'd expected questions, but not that. She mulled it over, turning it round and round. It was a logical conclusion.

"No," she said, and let herself relax a little. She'd expected him to be mad, ask what was wrong with her. She didn't know why. He'd never been like that. She supposed she just expected him to act like everyone else.

"You know you can tell me if they are, all right?" he asked. "I won't tell anyone, I'll just whoop the son of a gun for you."

A small laugh broke past her defenses. "You couldn't win a fight with an eighth-grade girl, Ez."

Ezekiel shook his head but didn't argue. "I'd bring my brother along to help. He's training to be a soldier, you know."

"It's fine," Kessie said. "No one's hurting me, I promise. I'd tell you if they were, but no one is."

One of Ezekial's muscles jumped. He sighed again. "Then what's wrong?"

"I'm scared," she murmured.

Ezekiel's eyes darkened and wrinkles formed between his eyebrows. "Why?"

"Let me handle it."

Ezekiel didn't look pleased, but he released her hand and sat back again. Something flickered in his eyes and he started to open his mouth, but he then closed it with a click of teeth. He paused for a moment and then asked, "Do you want me to walk you to your door?"

"I can handle it."

With that, she made her way to the house, key in hand. She kept her eyes to the ground and to the doorknob, avoiding any reflective surface.

She wished she could handle *it*, as in everything that was currently wrong with her life. But if she could just get rid of the haunting dog, maybe things would be better.

She sat on her bed, staring at her cracked door. The doorknob was missing. She focused on that for a few seconds, before settling back into the heap of pillows she'd collected. None of them matched, but they were all clean, and with them she could use her bed as a couch. She had an owl plushie she hadn't donated yet lying against her leg, and her ancient tabby cat with the uninventive name of 'Tiger' rested his head on her thigh. She stroked his ears and tried to pretend that she was comfortable, that she did feel safe. She should be good here.

It didn't help being home.

The ghost dog was increasingly angry. It growled, a whisper of a noise, and every so often she could see its mangy brown hide out of the corner of her eye. It was pacing, she thought. It was pacing around her room, unhappy with being trapped, stuck by her side. She wondered where it went when she couldn't hear it, couldn't see it. Was it always there? Had it always been there? She didn't know. She only knew that for the first time she was seeing it solid outside of reflective surfaces.

She wondered what would happen if it continued to be angry. Could it hurt her? She didn't know.

If it wasn't real – it couldn't be, right?

Then again, what was real? She could see four walls and the things inside her bedroom, but she could be in some asylum already, drugged and delirious, seeing what she wanted to see. Was there ever any proof that reality was reality? She didn't know, so she was scared, trembling as the dog stalked around her room.

Suddenly, Tiger was up, back arched and fur standing on end. He hissed at the air, green-hazel eyes stunned, and then ran off, skittering out of the room.

Kessie gulped. She felt hot breath on her throat, and a low growl brushed her ear.

She jumped up and ran. She rushed down the hall and ripped open the front door, much to the shock of her two younger siblings. They looked up at her with wide, perfect blue eyes from where they played a board game in the floor.

Kessie froze for an instant. Her mother called from the kitchen, asking what was up, and her step-father looked up from his paper where he sat on the couch.

"Where are you off to?" he asked, nose wrinkled. "Not a party, I hope."

I'm wearing sweats and a hoodie. Kessie had the feeling he didn't know much about parties, or about her.

"Out for a run," she said.

He nodded and went back to his paper.

Kessie heard the dog's nails clicking on the hardwood behind her. She swallowed and dashed off again, out into the dying sunlight of evening and down the stairs in one fell leap. She took off at a dead sprint, hoping her demons wouldn't follow.

She became a horse with blinders, seeing nothing but the sidewalk ahead and obstacles – driveways, cars, low lying tree branches, trash cans. Everything else blurred away.

That is, everything real. The dog's hot breath was on her ankles, and it nipped on occasion, a brush of teeth, steering her down its preferred streets like a collie would herd an unruly lamb.

When Kessie came to her senses, she was not in a good place. She'd run right into a bad neighborhood and, as far as she could tell, was in its decayed heart. Admittedly, her own neighborhood wasn't brilliant, but this one looked post-apocalyptic in the blood red sunset's light.

Most of the houses were vacant. Some were burnt-out husks, others had been eaten alive by kudzu and ivy, and one had had a tree dropped on its roof. Next to a rusty pick-up amidst a pile of trash, a harem of scarred, skeletal, feral cats eyed her warily. In an alley amongst the weeds, three boys around eight years old ignored her as one stuffed a cloth into a half-full liquor bottle and another played with a lighter.

She came to a grinding halt on the glass-littered, broken sidewalk and crossed her arms. She looked for a street sign, a familiar building, anything to tell where she was. While a twisted tree in a field down the road seemed somewhat familiar, she couldn't remember where she'd seen it before, or whether she ever had.

She sighed, shoulders slumping, and reached into her pants pocket.

She then tried her other pocket.

Then she tried the front pocket of her hoodie.

Empty-handed, she felt ill.

She'd left her mobile back at the house.

Stupid.

She pinched the bridge of her nose, sighed again, and ran a hand through her sweaty hair. At least *it* had left her a block back. With a little more clarity, she decided to go to the nearest nice house and ask where she was, or, better yet, find a gas station or store and ask if she could use their phone.

Either way, she didn't want to be where she was for long. When the moon went up, crime followed.

Still panting from her breakneck run, she headed toward the wider road at the end of the street, hoping it led someplace less decrepit and more populated. She'd only made it a few yards when she heard the growl again. Apparently she needed to quit lying to herself.

She felt that all-too-familiar hot breath, and then sharp, frigid-hot pain like needles stabbed deep into her calves. She let out a shrill yell and stumbled away, narrowly avoiding a face-plant. Her eyes watered, even worse than before because of the crushing sense of hopelessness. She felt the dog's fur brush her legs, guiding her again, but it disappeared for an instant and she bolted.

She managed to get to the nearest lived-in house's porch before she broke her internal pact not to cry and the dam went down. At the same time she decided to be more proactive, even as the growling returned. She'd call her mother, get herself home, and then tell her she'd gone crazy and needed pills before she wound up hurting herself or someone else.

She couldn't live like this anymore.

With the growls behind her, getting louder and louder, she raised a fist to knock on the door.

She then heard yelling, loud and horrible, inside.

There was a smash, a shatter of glass, and as her knuckles brushed the dark green door, it was ripped out of range and a tiny, absolutely petite woman appeared before her, sea-colored eyes wide with shock. One was outlined by a black and purple bruise, skin mottled yellow and green around it. Her cheek had a ruby cut and her mouth was popped open.

They gawked at each other for what felt like a solid minute, then the woman was jerked away, thrown onto a tan-green couch by a brutish, tattooed man who was wholly and completely *wasted.*

Kessie stepped over the threshold, hands balled at her sides and heart thudding, with absolutely no idea what to do. The house smelled like vomit and something dead. That was the last thing she noticed before a staggering pain ripped through her, heaving her midsection raw before a calm, contented daze befell her.

It was like she was out of her body, but perfectly aware. Only, while she panicked in her head, her body no longer gave any sign she was scared. Her heart slowed down more than it ever had, and as she moved farther into the house she didn't even sweat.

It was like she was at peace, praying or meditating instead of absently pulling her sleeve over her hand and picking up the beer bottle that had hit the wall. Its neck had broken off, leaving the brown glass jagged.

She was then compelled to the sofa where the drunken man kept the woman trapped. She let out squeaks of pain as he left bruises while slurring names and curses. She tried to placate him, whimpering all the while.

The man looked briefly over at Kessie in a drunken haze, apparently hearing her footsteps. However, he kept his bloodshot eyes on her knees.

"Damn dog, I thought you were dead," he said.

The woman took the distraction as opportunity and kicked him in the balls. He howled.

Kessie walked up behind the man, heard him growl, and heard him call the woman a whore. Kessie's arm moved, and she thought she knew what was going to happen. Her hand would twist and the bottle would shatter. After it hit the man's head, the glass would glitter like the shards on the curb and sidewalk, and he'd fall unconscious.

Instead, her hand *never* turned, and the sharp points of the bottle cut the soft skin of the man's neck like butter.

He choked and fell, thrashing.

Both she and the woman stared, dead silent.

Kessie came back into control and gasped in a sharp breath.

"What?" the woman asked, vacant eyes on her dead abuser. She then looked up, and Kessie saw the same expression that she herself had had when the ghost dog still let her see her face in mirrors.

The woman saw a monster.

Kessie thought of pleading, saying she hadn't meant to, that it was a mistake. She thought of telling the woman to be grateful, that Kessie had done her a service – but that would have been sociopathic.

So Kessie merely turned on her heel and left, hoping her hood had shadowed her face to obscurity, and was back to running, this time from something other than a ghost.

Kessie managed to get off the porch and down the road until she was near a dusk-shadowed, vacant lot full of wildflowers and tall grass. She bent over and tried to avoid retching. If she knew one thing, it was that if you became a murderer it was a bad idea to puke near the crime scene.

She winced, eyes shut. How could she have been so calm, yet

run off like a lunatic? Sure, there was the self-preservation thing, but she should have stayed, let the cops come and get her, and then let herself be institutionalized *because she truly believed a ghost dog had possessed her and forced her to murder someone.*

She let out a shaky breath, swallowed the extra saliva that had pooled in her mouth, and stood.

She saw a flash of brown and froze.

No.

It couldn't be back, not so soon. She shut her eyes. Strangely, no growling started. Instead, there was nothing, no noise except the wail of far off police sirens.

A thought hit her.

Her eyes popped open and she stepped off the sidewalk into the tall grass. Broken and dead, yellow eyes glaring blankly, was ghost dog's real body. She looked from the dog to the nearby house, and suddenly felt sick and a little giddy because *everything made sense.*

Everything made sense, for this was the dog that had haunted her. Haunted her because it couldn't protect its master any longer.

She shook herself. The dog stank and she needed to leave. If only it didn't feel like it was too late to go back.

When Ezekiel opened his house's flimsy door, he was wearing a ratty plaid bathrobe over sweat pants and an expression of confusion and concern. She smiled at him, hoping he'd ignore her wind-wild hair, blood-splattered sleeve, and general look of weariness.

It didn't work.

He looked her up and down, eyebrows drawn together, and backed out of the doorway. "Would you like to come in?"

She looked into the depths of his orange-lit shotgun home and nodded. "Please."

He let her into the tiny living room and had her quickly bundled up in far too many synthetic fiber blankets. When she asked why, he said for shock. He was far too perceptive.

He sat across from her in an ancient leather recliner and leaned forward, elbows on his knees and hands steepled in front of him. His eyes were cataloguing every detail. She'd rolled up her sleeves seconds after she walked in the door. It apparently hid nothing.

"Is that your blood?"

"Hm?"

"On the sleeves of your jacket, is it your blood?"

"No," she said.

His mouth twitched.

"I was out running," she explained. "There was a guy–"

Ezekiel scowled, probably mad at the guy more than the fact she'd gone out running alone at dusk.

"Okay," he said. "Are you all right?"

"Yeah." She nodded, and let out a breath through her nose.

"Would you like to tell me what's happening? You've been scared for weeks. My mind's been everywhere: abuse – though you claimed that wasn't the truth earlier – crime, drugs, pregnancy, sickness."

Kessie blinked. He was right on one account. Her new trouble was crime, crime she'd committed. She opened her mouth while she tried to think up something logical to say to explain things. She couldn't.

She could accept that her family might think she was crazy and maybe the rest of the neighborhood, but it had just truly hit her that if she went away, Ezekiel would be alone. Admittedly, a few girls vied for his attention because he seemed like a sensitive guy and maybe

C. M. Koenig

Ez could do better, but she had no idea how it'd affect him.

But she didn't want to tell him. Not tonight. Maybe tonight it was over. Doubtful, but maybe.

"Ez?"

"Yeah?"

"Come over here," she said.

He tipped his head but said nothing. He got his lanky body out of the chair and sat down on the sofa, keeping a safe distance away.

She scooted over and burrowed herself up against him. He glanced down at her, surprise clear on his face. She pressed her nose up against his fuzzy bathrobe and breathed in. This was what being safe felt like.

The ghost dog had never come when he was nearby.

"Ez?"

He hummed.

"What would happen if I wasn't around anymore?"

He tensed under her. "Excuse me? Wait. You're not *suicidal*, right? That didn't even get on the list." He paused for a split second and then added, "Not to make light of things if you are."

"Maybe a little," she concurred.

She played with one of the loose fabric ties on the bathrobe, thinking about it. She felt wretched, but she was relatively certain she didn't want to die. Then again, how was being kept in a padded cell getting drugged for a lifetime different from death? Not much.

Ez's muscles seemed to turn to lead in response. He let out a small, unhappy noise.

"I'm fine," she said.

"People who are *fine* aren't a little suicidal," Ez retorted, still bristling.

"It's over now, anyway," she said.

"What's over?"

"What was making me upset," she said. "I think, anyway."

Ez let out a long breath. "I hope so."

"Me too," she mumbled.

Her great-grandmother had seen dead people and dead things since she was little, according to all stories, and it had never stopped once she got the ability. She'd seen dead pets and wild animals, boy soldiers returned from war, and more. Supposedly she'd never managed to go through a cemetery gate until her death. She'd been too blindly terrified.

Plenty of people wanted to be special. All Kessie had ever wanted was to be normal. She'd wanted to *look* normal even if she learned quickly in kindergarten that she couldn't be like the princesses her friends worshipped, with their milk pale skin and blue eyes. She'd accepted she'd have to be abnormal, but she could get out of this one horse town.

Running couldn't solve her current problem. Only Ezekiel seemed to drive away the new demons, so she chose to clutch onto him with her life. She knew her nails were probably scratching him by now, but he just rubbed her back soothingly. It made her remember that maybe, just maybe, it was over.

"We should go out and eat sometime," she said. She didn't know why, maybe because that would be normal. Everyone said guys and dolls couldn't be *just* friends.

Ez's back rub broke rhythm for a second. "As a date?"

"Life is so short," she said. "We might as well enjoy it. It doesn't have to lead to anything. It just might be nice."

Ezekiel huffed. "I don't understand you."

"Well, that's good. I don't really get you either." She grinned up at him. It was weak but somewhat genuine. She felt both pleased and sick with herself, but she managed it.

He smiled softly back. "Okay. As long as you tell me what's been bothering you afterwards."

"Of course." Her stomach twisted and her mind rebelled, but it was only fair, wasn't it?

If this was over, she most certainly had quite the story to tell. She wondered if her great-grandchildren would hear of her exploits. Probably not.

She hadn't quite broken her second rule.

Earl and Bubba Save the King

Louise Herring-Jones

Mama's voice hit a fever pitch that vibrated the beer bottle in Earl's hand. She knelt on a plastic stool in front of a life-sized black velvet painting of the King of Rock 'n' Roll in his jewel-encrusted white jumpsuit. The black armband on her right sleeve contrasted with the faded blue of her denim house-dress.

"Oh, Elvis, if only I could hear 'Love Me Tender' from your sweet lips one more time." Mama lit a votive candle in a red glass cup with nubby bubbles forming its outer surface. Three other votives were already lit and set on the dollar-store shoe shelves stacked under the painting.

"Earl, we've got to go back and rescue Elvis from hisself," Bubba said, standing in front of the television and blocking his brother's view of *Cowgirls Gone Wild*.

From his semi-prone position on the recliner, Earl strained to look around Bubba's paint-spattered T-shirt. "Darn, what with Mama's caterwauling and your complaining, I can't watch my program."

"But, Earl—"

Earl slammed down the foot rest on his chair and pushed Bubba away from the TV screen. "You're both crazy, bro. Mama's got every Elvis song there ever was and we can't go back in time. That's for movies and weirdoes." He settled into his chair. "Have a beer. Miz Rhonda is making a guest appearance."

Earl watched the busty Rhonda ride into the TV show on a sorrel quarter-horse as the screen door at the front of the trailer slammed. Rhonda dismounted and leaned forward –

BZZZZ, the speaker spat as the TV screen devolved into gray and white snow flurries.

"Bubba!" screamed Earl. He downed a swig of beer and stomped out the door. Bubba rounded the corner of the trailer and Earl swiped at him with a free fist. Lurching to one side, Bubba grabbed Earl's beer-hand and turned the bottle over. Amber fluid flowed onto the dirt and Johnson grass that surrounded the cinderblock underpinnings of Mama's mobile home.

"What'd you go and do that for?" Earl cried.

"No more TV, no more beer until we rescue Elvis. Done hid the satellite dish. It's not even August yet, and if Mama's gone this batty already, I can't make it through another Death Week." Bubba crossed his arms over his chest. "You was always the smart one. Figure a way to take us back in time."

"No beer?" Earl's eyebrows rose and the corners of his mouth drooped.

"Thas right. No beer and no cowgirls neither until we find a way to save Elvis. We gotta make Mama happy again."

"Hmm." Earl pondered as he twiddled the beer bottle from his fingertips. "You don't happen to have no transmogrifier, do you Bubba?"

"I don't even know what one is."

"Me neither, but it shore sounds good. Guess if I had one, it'd be

236

repossessed by now anyways." Earl scratched his chin with the bottle neck. "Maybe we could do what Superman did?"

"You mean, fly arse-backwards around the world really fast and flip back in time?" Bubba said, his eyes wide.

"Nope, in that other movie, the one with the old-timey actress. You know the one, the girl with the blue-green eyes?"

"I don't think I saw that one, bro."

"No matter," Earl said, putting an arm around Bubba's shoulder. "I was about tired out from Mama crying all the time... like a hound dog, I reckon."

"You can do it, Earl."

"Yassiree, guess I can. Let's go look into Daddy's trunk."

"You got the key?"

"It's in Mama's purse. In the state she's in, she'll never miss it."

Both men walked back into the trailer, past their sobbing mother, and into the master bedroom that took up the whole other end. Mama kept the room as the primary shrine in the house, with nothing changed since her husband had disappeared in a Vietnamese jungle some forty years earlier.

Mama's and Daddy's bed was pushed up against the window alcove. Daddy's army trunk sat at the end, covered by an old quilt with a black and white MIA symbol sewn over pastel, interwoven circles. Mama's black, patent leather handbag leaned against the side of the trunk, a dark shadow against the faded, lime green shag carpet.

"Mama's not gonna like it much, us rummaging through their stuff." Bubba bobbed up and sideways, trying to see their mother beyond the half-closed bedroom door.

"Until her black armband comes off, she's not gonna notice," Earl said, raking his hand through the inside of Mama's handbag. He held up a long-handled key. "Here 'tis. Let's see what we can find in the trunk that'll take us back to 1972."

"Why 1972?" Bubba asked.

"Thas before Elvis totally messed up his life with pills. I'm thinking he'll be home, but not Priscilla and Lisa Marie. Mama told me about how she left him when we visited Graceland last Death Week."

"How we gonna get to Memphis?"

"I got that figured out, too. Shut the door, Bubba." Earl lifted the MIA quilt and unlocked the trunk. At the top were Daddy's blue jeans and boxer shorts, pressed and creased. His white T-shirts were next, along with two pairs of white, rubber-toed sneakers with matching crew socks, all ready and waiting for the warrior's hoped-for, but much delayed, return.

"You sure this is okay?" Bubba took one last look toward the living room and closed the bedroom door.

"Daddy won't mind. Good thing he was always a big fella. Otherwise, these clothes might not fit." Earl handed Bubba a pair of jeans. "Put these on, and the rest of the outfit too. If I'm right, Mama's wedding dishes are in the bottom here. They're jus' like the ones Elvis used at Graceland."

"What does that matter?" Bubba took the jeans and pulled off his own.

"Here, put on some of Dad's boxers too."

"What ever for?" Bubba asked, standing naked except for his jockey shorts. "Don't seem right, wearing Daddy's underwear."

"Jus' do it. If'n you want to be transported back to 1972, we got to be authentic all the way down to the skin."

"This is crazy, Earl." But Bubba snatched the undershorts and turned his back. Earl nodded. Bubba mooned him as he stepped into Daddy's striped boxers. Earl changed quickly.

The brothers faced each other, dressed in their father's vintage clothing. Earl combed his own hair straight back and used Mama's hair spray to hold it in place. He pulled his brother's hair into a passable Seventies style. It helped a good bit that Bubba seldom had his hair cut and hadn't bathed for a few days.

"What about my smokes?" Bubba held up a pack of cigarettes, unfiltered Camels in classic box packaging.

"Look fine to me." Earl folded the box into the sleeve of Bubba's T-shirt.

"Ready to rock 'n' roll?" he asked. "Think about Graceland now." He held up a dinner plate from Mama's and Daddy's wedding set. Both brothers stared at the shiny red apples painted on the dish.

"We, Earl and Bubba, are now in the dining room at Graceland," Earl said. "It's July 16, 1972."

"Shouldn't you say Graceland in Memphis, Tennessee?" Bubba asked.

"Hush now. We, Earl and Bubba, are now in the dining room at Graceland, Memphis, Tennessee. It's July 16, 1972."

Bubba pulled at Earl's shirt. "Why July 16, 1972? I thought Death Day was August 16, 1977?"

"That's right, Bubba." Earl set the plate on the bed. "You know well as I do after thirty-sumpthin' years of Death Weeks with Mama. But if'n we show up on the day that Elvis died, we'll be too late."

"Good thinking, bro."

Both brothers stared at the dinner plate while Earl repeated, "We, Earl and Bubba, are now in the dining room at Graceland, Memphis, Tennessee. It's July 16, 1972."

Bubba closed his eyes. Earl pushed the plate on top of the MIA symbol, pining for his missing father. Remembering their quest, he shifted his focus back to the Presley dining room in Memphis. He grabbed onto Bubba's arm as the lights flickered, once, twice, and all went dark.

"I don't think we're in Clayhill County no more." Earl let go of his brother's arm and stared at the glass-front china cabinet holding red apple dishes identical to his parents' wedding set.

Bubba opened his eyes and steadied himself against a chair. A sandwich sat on a plate near the head of the long table. He lifted the top slice of bread.

"Peanut butter and banana with bacon and mayo. I think we've done arrived."

Earl nodded. "Now we got to explain why we're here. Don't want to get stuck in no Memphis jail."

"You didn't think of that afore we left?" Bubba shook his head. "Can't we jus' tell the truth?"

"What, that we're visiting from the future and we're gonna save Elvis? That'll go over real big."

Bubba blinked as Elvis Presley ambled into the dining room and sat at the head of the table. The chair rocked as his shoulders pressed the back. He was broader now than the gangly kid who once recorded a ballad for his mother. Longer sideburns framed his pale face, and his signature curl, as black and thick as ever, fell forward and divided his brow. The King picked up the sandwich and chewed with vigor. Halfway through his second bite, he looked up at the brothers.

"What you boys doing in here? I thought we were going out."

"Where to?" Earl asked, his trembling voice shaking all the sense from his head. But, with his thoughts wandering about like stray cats, he couldn't save Mama from Death Week drama and Elvis from his own folly. He collected his wits, smiled, and leaned on the table. "I mean, where you wanna go?"

"I've got a hankering to see my brother's grave," Elvis said. "Feel up to a trip to Tupelo? The Colonel said to be sure one of you guys drove."

"Sure, Elvis, anything you say," Bubba said, sweeping back his greasy hair with a toss of his head. "Got any more of those nanner sandwiches?"

"Help yourself. Everything's in the kitchen. Pauline makes sure I've got what I need before she goes out."

"Is Priscilla gonna come with us?" Bubba asked. Earl punched him in the ribs. Bubba escaped to the kitchen.

Elvis shook his head. "Naw, she took the baby and went to L.A. I just don't understand why she left me for that other guy. Karate instructor, hmph. She don't want me to have any fun, but it's okay for her to mess around."

Earl started to answer, but stopped as Bubba returned with a plate of sandwiches and three bottles of beer. He set the haul on the table and started eating.

"Maybe jus' one for the road," Earl said, and tried to twist the cap off a beer bottle. The lights in the chandelier sputtered. Elvis laughed and handed over a key-ring with a bottle-opener fob.

"You might try this church key. Otherwise, your teeth'll do." He laughed as Earl chewed on the cap. The lights blinked again. Earl gave up and used the opener.

He had chugged about half the beer when Elvis said, "Slow down, bud. Won't do me no good to have a driver if he's drunk." He pointed at Bubba. "How about you drive, brother?"

"Shore nuff, Elvis," Bubba said and took the keys from Earl. "Let's go."

As Elvis walked toward the front hallway, Earl leaned toward Bubba and whispered. "Good thing we're going. I figure those other guys will be here soon."

"No prob, Earl. I already told them to leave. They came while I was in the kitchen."

"And they jus' left?"

"Yep. It seems like the King's road trips can get a body into a heap o' trouble."

Elvis yelled from the front door. "Let's get moving. I know a little place that'll still be open, got the best dry-rub ribs south of Memphis."

"We's a comin'," Bubba said, leading Earl out the door. A few stars were just starting to twinkle above the Memphis skyline in the distance. A red two-door Cadillac Eldorado with a white convertible top, matching leather interior, and dealer tags waited on the circular driveway.

"The Lincoln's in the shop, but a dealer sent over this one," Elvis said. "You got the keys." He slid into the back seat and donned chrome aviator sunglasses, even though it was already dark. Bubba got into the driver's seat and Earl took the shotgun slot as his brother started the car. The Eldorado roared like a tiger on steroids.

"Just press that button to take down the top." Elvis leaned over the seat and pointed. "All these new models got automatic everything." Bubba obeyed and the roof of the car folded into an alcove behind the back seat.

"Let's go, y'all. The night is young and we are beautiful." Elvis patted the back of the driver seat.

Bubba saluted and drove the Caddie down the drive. The music-grilled iron gates opened at their approach. Elvis and Earl leaned back into the leather seats.

The Caddie sailed down Poplar Avenue with Earl spying on Elvis from the visor mirror. Just south of Midtown, Elvis pulled a prescription bottle out of his pocket and jerked open the top. Pink pills scattered across the dark carpet. Elvis opened an ashtray that was set in the door handle and a light came on.

Earl reached over the seat and started grabbing pills. "What, no child-safe top?"

The ashtray light went out. Elvis flicked it back on with his finger, looked up, and scowled. "These aren't kiddie aspirin," he said, holding out his hand.

Earl held the tablets over Elvis's palm. "You shore you want to ruin a good time?"

"What's to ruin? Just calms my nerves, makes my back ache less."

"Man, you're too young to have aches and pains," Bubba said, his bottom lip pouting as he maneuvered through the sparse but steady evening traffic.

"Ain't you boys ever been to one of my shows? You'd have back aches too if you were the Pelvis. But y'all sound just like my Mama, God bless her soul."

Earl shrugged and dropped the pills. Elvis popped several in his mouth and swallowed them dry.

"Not nagging you," Earl said, wagging a finger. "Jus' wondered if you always take so many pills."

"Sure, why not?" Elvis leaned forward and spread his forearms across the top of the front seat. "I can get all I want."

"You can get real sick that way," Bubba said.

"Won't happen to me." Elvis laughed. "The colonel's got too many docs watchin' out."

"Well, thas good," Bubba said. "Where we going?"

"Little place just before the state line called the Last Chance Diner. Last chance for liquor too, before you get to Mississippi." He winked. "Even on Sundays, if you know who to ask."

"I suppose you do?" Earl grinned, but wondered how he could get Elvis to slow down, not just tonight, but permanently.

"Sure do." Elvis leaned back and put his hands behind his head. "Y'all just follow this highway. It's not too far."

"Yas, sir," Bubba said. Earl kept his thoughts to himself as the street lights died away and the dark countryside below Memphis sped by. The Cadillac hummed through the hot, humid night, and the wind tousled their hair with the sweet perfume of honeysuckle vines in bloom.

"Pull in right here," Elvis mumbled as they approached the neon sign proclaiming that the Last Chance Diner was open for business. As the car skimmed over the gravel parking lot, Elvis pushed the seat forward, jamming Earl into the dashboard. The King halfway fell out of the car and Bubba hopped out to steady him. Freed from the seat, Earl helped Bubba push Elvis through the glass doors into the Last Chance.

"Daddy's home," Elvis bellowed, shaking off the brothers and pulling off his sunglasses in one fluid motion. "What's cookin'?"

"Woohee, it's Elvis, Garvin. Pull some beers." A stout woman stepped out from behind a counter, a cigarette dangling from her right hand. Elvis walked into her arms and grabbed Mabel around her substantial waist.

"Brought ya some new customers, sweetheart," Elvis said, lifting the woman off her feet and setting her down. "Put 'em on my tab." He kicked a chair out and sat at a table.

Earl leaned against a glassed-in phone booth set apart in a nook by the entrance and absorbed the classic mix of diner aromas. Coffee. Cigarettes. Deep-fried animal fat. He felt a tremor, as if the world had shifted under his feet, but the feeling passed.

Bubba sniffed the air like a bird dog on point. "Onion rings," he crooned.

Mabel laughed, struggling out of Elvis's grasp. "What's your names?"

"Bubba."

"Earl."

"Y'all will fit right in," Mabel said. She blew each of the brothers a kiss.

A thin man pushed open a swinging door. He set a six-pack carton of cold beer bottles on the table and shook Elvis's hand. "Where you boys from?" Garvin asked.

"Bama," Bubba replied, taking the chair next to Elvis. He pulled his Camels from his rolled-up shirt sleeve and turned over an ash tray. "Must be the smoking section."

The fluorescent ceiling lights and the neon beer signs over the bar hummed ominously. Garvin and Elvis stared at each other. Elvis shrugged.

"Not from around here, that's for sure," Garvin said.

Earl took the cigarette from Bubba and twisted it out. "I don't think more beer's a good idea."

Elvis ignored him and opened three bottles.

"Come on, now, somebody's got to be the deg'nated driver," said Earl. The neon lights over the bar dimmed, but brightened when Bubba joined Elvis in the round.

"The beer done made Milwaukee famous," Bubba said. He lit another Camel and puffed smoke rings.

"Schlitz was my Mama's favorite." Elvis clinked his beer against Bubba's frosty bottle.

"To the King of Rock 'n' Roll," Bubba said. He wiped foam from his mouth.

"To your health," Earl added, not forgetting their mission.

"Naw, to yours." Elvis drank and set the bottle down with a clunk. "Have a beer."

Earl set a chair backwards against the table and plopped down, his hands on the chair's vinyl upright. "Naw, really. It's your health we want to talk to you about."

"Naw, let's toast your health again." Elvis spluttered beer suds as he laughed.

"No, sir. Not our health, your health. The health of Elvis Presley."

"Well, get in line, you and my doctors and that other passel of quacks the Colonel sends around. Ain't nothing wrong with me that some sweet-lovin' lady can't fix. Already got my eye on some local beauty queens, ones with true spirit. I like a gal who can think for herself, you know what I mean?" He saluted Mabel with his bottle and chugged the rest of his beer.

"Your eyes shore look funny," Bubba said. Elvis stared at him, his pupils pinpoint dots in his blue eyes.

The King shook his head. "Y'all are just old women. Might as well look up Pris and get a lecture." He stood, swaying.

"Naw, naw," Earl interrupted. "Bubba didn't mean no harm by it. This is a road trip, no rules. Where ya wanna go next?"

"Tupelo," Elvis said. "Anyone in the mood for a séance?"

"Shore." Bubba poured another beer. The foam head spilled over the top of his glass. "What's a séance?"

"Way to say hello to my twin."

"He's got a twin?" Bubba asked, licking the foam off his lip.

"Yep. A dead one," Earl muttered.

The King chugged until the last drops of golden liquid slipped away.

Elvis stayed in the back for the long drive south to Tupelo. He leaned his head against the high leather seat, his eyes star-wards. Soft snores floated away on the warm breeze.

"He's done checked out," Bubba said, glancing into the back seat and then skyward. "What we gonna do once we get to Tup'lo?"

"Play along," Earl said, sobered up and taking his turn driving down the dark highway. "I figures we can use this séance thang to help out." He drummed his fingers on the padded leather steering wheel. "You can play his brother."

"I ain't dead," Bubba protested.

"Naw, but you might as well be if we got to listen to Mama caterwauling about her Elvis being both dead and gone." The dashboard lights flashed. He looked over at his brother. "I jus' can't stands it no more."

"Calm down, bro," Bubba said, patting Earl's shoulder. "I'll play the part of the dead kid. What's his name?"

"Don't rightly know, but you better find out."

"Me? But, but – Elvis, he's sleeping."

"Use your head for once."

Bubba pounded his head on the back of the seat. "I'm thinking, I'm thinking," he repeated.

"Jessie," sighed Elvis, talking in his sleep.

"That's using your noggin for sumpthin' sides a cap stand," Earl said, slapping the steering wheel. "You jus' climb up a tree and pretend to be Jessie."

"I don't like high-ups," Bubba protested.

Earl gave his brother *the look*, piercing eyes melting into a curled lip.

"Hell, okay, jus' hope there's a tree."

"It's Miss'ippi, brother. Ain't nuthin' else."

"Wake up, Mr. Elvis," Bubba said, pulling on the King's jean-clad knee. "We's in Tup'lo."

"Gotcha." Elvis rubbed his eyes and sat up. "I know where I am. Turn down there. We got to go to the Priceville graveyard, just outside town."

They drove on until Elvis said, "This is it." Earl turned toward a grassy patch dotted with tombstones and crowned by a spreading live oak garlanded with Spanish moss. As Earl parked, Elvis jumped out of the car. Earl gestured to the tree and grabbed Bubba's shoulder.

"Here, now," he whispered into his brother's ear. "He won't see you behind all this tree hair."

"Okey dokey." Bubba slipped out and slunk behind the oak's wide, ridged trunk. Earl left the keys in the ignition and joined Elvis.

"He's buried somewhere round here," Elvis said. Starlight shone through the dangling moss and illumined a few crooked tombstones.

"I'll look for the marker." Earl followed the King, his eyes downcast.

"Ain't no marker." Elvis kicked the dirt, spraying pebbles over Earl's sneakers. "Mama and Daddy couldn't afford one."

Earl stared at the King's fancy gold necklace with the "taking care of business" TCB initials and lightning bolt emblem. His raised eyebrows asked the question more poignantly than if he'd spoken.

"I know. I should do it. Just can't find the grave."

Earl nodded and looked up. A few dark, oval leaves floated down. Bubba had climbed the tree.

"Here's close enough." Elvis took off his sunglasses and closed his eyes. He sang. Rich, mournful notes echoed through the trees and off the stone memorials.

Elvis dropped to one knee. "Jessie, if you're here, touch me, brother. I'm feeling mighty lonely with my family gone. What can I do?"

The King bowed his head.

"Elvis!" yelled Bubba as he plunged head-first out of the oak, trailing moss. The two men crumpled together, and Elvis's head hit a broken chunk of granite. Bubba jumped to his feet. The King lay still as death.

"You kilt him," Earl yelled, shoving his brother's arm. "Do sumpthin'."

"Like, like, like what?" Bubba stammered.

"CRP, artificial perspiration, anything."

"I don't know none of that stuff," Bubba cried.

"You seen it on TV."

"What the heck, but don't you go tellin' nobody I done kissed another man."

"Even the King?"

"Well, maybe." Bubba plucked moss from his shoulders, knelt beside Elvis, and turned his head to one side. He leaned down and smacked a kiss on the full lips, but nothing happened.

"You gotta breathe in," Earl insisted, leaning over for a better look.

"You mean tongue?" Earl skittered back on all fours, crab-like. "No way."

"Then move aside." Earl pushed his brother out of the way and crouched beside Elvis. He took a deep breath, pressed his mouth against the mouth of the King of Rock 'n' Roll, and just blew. Elvis gasped, batting at the air.

"That you kissing me, Earl?" he asked, wiping his mouth.

"Naw, that was me," Bubba said.

Elvis turned his head and spat on the ground. "You Alabama boys are sure strange." He reached out and Earl yanked him up. A purple bruise was forming on the King's forehead, but his skin remained unbroken.

"I've had a vision," he said.

"You sure you okay, Elvis?" Earl asked. "You must've fainted, maybe them pills?" he added, winking at Bubba. Bubba winked back.

"Naw, I'm fine," Elvis said, reaching up to touch his brow. "Ouch. I'm goin' have a goose egg tomorrow." He reached in his pockets, but produced only bottle caps. "I think I saw a phone booth down the way a bit. Either of you boys got a dime so I can make a call?"

Earl and Bubba looked at each other and asked together, "Quarters?"

The air shimmered around them as the starlight blinked out. *POOF*, the brothers disappeared and the stars returned, blinking steadily in the clear, midnight-blue sky.

Dust and something more, something ethereal, swirled down from the Spanish moss.

"Dang it," Elvis cursed, turning in a circle. "Earl! Bubba! Where'd you boys get off to?"

The lightest of taps on his shoulder stopped Elvis in mid-pirouette. Two men now faced each other across the graveyard. Elvis stood tall, substantial as home-cooking. His twin only echoed the living man, yet Jessie was as real to his brother as the aroma of buttermilk biscuits. They embraced for the first time.

Together, they walked to the Cadillac. "Guess I'm driving home," Elvis said. The King held the passenger side door open. "It's just you and me, Jessie, all the way back to Memphis."

His twin brother's ghost slipped onto the seat with a soft purr like a contented kitten. Elvis shut the door and walked around the car. Settling into the driver's seat, he turned the ignition. Elvis, and Jessie, left the cemetery.

Even though the King had grown unaccustomed to driving, the long trip to Graceland flew by in a dream. Elvis chatted, laughed, and wept the whole way. The twins had a lot of catching up to do.

"Oh Lordy, that was some coaster ride," Earl cried as he landed in his front yard.

"Yeah, man!" Bubba ricocheted off the polished rear wheel of a car parked in Mama's gravel drive.

"What the Sam Hill?" Earl snorted. "There's two of the durn things." Matching pearl-white Cadillac coupes gleamed in the dawn sparkle.

The screen door of the double-wide trailer jerked open and Mama stepped onto the front stoop. No black armband disturbed the pale pastels of her flowered housedress.

"Get in here and have some breakfast, boys. Stayin' out all night, again, eh? If y'all were any younger, your Pappy would whup ya."

"Daddy?" Earl croaked, his eyes wide with longing.

"Pappy's late for work down at the VFW, waitin' for y'all to get yor carcasses home safe. Now, git in here and eat."

Earl whispered to his brother. "We wore Daddy's clothes to Graceland. Do you think that brought him home?"

"Who cares?" Bubba said, jumping up.

"Where'd these cars come from, Mama?" Earl yelled.

"Earl, you cat-er-wail at me like that again and you're goin' to the lake of fire for disrespectin' your mama. Am I gonna have to read you the commandments again?"

"Naw, Mama, but how come there's two Caddies parked in our front yard?" Earl asked, gathering all the respect he could muster on short notice. He would prefer a beating over Mama's dramatic reading of the Ten Commandments any day.

"That Mr. Presley sent 'em, same as always. I jus' don't know why you boys hang with that rocker-billy, 'ceptin' for these here cars."

"Save some biscuits for me, Daddy," Bubba said, climbing the concrete stairs to the door and pushing Mama inside. "You comin', Earl?"

"Jus' a minute, bro. Got to take it all in." Earl rubbed his hand across the shimmering hood of the coupe nearest him.

"It's good to be friends with a King," Bubba said, smiling his best stink-eating grin. "Hey, Daddy-o!" he screamed, slamming the screen door. Mama jabbered after him to mind his manners.

Earl patted his new Cadillac. He wiped a tear from the corner of his eye and hurried inside before Bubba and Daddy polished off all of Mama's biscuits.

Summer Forever

J. M. Gruber

Simon drove home from school on a Tuesday. Sunset slipped between the trees flanking the highway and stabbed at his eyes. His dollar store sunglasses weren't much good for fashion but they could protect him from the light, and that was all he really needed sunglasses to do, if he thought about it. He thought about it again as he drove; after four hours on the road, he was running out of new thoughts.

The school was Sewanee, the University of the South. During term it could pass for Cambridge or Oxford, a serious place for serious people. In the summer it was a different story. Set in a vast expanse of countryside with nothing nearer than an hour's drive, summer at Sewanee meant stewing in beer sweat in a tent somewhere.

He'd left because he had a plan. It went like this: Wake up at six A.M. Work from seven to three thirty, pausing to eat a sandwich. On weekends, study for the LSAT. Do not spend money.

The sun was gone but its heat still lingered, a fraction of a degree lurking within each droplet of humidity, when he pulled up to a tar-roofed cabin. The crunch of gravel under his tires was a particular sound that no other gravel made. Over the tick of the cooling car he could hear the creek at the bottom of the hill, though he couldn't see it.

His dad was in the kitchen, stirring a pot from which rose steam and the sweet bite of tomatoes stewing with Vidalia onions. The screen door slammed behind him as he came in, swirling flies into the room in his wake.

"Hey, son," his dad said, and dropped the spoon to shake his hand. His dad called every boy "son," whether he was scolding or praising him, and even if he'd never met him before.

Simon's phone rang. After he saw who was calling, he let it go to voicemail, knowing that Martin would leave a thorough message, as always. It was easier to let him say what he wanted than to try to have a conversation, and Simon had an early start in the morning.

He saw the ghost the next day before he left for work. He was drinking his coffee with the kitchen door open, in those magical few hours when the sun was up but the dew still on the grass, the few hours in a Tennessee summer when the air wasn't thick with heat, and he found himself walking down to the creek. He felt guilty for sitting inside on such a nice morning.

She stood knee deep in the water, and he only knew she wasn't there because the current didn't touch her pleated blue skirt. He never considered that he might be seeing things. Simon trusted and treasured his mind above all else. It didn't take him long to come to the obvious conclusion that this girl, in her old-fashioned but still somehow current skirt that reminded him of a particularly conservative school uniform, was a ghost.

Ghosts had rules. They didn't pop up like mushrooms. If there was a ghost, there was a body, a body of a person with a problem. Simon knew his grandparents had built this house. He wondered what they hadn't told him about, and entertained visions of hushed-up deaths and skulls uncovered from Indian burial grounds.

Ghosts had rules. If he traced them back, he would find the source of this apparition. He was inspecting her for visible wounds, a cause of death, when she spoke.

Her voice was distant, like his dad's on a Saturday morning, calling him in for breakfast.

Her voice was friendly, but there was a chill riding on her words. With the heat of the day bleeding in at the edges of the shade, the shiver was refreshing, like a flipped pillow on a hot night.

Her voice was casual, not at all the sepulchral moan he'd been expecting.

"You didn't scream," she said.

"Did you want me to?"

Her laugh had a tinge of the tomb, or so he told himself. His first ghost, much like his first job interview and his first sexual experience, was not meeting expectations. It was not following the rules. If you had the right qualifications and a professional demeanor, you got the job. If you slept with a willing partner after careful consideration, the encounter would be pleasant and end amicably.

And ghosts were scary and had unfinished business. They didn't plop down next to you where you'd fallen to the bank, spilling your coffee and not caring, though you usually hated waste. Except in her case it wasn't a plop so much as a soft *foof*, as if her movement pressed breath out of the world's lungs.

"I don't really care whether you scream," she said, "but it's expected, isn't it? Do you see a lot of ghosts?"

"No," he said, "but I'm seeing one now. It's the unknown that scares people, but you're right here in front of me."

She sighed but otherwise stayed silent. Her eyes twitched. They were a translucent green, translucent in the human fashion, not in the sense that he could see the trees through them. After a long moment of observation he decided she was trying to roll her eyes. He wasn't sure whether she realized she was failing, but was prudent enough not to ask. Proprioception would naturally be difficult for the incorporeal. That, at least, made sense.

"I won't be here for long," she said. "It's getting hot."

"I don't know what that means, but I have to get to work anyway." Still, he felt a pang of regret, the wind of a door closing. He pushed it away. He didn't have time to chat with ghost girls.

Work at the automotive plant was the same as it always was. It was only a summer job anyway, something to get him away from Sewanee.

He stamped parts and kept to himself, speaking only when spoken to, enduring his new nickname of "Doc Hollywood." He had let slip that he was headed back to college in the fall, and less than an hour later it was as if they'd forgotten his name. What they called him didn't matter. They didn't matter.

The ghost didn't matter either, but he looked for her at the end of the work day, which was still mid-afternoon. He thought he saw something like a heat haze move across the water, but it wouldn't answer him.

Martin called at five on the dot. Simon was making sweet tea and thinking of nothing at all, and the call took him by surprise so he answered.

"You off work, man?"

"I get off at 3:30. So yeah, I'm off." Simon kept his words clipped, irritated. Martin appeared not to notice, as usual.

"Cool, cool. Listen, you coming up next weekend? We're going to the lake!"

"No, I don't think so. I don't really have the money."

"Oh, please," Martin said. Simon could have told him that aliens had come in the night and dissected his parents, and Martin would have objected in the same tone. "I know you're sitting on piles of cash over there, Scrooge. Come on, everyone's going to be there."

"Great. I can spend a hundred dollars on gas to come get drunk and have the same conversations we always do. Sign me up."

Martin may not have noticed irritation, but he always picked up on sarcasm.

"What are you going to do instead, get drunk by yourself? Talk about the good old days with your folks? Come on, Simon! You want to come, I know you do."

"That's where you're wrong," Simon said.

"One weekend, dude. Then I'll leave you alone. Though I won't need to, because you'll want to come back every weekend because this is going to be awesome."

"Nope."

"But–"

"My parents just got home. I have to go."

It wasn't as final to hang up on someone with a cellphone, but Simon made the best of it. His mom had been home all day and was napping in the living room. His dad wouldn't be home from choir rehearsal for another few hours at least, but the lie didn't bother Simon. If he hadn't come up with something, Martin would have kept on until his phone died or his voice gave out.

Simon's mom woke up dull from her nap and was halfway through her supper – a spread of canned vegetables, lovingly heated by her son as a favor – before she started asking questions.

"Are you going out tonight, hon?"

Simon swirled his last few pinto beans around in the juice from his turnip greens.

"It's a work night, Mom."

She shook her head. "I swear I'll never understand my children. We were lucky to catch a glimpse of your sister last time she was home."

After supper, they drank the sweet tea on the front porch, sitting in wicker chairs with sticky vinyl cushions. A breeze rustled the trees off somewhere in the dark, but it was swallowed up by the hot stillness surrounding the house.

Simon pushed his hair back off his forehead, where it lay heavy and curled, and watched a spider wrap a fly in the glare of the porch light. Sometimes, on a night like this, it seemed like too much of an effort to speak. The only sound was the click of ice settling in their plastic cups as they sipped in an unconscious rhythm.

"How about this weekend? Got big plans?" Simon's mom was like that. She'd drop a topic only to pick it up later as if there'd been no pause. Perhaps because she wasn't a woman of many words, it seemed natural.

"Nope," he said. "I don't really keep in touch with anyone around here anymore."

"That's a shame. How about at school? Why don't you visit your friends there?"

Simon set his glass down carefully next to his phone and walked away.

He didn't need the susurrus of water over rocks to find the creek.

He'd run this path nearly every night as a kid, in that last half-hour before he had to go in. When he'd had a bedtime, every minute of those thirty was precious. He could have been ready to kill his friends out of boredom or overexposure, but going in early was out of the question. It had never even been suggested. Lately, sunset was little more than a reminder of how little time was left in the day.

He felt the chill before he heard her. Her voice was little louder than the wind that was still sighing through the trees, somewhere too far away to do him any good.

"It's a nice night," she said.

"How can you tell?"

"I can feel the wind. That's all."

"Oh," he said. Then, "Why are you here?"

"Because I'd never been here before."

It could have been flippant, but he thought there was more to it than that. He pushed, and she evaporated as the breeze reached him, brushing at the sweat on his face. He wanted to call for her, but didn't know her name.

When Saturday came, Simon was up and out of the house before the sun was fully up. The cuffs of his pajama pants soaked up dew as he crossed the yard. He took a pot of coffee and a bacon sandwich to the creek and sat on a rock. The crickets had gone to bed, and the birds were warming up their voices, calling to each other from tree to tree. As the light went from red to gold she appeared as if painted on the air, melting into existence in streaks and splashes.

"Good morning," he said. "I would have brought you a sandwich, but I didn't think it would do you much good."

"No," she said, smiling.

"So you forgive me?" he asked. Simon took care to be sure about feelings. There was too much room for error.

"I wasn't angry," she said. "Night isn't my best time. I'm fragile."

"Because you left the place where you died?"

She frowned. "Why would that matter?"

It was bad enough that she didn't follow the rules; her ignorance of them was worse. He explained it to her, that ghosts were supposed to haunt the place where they'd died until their unfinished business was resolved.

"That's silly," she said. "No one ever told me that. I wanted to leave, so I did. And I don't have unfinished business. What difference would it make? I'm dead. Nothing I do can change my life."

She told him about that life. Her name was Becky and she'd grown up in Opp, just north of the Alabama-Florida border. Auburn for college and a teaching job at the high school back home after graduation. A husband whom she didn't miss.

"He wasn't a nice man."

He asked her if that was why she'd left. She told him it wasn't, that once she'd realized what was going on she just didn't see any reason to stay in one place anymore. She'd lived in one little slice of Alabama her entire life. She went north, as far as Birmingham, and spent a few years haunting the theaters.

"You'd be surprised how many there are. Those were good years."

In her third year, she started to fade.

"Fade?"

She started to answer, but the jangle of his phone drowned her out. With her watching, he couldn't screen the call. He was sure she wouldn't understand.

"Hello?"

"One week, dude. You ready?"

"I'm not coming, Martin."

Martin sighed. It was a heroic sigh, to be loud enough over the phone that Becky heard it. She giggled, and Simon wondered if ghosts could be heard over the phone. It didn't matter, because Martin was already talking again.

"Look, I know you're going to be a big time lawyer one day. I say 'I know' because even if you aren't sure of it, I am. One weekend isn't going to change that. And you won't have time to party once you lawyer up."

"Goodbye, Martin."

He wished he had a flip phone, so it would at least click shut when he hung up.

"I don't think I've ever seen someone so angry that his friend wants to see him," Becky said.

Simon cleared his throat. "You were saying about fading?"

She hesitated. "Well, if I stay too long anywhere – I don't know how to describe it. It's like falling asleep. Falling asleep on the couch when you don't want to. It pulls you down and you don't even notice until you jerk awake."

"How did you figure out what was causing it?"

A person would have blushed. Simon realized that he was probably indulging in some species of prejudice by thinking of her as other than a person, but he didn't know what the correct term would be. Ectoplasmic-American? Whatever the terminology, she was embarrassed and lacked the flesh to express it. Again, she didn't seem to notice the lapse.

"I was scared. I ran. It woke me up for the next year or so. Then

261

I started to fade and had to move again."

The coffee was cold – as cold as it could be when the temperature never dropped below eighty degrees – and half the bacon sandwich was gathering ants. He glanced at it and let it go, only cringing a little at the waste.

"Why didn't you go somewhere interesting?" he said. "West Tennessee isn't exactly a tourist hotspot."

She paced out into the water, kicking at it without a splash.

"I realized after the second move that I couldn't go back to anywhere I'd been before. I don't want to use places up faster than I have to."

Simon took a sip of the cold coffee and grimaced. She was on the other side of the creek, wandering up the bank and showing no sign of stopping. He was afraid he'd lose her; still, he untied his shoes instead of shucking them off, and draped each sock carefully across its shoe before following. Pine needles stuck to his wet feet.

He was supposed to be studying for the LSAT. The procrastination gave him a sick feeling of panic, but he stopped thinking about it with a shake of his head and a few deep breaths. It was easier to relax out of sight of the house, with the trees and a dead girl and the thorny vines that let off a warm green smell as he tore through them with each step.

He'd left his coffee, sandwich, and phone at the creek, and everything else in his bedroom. He didn't wear a watch. He couldn't see the sun through the canopy, though he felt its warmth, and so time seemed not to exist. For once he didn't feel the minutes racing by, minutes that once wasted could never be called back. Out there, beyond the woods, someone was using those same minutes to pull ahead of him, to take his place. And he didn't care. In the silence of the forest, the thought was almost enough by itself to worry him again, so he spoke.

"How long do you have here?"

She stopped her steady, quiet progress. Every so often a leaf blew out of her path, but otherwise there was no trace of her passing.

"Not long. It gets shorter everywhere I go, as if something's hunting me, getting closer and closer."

He shivered, and not entirely from the now familiar chill of her voice. "That's, um... horrible. I'm sorry. What will happen when it catches you? I mean if, if it catches you. Sorry."

"I don't know," she said, and once again she defied expectations: he'd never thought he'd see a ghost scared. "It doesn't feel like they say, like there's a tunnel of light or anything."

"Well," he said, "that's actually been shown to likely be a physiological reaction to near-death, and since you're actually dead..."

"What I mean," she interrupted – interrupted by a ghost, he thought, and had to stifle a laugh – "is that it feels like, well, fading. Not like heaven or anything. Like I'll just be gone. I don't think I'm ready for that."

"How long?" he said.

"A couple of weeks, maybe."

"Where will you go?"

She turned her head. He couldn't tell what direction she was looking; he didn't even know which direction home was now.

"I want to go north. The heat here stifles me, but I need the sunlight or I'm just a voice. So I want to go north. Maybe somewhere in Maine. I hear it's beautiful. I want to go there, or as far as I can."

"Maybe the fading is what's supposed to happen. It has to be, right? Otherwise the world would be covered in ghosts."

"Sure," she said. "That doesn't make it any easier."

He spent the heat of the day studying, glancing out the window now and then, though he knew he couldn't see her shimmer from his desk. In the afternoon, he went grocery shopping with his parents. They were surprised to have him along, but happy, and they showed it by letting him pick out his favorite foods as if he were nine again. He didn't mind. They'd never learned another way, and besides, frozen pepperoni pizza was still good no matter how old he was.

He visited her again that evening, with a tall glass of whiskey and water replacing his coffee. He'd taken an entire practice test and reviewed the answers, and felt he deserved a drink. Since he couldn't see her at night, it was easier to answer when she asked about Martin.

"He wants me to come to some party next weekend. I really don't have the time or the money."

He felt sure she'd shrugged, though he couldn't see her. Her answer sounded like a shrug, her tone bored.

"I have all the time in the world, and I don't need money, and I don't have any friends to bother me. It's not as nice as you'd think."

"That's not what I mean," he said. "It's just that sitting around on a boat drinking beer – what good does that do? I need to save money this summer so I don't have to work in the fall. If I don't have to work, I can concentrate on my grades, and then I stand a better chance of getting into a quality law school. Once I've done that, once I graduate, then I can start relaxing. Until then, I don't have the time."

Her voice faded into the murmur of the creek. "You won't have summer forever."

He took her swimming the next morning. She couldn't ride in the car, but there was a block of cheap apartments only a mile or two away, and she had a long stride and endless endurance. He knew from one disastrous attempt at reconnecting with a high school acquaintance that the apartments had linoleum floors in their kitchenettes and cigarette burns in their carpets, but they also had a pool, and the residents who weren't working on a Sunday morning were at church or sleeping in. He climbed the fence; Becky simply walked through. He thought it was unfair until he remembered that she wouldn't be able to feel the water on her skin.

The pool was bathwater warm. Simon sank until it covered his mouth. Tiny waves lapped at his ears, and he let his feet drift until he was floating on his back. A child's shout filtered through the water, metallic and strange over the drone of the blood in his head. Becky watched him with a mournful smile. He felt guilty for pointing out what she couldn't do. Then again, why couldn't she?

"Have you ever tried floating?"

"I don't think I have. I'm afraid that if I leave the ground I'll fall through it when I come back down."

"Then you'll end up in China," he said, righting himself. "Well, actually somewhere in the Indian Ocean, but you've never been there, right?"

He wasn't used to making girls laugh. It was nice to hear, and nicer still when she spread her arms and laid back, lifting one leg and then the other until she floated a few inches below the surface.

"Close enough," she said. It left a skim of ice on the surface of the water, which melted almost at once. A tension in Simon's chest that he had grown used to eased, and he laid back again, the water filling his ears and transforming the sound of the world. Her voice remained the same, friendly and distant.

She said, "Remember this."

He opened his eyes to a sky without a trace of cloud, the moon hanging ghostly overhead. He couldn't see Becky, but he knew she was there.

"Remember this," she said. "You can't plan a memory. All you can do is hold on to it when you find it."

Law school had never felt so far away. It had always seemed like the summit of a mountain, and he'd picked locations for base camps and packed equipment and despaired of reaching the top. On this long summer morning, trespassing in a concrete basin filled with over-chlorinated water, it was a mountain far off to be admired for its beauty. He meant to climb it, but the mountain wasn't the world. There were other mountains, and there were valleys and plains and the Indian Ocean. There was Opp, Alabama and Oakfield, Maine, and everything in between.

He saw her for the last time at the window to his room. It was past his bedtime on a Thursday night, and that wasn't in the plan. The plan was shifting around him, and he let it. He opened the window to let her in. She slipped through the sill as if to prove a point, perhaps to point out their differences. He chose not to notice it.

"I'm going to the lake," he said as soon as she was inside. He'd wanted to tell her, but up until now he'd told himself it was still just a thought.

"The lake?" she said. She didn't seem to be paying attention.

"With Martin and the guys. And the girls, or so I'm told. I'm taking tomorrow off and I'm going for the weekend."

"Ah," she said. "That's good, Simon. I'm proud of you."

That, he was used to hearing, but about straight A's and college acceptance letters, not about having the same old conversations over the same old drinks with the same old friends. But he was proud of himself, too. Why shouldn't fun be part of the plan? He could budget time for it like anything else.

She wasn't smiling. It wasn't usual for ghosts to smile, with the possible exception of creepy grins, but he had grown accustomed to her face. He missed the smile. Its disappearance was a mystery, a problem, and he was nothing if not a problem solver.

"What is it?" he said. "You've never climbed in my window before."

He couldn't blame her. It wasn't much of a bedroom since he'd moved out. There was a dresser, not his, and a bed, not his either, and the mallard ducks that his mother had stenciled in a border just below the ceiling had been painted over years ago. The creek was far more scenic, and anyway he had an idea that she might possess an old-fashioned sensibility about coming to a man's room after dark.

"I'm fading. I have less time than I thought."

"When?"

"Sometime this weekend."

"I guess you'll be moving on, then." He was happy for her, he decided. They were both moving on, both exploring the world outside their small towns.

"I don't know," she said. "I've been thinking about your plan, about how your life has a point. How you can still change things. You can go to the lake, or not. You can go to law school, you can kiss a girl, everything can be different for you between one moment and the next. Maybe it's time to find out what's next for me. I can't stay forever, and I can't change anything about my life. It's over.

267

Maybe it's time to accept that."

Simon wasn't prone to impulsive decisions. He always considered each ramification of the road not traveled, the pros and cons, a cost/benefit analysis over his choice of breakfast cereal.

"I'll stay. Whatever you decide, I'll stay."

"No," she said. "No, you have to go. I really think you do."

"You don't get to make that decision," he said. "What are you going to do, make me leave? You're a ghost."

There wasn't much to say after that.

He went back to school, leaving behind his summer job and his schedule, if only for the weekend. He'd gone looking for Becky as soon as the sun rose, but she wasn't there. Whether she'd faded, moved on, or was simply hiding from him, he couldn't say. He decided to be a gentleman, packed his bag, and drove away. He'd never seen his parents so happy to see him leave, but he thought he understood.

He stopped at a gas station on the edge of town. Some part of him felt guilty about the time he was wasting, his departure from the plan, but it wasn't as bad as he'd expected. He laughed and sipped his Gatorade, then called Martin.

"I know two things right now, Simon. One is that it's an ungodly hour when no one should be awake, and the other is that you're a crazy person. So I assume you're coming?"

"Yeah," Simon said. There was a heat haze hovering above the blacktop, and he smiled at it. "It sounds like fun. See you in a few hours."

Hurricane Season

Jared Millet

Lindsey Destrehan huddled on the couch in front of her dead grandmother's RCA while Brad raged and screamed outside. He rattled the windows, hammered the door, kicked the siding, and shouted through the walls while Lindsey flipped the channels and wished he'd go the hell away.

What a stupid thing it was to give a storm a name.

The weatherman on the national broadcast gushed with excitement as his reporter in the field pulled a hood over his rain-drenched face. The Pensacola station had live video of trees whipping and surf pounding, while on the Mobile affiliate a coffee-powered anchorwoman insisted that Brad had weakened to a mere tropical storm. Lindsey didn't believe it. It was as if someone had scooped the entire Gulf of Mexico into a bucket and was pouring it directly over her house.

She remembered as a child watching Andrew plow through the middle of the country on TV, but where she grew up in Indiana it seemed no worse than a regular thunderstorm. Katrina provided an annoying day or two of rain at her campus in Bloomington before the horrifying truth of it poured from the images on the news. Even so, it never occurred to her when she took possession of the old family home, twenty miles from the coast in the small town of Craft, that the threat was more than pictures on a screen.

The lights flickered and something like a herd of gazelles stampeded along the side of the house. Lindsey parted the living room drapes to watch her garbage bin tumble across the lawn. It bounced off one of her oaks, plopped on an azalea bush like a beanbag, then rolled until it hit her wrought iron fence and stuck. She hoped it would stay, or else she'd have to hunt for it later and explain to her neighbors why she hadn't the brains to bring it inside.

A shadow drifted on the other side of the fence, small, hunched forward, and moving against the wind. Lindsey gasped. It was a child, and far too young to be alone, storm or no storm. She looked up and down the street, what little she could see of it, hoping there was a parent nearby. There wasn't.

Damn it.

Lindsey liked being dry. She'd planned to stay that way until the storm passed, but there was nothing for it. The lights dimmed again as she slipped into the decades-old poncho that hung in the utility room. With no time to hunt for a flashlight, she stepped out to the carport, shutting the door behind her and bracing for the worst. The wind had slackened, but the rain was still sheeting down.

She jogged to the end of her driveway, keeping her back to the weather. Within seconds her shoes were heavy with water. The child, a boy, wasn't far down the sidewalk. He was small, black, no more than five years old, and drenched to the skin. Rain was so thick on his face that Lindsey wondered if he could even see.

"Hello?" she said. "Are you lost? Can I help you get home?"

She did what she could to block the rain. In the moment's respite, he wiped the flood from his eyes and looked up at her, scrunching his nose.

"Are you the piddy lady?" he asked.

"Am I what?"

"The piddy lady told me to come."

"What? I don't … Look, kid, where are your parents? Are they around?"

"I dunno." The boy shrugged. "The piddy lady said to go this way."

Oh, for god's sake, she thought. Lindsey was already shivering and she didn't have patience for preschool mind games.

"Look, come out of the rain. I think the phones are still working. Do you know your number?"

He shrugged again. Lindsey took his hand and led him to her carport while looking over her shoulder to see if anyone was watching. She had to do something, but she wondered what kind of trouble she'd get in for dragging a strange child into her home. If the kid didn't know his number, she wouldn't have any choice but to call the police.

"Is this the piddy lady's house?" the boy asked.

"Yes," she said. "A very pretty lady lives here. A wet, pretty lady." *Come inside, darling.* "Come inside, darling."

She almost had him across the threshold before she stopped herself. Why had she said that? That didn't even sound like her, and had she faked a Southern accent?

But the door was open. She'd closed it, she knew she had. She let go of the boy's hand and something shifted in her belly. Someone was in the house. They must have slipped behind her as she'd gone to the road.

"Hello? I know you're there. Hello? I'll call the cops." She reached in her pocket for her phone, but it wasn't there. Of course not, she'd left it in the living room. "Hello?" she said once more, then listened.

A chair in the kitchen scraped the floor.

"Get in the car," she said.

"But the piddy lady–"

"I said get in the car." She opened her Beetle and lifted him in. She didn't have a child seat, so she buckled the belt across his lap and hoped it would be enough. She climbed into the driver's side as fast as she could, only taking her eyes off the carport door when she had to. She found the key by touch and started the engine.

"Where do you live?" she asked, as if a five-year-old would know that. There was a hospital on the other side of Craft's downtown. She decided to take him there and let someone else figure out what to do. Water spun from the tires as she backed too quickly into the street, and the brakes made a wet groan.

There were already police at the hospital, keeping dry and waiting for emergency calls. To her relief they took her seriously about the intruder, though they asked so many questions about the boy that she was afraid they were going to arrest her.

His name was Ray. As soon as the officer asked, Lindsey felt bad for not doing so herself. The dispatcher reported that a child matching Ray's description had gone missing, so one of the patrolmen left to collect the boy's father while another, Officer Rice, offered to follow Lindsey home.

The rain slacked off on the way back, but the ditches on both sides of the road were full to the brim. Rice pulled into the driveway behind her, but Lindsey veered off to the side so she could leave in a hurry if she had to.

Through the rain-frosted window, she watched Rice hurry to the carport. The door was still open; she could tell from the blurry rectangle of light. The policeman's shadow passed through it, and the rain gods turned the nozzle back on. Lindsey settled into her seat and waited.

That's when she saw her: a golden-haired woman in a white dress walking across the lawn. Whoever she was, she didn't care about the rain. She moved slowly, casually, looking up at the sky as if on a clear summer day. The windows of the Beetle were too fogged to make out her face, so Lindsey rubbed a clear patch with her sleeve.

As soon as she did, the woman was gone – or rather, the illusion that it had been a woman at all. A stray beam of sunlight broke the clouds, and it became clear that all she'd seen was the siding of the house next door, glimpsed through the gap of two low-hanging willow branches.

Lindsey sighed; she was way too on-edge. She took a breath to calm herself, then jumped out of her skin when Officer Rice knocked on her window.

"Miss Destrehan? The house is clear, but you definitely had a visitor. You'll want to come see if anything was taken."

The sitting room just inside the door was untouched, but in the kitchen her grandmother's collection of spoons had been knocked off the wall and scattered across the floor. The living room was also a shambles: the couch was turned on its back, the lounge chair on its face, and the TV stand had been shoved several feet to the side. All of her grandmother's oddments and knickknacks seemed to be in place, but even after living there for several months, Lindsey still hadn't memorized all of the house's flotsam.

"She was a nice woman, your grandma," said the policeman.

"Never knew her. I mean, she came to visit a few times when I was young, but my mom never brought me down here."

"So how'd you come to own the place? If you don't mind my asking…"

"No, it's all right. My mom passed away several years ago and I was the only grandkid. I thought about selling, but I needed a break from my life up north. So here I am."

"You get a job in town?"

"I work part time at the Art Center, but mainly I edit copy for a magazine in Chicago. If not for email, the commute would be a killer."

Something rumbled, probably thunder or a transformer about to go, but it sounded more like a growl. Lindsey rubbed her arms, but she couldn't relax.

"Look," said Rice, "if you don't feel safe here, there's a hotel off of I-10 where I can get you the police discount."

"No, that's alright. I'll just make sure all the doors are locked. Twice." She didn't relish the idea of going back into the storm any more than the thought of another break-in.

"Okay, but I'll be in the area. Call my dispatcher if you get to feeling uncomfortable."

She nodded, smiled, and showed him out.

Something growled again as she closed the door. Her imagination put the noise in the living room, though she knew that wasn't possible. It might have been easier to leave, but she knew that if she didn't stay home and bear through the panic, she'd be jumping at every creak the house made for a month. She'd be better off if she just made some tea, set the couch upright, and went back to surfing channels.

The Craft Community Arts Center was in an old theater building run by Mrs. Maddy Babineaux. Part of the Center doubled as a day care in the summer, and Mrs. Babineaux also owned the ancient beauty parlor next door, which was currently serving time as an antique store. Lindsey was late for work that afternoon, but she found herself staring at the beauty shop window.

On the other side of the glass was a lovingly arranged setting of a small, round table and two high-backed wooden chairs. The table was covered with an old patterned cloth that retained most of its vibrant green, set with plates and silver for two. Draped across one chair was a tweed jacket, and on the other hung a short-brimmed woman's hat that hadn't been in style since the Roaring Twenties.

Behind the display were shelves lined with figurines and curios just like Lindsey's grandmother's. Tiny porcelain cherubs lounged on sculpted clouds while petite, painted toddlers played endless games of hopscotch. How many people still collected such things, she wondered, and what would the grown children in the day care do with all those knickknacks once the generation that cherished them had gone to dust?

A reflection over her shoulder snapped her out of her daydream. He was a black man with medium-light skin, maybe thirty or forty years old. His nose was narrow, his face angular, and he had a sheepish smile that refused to break into a grin. She didn't know him, but there was something familiar about his eyes.

"Excuse me," he said, "are you Miss Destrehan?"

"Yes?"

"I want to thank you for finding my son. I'm Tony Allen, Ray's father."

"Oh! Sure, no problem. I mean, I'm just glad he's safe. How is he?"

"He's doing fine. He keeps talking about the pretty lady he met in the storm."

"Well, I'm glad I made an impression." It suddenly clicked why Mr. Allen was there. "Wait, is Ray one of the kids in the day care? I must have seen him all summer and I didn't recognize him."

"Do you work with the kids?"

"No, just with the art gallery, and I'm... Why don't you come inside and have a look?"

They entered the theater just as the kids and their teenage herders had gathered in the lobby for their parents to pick them up. Ray ran to his father with a piece of art of his own – a paper face made of dry macaroni that looked oddly like a Picasso. Tony picked him up and the boy draped his arm over his father's shoulder.

"Hey Ray, look who's here."

Lindsey waved. "You remember me?" Ray shook his head.

"Yes you do," said Tony. "It's the lady from the storm."

"That not the piddy lady. The piddy lady's in the pitcher."

Tony shrugged. "Don't mind him. I don't know what's going on in his head."

"You want to see some art, Ray?" Lindsey put on her best talking-to-kids smile and hoped she didn't look like the Joker. The kid nodded.

The gallery was in the theater hall itself, where the seats had long been removed and the paintings were laid out in a maze.

"This is nice," said Tony as he set Ray down. "We've only been in town since last Christmas. I didn't even know this was here."

"We're getting ready for a show in September. Weather permitting, we'll move everything out to the city park, but right now this is the only place to store them."

"Daddy!" shouted Ray. He'd ignored the paintings and gone behind the stage curtain. "Come lookit! It's Heaven Man."

"Heaven Man?" asked Lindsey. "What's that, some new super-hero?"

"I don't know," said Tony. "He's real smart, and all summer he's been making stuff up. His teacher says he ought to go into acting."

"Well, this is the place for it."

"Daddy, lookit Heaven Man! He's got a skull."

"Ray?" said Lindsey. "What are you getting into, honey?"

She and Tony stepped around the curtain to find Ray beaming up at an old poster from a local production of *Hamlet*. The theater was full of them and they were something of a joke, since the printer had inserted the wrong dialog over each scene. The one Ray had found was of Hamlet holding Yorick's skull, but the caption read *There are more things in heaven and earth, Horatio, than are dreamt of in your philosophy.*

"Heaven Man," repeated Ray.

"Why are you calling him that?" asked Lindsey. Then it struck her. "Ray, can you read what it says?"

"More fings in heaven and earth."

"Told you he was smart," said Tony.

"You weren't kidding."

"I's smart as a button," Ray declared. "That's what the piddy lady says."

They dragged him away from the stage and back to the gallery. Something itched up Lindsey's spine, and Tony must have felt it too from the glance he gave her.

"Son, does the pretty lady work in your day care?"

"Naw, she's in the pitcher. She only comes out when it rains. That's cuz she's made of water." Ray giggled and pointed at a painting. "That one's funny."

An imaginary friend could be healthy at Ray's age, Lindsey thought, but not if he used her as an excuse to run away from home. That assumed, of course, that the fairy tale wasn't true.

"Tony," she said, "I'll keep my eyes open and see if I can figure out who he's talking about."

"I'd be thankful for that," said Tony. "Come on, son, it's time to go."

It didn't rain for weeks, not until Tropical Storm Drake came on shore between Fort Walton and Destin. Craft didn't even bother to close down, but the western angle of Drake's path brought a deluge all the same.

Lindsey volunteered to cover for one of the teens at the daycare. Attendance was low; only the children of people who had to work had turned up. It wasn't easy to keep an eye on Ray, what with the constant distraction of other kids who needed help with their art projects, or were getting in fights, or needed to potty. Ray didn't beg for attention. For the most part he sat on a bench by the window and looked out. Occasionally he would wave. When Lindsey went to see what he was looking at, there was nothing but rain and bushes.

By the end of the day, as she tried to keep her charges from tearing the theater lobby apart, Lindsey had developed a new respect for people who worked with children. Next to the exit, a poster of Hamlet's ghost leered down with unmitigated menace. *Angels and ministers of grace defend us*, read the caption, which Lindsey found completely appropriate.

Eventually Ray was the only child left and Mrs. Babineaux was getting pissy. Lindsey worried. It wasn't like Tony to be late, but in the backwash of a tropical cyclone there were plenty of reasons for tardiness, none of them good. As if to punctuate her fears, a miniature whirlwind twirled like a ballerina down the road outside. The phone rang and Mrs. Babineaux answered.

"Hello? Oh, Mr. Allen. Yes, he's still here. No, I'm afraid it's against our policy to stay later. You'll have to be charged a fee for every five minutes after four o'clock. I understand about your tire, sir, but we can't bend the rules."

Why don't you take him home?

"Why don't I take him home?" Lindsey asked. "Give Tony my address and he can pick him up later."

Mrs. Babineaux scowled. "I'm afraid that's also against policy. Day care staff–"

"But I'm not staff, I'm just filling in. And besides, I'm a friend of the family." That was a stretch, but she hoped not too much of a lie. She slung her bag over her shoulder and picked up Ray with the other arm. "It'll be fine, just tell him to come by my house when he can."

She buckled Ray into the back seat. Hopefully the cops would be too busy to pull her over. For that matter, there were more than a dozen reasons she might get in trouble for running off with another person's child. She hadn't even asked Tony's permission. What had she been thinking?

It didn't matter now. The day care was closed, the theater locked, and there was a toddler she barely knew warming the seat of her car. All she could do was head home, order some pizza, wait for Tony, and hope he wasn't angry.

The wind picked up just as she turned into her driveway. The carport was dark, so she bundled Ray out of her Beetle and told him not to run off while she fumbled for the house key.

Ray giggled. "Hey, piddy lady!" Lindsey smiled, turned the knob, and opened the door.

GET THAT TRASH OUT

The force of the command pushed her backward two steps. It was deep, angry, like a boom of thunder. The inside of the house was cold and black, but what really made her want to run was that there hadn't been a voice at all, just words resounding in her head.

I SAID GET THAT TRASH OUT

Ray giggled and ran for the door. If he went inside he'd die, somehow Lindsey knew it. She dove after him and threw her arms around his shoulders as they both fell to the floor. He cried in surprise and started to wail. Lindsey looked around for the intruder and prayed that they still had time to get away.

On the far side of the room, a porcelain vase lifted from a table on its own, angled as if someone were about to swing it, and flew through the air.

In the last possible instant, she twisted and sheltered Ray. The vase smashed against her head and light exploded in her eyes. Something else parted the air with the stealth of a baseball and struck her back. A third object, sharper than the others, jabbed her shoulder and fell to the floor. A wind like the breath of a giant gathered behind her, to the sound of glass, pewter, and plaster cracking, clinking, and taking aim. All along, the deep, dark voice hammered her mind.

OUT OUT OUT

Lindsey flew out the door, Ray screaming in her arms. She tossed him into her car and didn't bother with the seatbelt as she cranked the startled engine and floored it in reverse. The back of her head was warm and wet, and she felt like she was about to pass out. She slammed her brakes at the end of the drive and sat with her eyes on the house while her fingers scratched 9-1-1 on her cell.

The dumbest thing anyone did in scary movies was not to leave once they learned their house was haunted. Lindsey didn't mention the ghost to Officer Rice, but stuck to her story about an intruder. The police didn't keep her for questioning – there were too many "stupid people driving in the rain" calls that evening – but they did seal her house and return Ray to his father. Rice didn't get on her case for taking the kid home; the disappointed look he gave her was enough. He asked her not to leave town until they'd had a chance to chat, and repeated his offer of the police discount at the hotel. This time she took him up on it.

She didn't sleep. The hotel never lost power, so she flipped between weather reports while shivering under the covers. Her chill was only partly from the ice pack on her head.

The next day was as clear and blue as he could want. All Lindsey's possessions were locked in the house, so she bought a change of clothes at Wal-Mart and headed to the Art Center to hand in her resignation.

Mrs. Babineaux's office looked more like a place for having afternoon tea than conducting business. An antique roll-top hid the day care's pesky paperwork, and a light green tablecloth draped the desk. There were even lace doilies.

Lindsey told the story of the attack as briefly and vaguely as she could. Mrs. Babineaux took it with a show of concern, but not surprise. Lindsey explained that she was too shaken by the incident, on top of the one before, and that she was just going to sell the house and move back home.

"Was it the father?" Mrs. Babineaux asked. Lindsey couldn't

make sense of the question.

"The father. What, you mean Mr. Allen? Absolutely not. How could you think such a thing?"

"That's not what I meant at all dear. I'm sorry you misunderstood."

"Misunderstood what?"

The older woman sighed. "Never mind. Best to let old ghosts lie."

Old ghosts. Maddy knew something, but Lindsey didn't want to ferret it out. That could only dig her deeper into a mess she wanted out of, so she decided not to press.

"Well," she said, "I guess I better get going. I need to see about a real estate agent."

"You do that, dear. Let me know if you need any recommendations."

She slipped out the door and headed to the lobby, thinking this was the last time she'd ever see the place. It was a shame; she'd been looking forward to the art show. She glanced at one of the misquoted *Hamlet* posters and wondered if she should steal one as a memento.

She froze at the image: a young woman in white with straight, yellow hair and an ethereal look as she lifted her eyes to the stage lights. The character had to be Ophelia, but she bore a striking resemblance to the woman Lindsey had seen in the rain. The caption on the poster read, *That he's mad, 'tis true, 'tis true 'tis pity.*

"Tis pity," Lindsey read aloud. "The pity lady. My god, *the pity lady.*" She turned and ran back to Mrs. Babineaux.

"Why, that was your aunt Savannah," was her answer to the obvious question. "Didn't your mother ever tell you about her?"

"My mother never told me anything." She didn't mean to sound as bitter as she felt, but there was no helping it.

"Well, your aunt was quite a bit older. She did that play when your mother was just a child. After that, she left town for a year or two, and it was quite the scandal when she came back."

"How so?"

"You sure you want to hear this?"

Lindsey nodded.

"Now you got to understand, your family's one of the oldest in Craft. Not rich, but respected. Her father, your grandfather, felt he had a certain reputation to live up to. I wouldn't call your aunt a hippie, but she was certainly a free spirit and the gossip was that he didn't like the kind of company she was keeping."

"You mean actors?"

Maddy smiled. "Just so."

Come to think of it, her mother had never talked about her grandfather either. In her grandmother's house, there weren't even any pictures of him. It hadn't struck her as odd until now. She knew he'd died before she was born, but her mother never said how and Lindsey never thought to ask. Mrs. Babineaux leaned forward, as if someone might try to listen, and went on.

"This was the summer of '79. Your aunt came home from wherever she'd run off to after high school, and the next door neighbor heard quite a row. Miss Savannah was seen driving off in some beat-up old Pinto and Mr. Destrehan drove off himself not too long after."

"What did he do?" she asked. Horrid speculations were already swirling in her mind.

"No one knew right away. They found your aunt washed up in a storm drain, but at first everyone thought she drowned because of Frederic."

"Who's Frederic?"

Mrs. Babineaux paused. "Hurricane Frederic, dear. Then it came out from the coroner that she hadn't drowned, she'd been strangled. And before the police could ask your granddaddy about it, he went and shot himself."

Lindsey couldn't believe it. Why hadn't she ever heard any of this? Her mother must have been there for the whole thing, even if she was just a kid.

"Where did he shoot himself?" she asked.

"In the head, dear."

"No, I mean where was he?"

"Oh, he was in the living room."

"Jesus. So you knew my house was haunted all this time?"

"Now don't raise your voice. I didn't know any such thing; I just put two and two together. Your gran kept a lot of old memories in that house, and to tell the truth I've seen Savannah myself from time to time."

"But you said you didn't know the house was haunted."

"Your aunt doesn't haunt that house, dear. She died in the rain, and that's where people see her."

Leaving Craft wasn't as easy as Lindsey hoped. Yes, she could have jumped in her car and hit the road, but there were bills to pay, utilities to shut off, and mail to forward, not to mention the tax issues of a two thousand square foot home that was no longer a primary residence. After all, what did the wrath of a murderous spirit matter compared to her credit rating?

Eventually Mrs. Babineaux talked her into staying through the art show on Labor Day, in an apartment above the theater's dressing room that had once belonged to the building supervisor. The floor was bare save for a carpet of dust, there were no springs for the mattress on the old single bed, and the window unit had died in its sleep years before. Still, there was a shower with hot water, the electric worked, and if she opened the windows, the breeze made it cool enough to sleep. There was even a working mini-fridge with three forgotten cans of beer.

At first she tried to avoid Mr. Allen whenever he came to pick up Ray, but eventually she gathered the courage to apologize. She didn't feed him the lie about an intruder. Instead, she told him the truth. He took it better than she'd hoped. At least he didn't call her crazy to her face.

"So this *pity lady* Ray's been seeing?"

"I'll show you," Lindsey said, and took him to the poster of Ophelia.

Tony jerked back, then reached forward and brushed the blond woman's face with his fingers.

"I know her," he said. "I've seen her, I know I have. Does she still work in the theater?"

"No, that's what I'm telling you. That's my Aunt Savannah. She died over thirty years ago."

"And Ray's been seeing this... ghost?"

Lindsey nodded. "I've seen her too, but that's not what's in my house. That was something meaner."

"This is crazy." There it was. "No, I believe what you're saying, but I can't see why this is happening. Why should my boy have a connection to this woman? We're not even from here."

"What made you move here?"

"I don't know. Had to move somewhere, and this place just felt right for some reason."

"Do you mind if I ask," said Lindsey, "where's Ray's mother?"

"At a rehab clinic in California. I think."

"I'm sorry."

"We're making it. My daddy raised me by himself, so I'm doing the same for Ray."

"But maybe if he's looking for a mother figure, that's why he's drawn to her." Lindsey shook her head. "I don't know. Why should any of this ghost crap make sense?"

"I'm sure it makes sense to somebody," Tony said. "But whoever that is ain't me."

The art show drew closer. Lindsey found an agent to take care of her house and hired a cleaning service to tidy up and bring out her belongings. She didn't tell them why she wouldn't go in herself, or else she'd have to hire a priest as well. Would that even work?

Meanwhile, she picked up a storm-tracker and began checking the weather obsessively. In August, Tropical Storm Evelyn formed off the coast of Puerto Rico and made its way toward Miami, but it veered north in the Bahamas and bounced harmlessly into the Atlantic. As soon as it was gone, Fritz developed overnight in the Gulf, but the winds blew it west before it gained any strength.

Gertrude was the one to watch. She came to a boil in the deep Caribbean and was already a Category Two by the time she swept Honduras. Labor Day was approaching, but so was the monster. The longer Lindsey tracked it, the more she grew convinced that this would be the big one.

She'd meant to leave before it hit. She had planned to be well on her way to Indiana, or at least Birmingham, and would have been if not for Mrs. Babineaux's sudden heart attack on the eve of the evacuation. The ambulance got her to the hospital in time for the doctors to stabilize her, but they didn't dare move her from the ICU, storm or no.

That left Lindsey to ready the gallery. The art show wouldn't happen, of course – delayed indefinitely on account of God – but someone had to protect the artwork. The theater was sturdy, but the roof couldn't be trusted. Once she knew she'd be staying until the last minute, she phoned Tony and told him to get Ray the hell out of Craft.

The first rain band hit as Lindsey triple-bagged the last of the canvases and sealed it with duct tape. There wasn't any thunder, just an insistent, gentle hammering. On cue, the radio let out three high-pitched beeps and the robotic voice of the National Weather Service announced Gertrude's location.

Tell me something I don't know, she thought as she stacked the last canvas in the ladies' changing room, which was the closest thing in the building to a vault. When she closed the door behind her, the box office phone rang.

"Art Center," she answered.

"Lindsey? It's Tony. Have you seen Ray?"

Ice ran down her throat. "I thought I told you to get out of town."

"I work for the power company; I don't get to leave. I gave him to my neighbor to take with her kids to Atlanta."

"And?"

There was a pause. "And I called to check on him, and she doesn't know what I'm talking about. Says she hasn't seen me in a week. But I know I sent Ray with her. I remember putting him in the car." There was a tremor in his voice, like he was trying to convince himself.

"You're not sure."

"I'm not. I don't know what's going on. I've been dreaming

about that woman you showed me. Do you think maybe she got in my head?"

Lindsey was already pulling on her poncho. "Look, we know where Ray's going. I'll meet you at my house in ten minutes."

The rain wasn't hard yet, just a statement of intent. Her grandmother's house hunched beneath its surrounding oaks with no lights, no cars in the drive, and its lawn not cut in weeks. The place looked downright sullen. Lindsey stopped just short of the carport and waited. There was no sign of Ray. She'd called Officer Rice's dispatcher, but there was no sign of the policeman either.

Tony pulled up in his company truck and together they approached the house. Something growled inside and this time Lindsey didn't pretend it was the weather.

"You think he's in there?" said Tony.

"God, I hope not." The last time, she'd been certain Ray's life was in danger. She hoped they weren't too late. The door was locked, thank goodness, so she turned the key and pushed it open.

Cool air washed over them with a smell of alcohol and tobacco. Someone was shouting in the distance. Lindsey couldn't move, but Tony took her hand and the connection snapped her out of it. Together, they squeezed through the door.

"Get that trash out of here."

"Trash!" Savannah clutched the wriggling bundle to her chest. "That's your grandson, you stupid old man."

"That thing is no blood of mine, and you're no daughter. You should have stayed in California. You should have died in some drug den with the rest of the filth. That would have been better than

bringing this disgrace back to your family."

Silent, Savannah's mother wept. Her little sister, Lindsey's mother, huddled in the corner and whimpered. In Savannah's arms, a baby bawled. They were all drowned out by her fury.

"You. Evil. Bigot. You pathetic little man."

"Get out." He lifted a vase and smashed it against the wall. Savannah's mother screamed and lunged for his arm, but he shoved her away. With his other hand, he held a porcelain shard like a knife. Savannah didn't back down.

"Oh, I'll get out. I've got my own family now, and once Ray and I start showing our baby boy around town, everyone's going to know what a black-hearted bastard you are."

Lindsey's grandfather roared. The sound wasn't human. He charged, makeshift dagger in his bleeding fist, and Savannah spun around, fear finally showing in her eyes. She barreled past Lindsey and Tony as Savannah's sobbing mother shouted, "No! It isn't safe! The storm..."

They staggered back outside.

"What the hell was that?" said Tony.

"Memories." The house was full of them, more so than Lindsey had realized. She looked at Tony anew, suddenly understanding – the thin nose and angular face, a dusky reflection of her aunt. The familiar set of his eyes, just like the ones she saw in the mirror every day.

"My god, Tony," she said. "You're my cousin."

He shook his head, more in shock than denial. "My mama."

"You said your father raised you alone. What was his name?"

"Ray," he answered. "My mother died when I was a baby, and Pop said I was better off not knowing about her." The ghost of their grandfather roared in the house, and under the carport rain began to pelt as the wind blew it sideways.

And there were Tony's mother and son, standing in the yard. Little Ray wobbled in the wind, but somehow managed to stay upright. His face was as slack as his rain-drenched clothes and his eyes were unfocused. Beside him, her white dress untouched by wind or water, Savannah Destrehan ran her nails lovingly through his short, black hair.

"Mama?" said Tony.

With his shroud as the mountain snow, she said, *larded with sweet flowers, which bewept to the grave did go with true-love showers.*

"Enough with the Shakespeare," said Lindsey. "What do you want?"

I want my baby. She pulled Ray in close. *He's gotten so big.*

"He's your grandbaby, Mama," said Tony. "I'm standing right here."

The ghost cocked her head. Lindsey didn't think that her aunt understood. How could she, when she was nothing but a memory?

Let's go see your granddaddy, baby, she said. *I can't wait to see the look on his face.*

"No," said Lindsey. "You already did that, remember? He killed you for it."

The ghost took Ray by the shoulder and walked him slowly toward the house. Tony grabbed him, but a blast of wind blew into the carport, bowling Tony over and howling through the open door. Lindsey fell to her knees as a sheet of rain sharp as needles stuck her face. Through the blur, she saw her aunt pick Ray out from Tony's arms. The door flapped like a monster gnashing its teeth.

Lindsey dove at Savannah. It was like wrestling a waterspout.

The storm rushed into her lungs and for an instant she was drowning. Then the ghost gripped her by the hair and yanked her back. Rain cascaded down Lindsey's face and poured from her sodden clothes.

Don't keep me from my baby.

"I'm your baby, Mama." Tony rose to his feet again. "I'm your baby, not Ray. I'm sorry I wasn't here for you, but you gotta let him go."

Something clicked behind the ghost's eyes and all the rage drained out of her. *Tony? Little Tony?*

The door slammed shut and Lindsey looked around. "Oh God, where's Ray?" She already knew the answer.

The wind held the door closed. Lindsey braced her foot on the frame and pulled will all her strength. It ripped open for a split second and she darted inside before it sealed again.

"Ray!"

Windows rattled. Anger seethed around her, filling the house with shadow. She flicked on the lights, but they barely broke the gloom. Something heavy crashed in the living room and she was there in a heartbeat.

The child lay on the floor, unmoving. He stared upward as his brown skin took on a hue of purple. Lindsey's heart lurched as she realized he couldn't breathe. She ran to pick him up, but an unseen force flung her back. Her head slapped against the wall and her ears rang from the impact.

GET THAT TRASH OUT

"He isn't trash," said Lindsey as she tried to orient herself. "He doesn't even know who you are. Why can't you let him be?"

NO BLOOD OF MINE

"That's right." She lunged at Ray again, and once more the thing in the room flung her away. She could see it now: a hulking shadow like a child's drawing of an ogre. Its humanity gone, there was nothing left but the memory of hate.

Memory. The house rattled again, and as Lindsey braced herself, she saw that none of her grandmother's knickknacks moved. Despite all the violence, not one of them was scratched. If the house was full of memories, here they were in solid form.

On an end table sat a clock with a bronze frame. She picked it up and threw it at the shelf of figurines above the television, smashing them into ceramic dust.

Her grandfather roared. He swept toward her, so she grabbed the nearest lamp and swung it at an arrangement of commemorative bottles. They shattered with the smell of an old man's mouthwash.

The shadow thing pushed her off her feet, but it was weaker than before. Lindsey pulled herself up, then grabbed the padded footrest next to the lounge chair and swung it at a curio cabinet full of photos and dolls. It smashed, sending bits of glass into her knuckles as its contents tumbled to the floor.

The shadow ripped the footrest from her hands and flung it across the room, then struck her in the chest with all of its unseen force. Her breath blew out of her as she fell back on the coffee table. Instinct taking over, she rolled to the side as another blow made the low table shudder. With all her strength, she lifted the heavy slab of oak and threw it at her grandmother's wall of shelves, crushing snowglobes, vases, candle holders, and old school trophies, sending the whole mess to a broken pile.

Ray cried out as the thing let him go. Lindsey scooped him off the floor and darkness swarmed around them as she dashed through the sitting room. Shadows tightened around her throat, pulling her to a halt just short of the door. She couldn't reach it without dropping Ray. The thing that had been her grandfather tightened its grip. Her eyes swam and her lungs emptied and her knees began to shake and the child was so heavy.

Light flung open the door. A mother's anger in the shape of Savannah whipped through the air, and the shadows let Lindsey go as the whirlwind tore the old ghost away. The howls of battling spirits mixed like the roars of two steam trains. Lindsey dared a glance behind her, and the house began to *grind* as couches, tables, lamps, and the old RCA lifted and plowed into each other in the ever-growing maelstrom. The very ceiling trembled and the walls began to bow.

Tony stood in the doorway and shouted, "Come on!" Behind him, police lights flashed – her knight in blue arriving too late for the rescue.

Lindsey didn't need any urging. Her nephew in her arms, she ran past his father into the light of the oncoming storm.

Despite the destruction, the Destrehan property glistened in the sun. The house was a broken pile of rubble, flattened save for mounds where appliances lay buried. Bits of wood, brick, and drywall were scattered across the yard. The trees were as bare as winter, the force of the storm having torn off their leaves, but the green grass and azaleas twinkled with the first early dew of autumn.

Ray played with a toy truck in the driveway where Lindsey kept an eye on him while Tony surveyed the damage. After telling Officer Rice the truth – the *whole* truth – he'd closed her case file and promised to keep it under wraps. Even with Gertrude a week behind them, most of Craft was still without electricity. Tony had managed to get away from fixing power lines only long enough to see her and Ray off.

"Thanks for taking him," he said. "I'll still be at work a month before they let me go."

"You turned in your resignation?"

He nodded. "We can't stay here. I'd be too worried."

Lindsey understood. Despite the house being wrecked, who knew what phantoms still lingered? Better to take the insurance money and sell. Maybe the land would make a good place for a gas station. She didn't know or care. She planned to give the money to Tony for Ray, but she hadn't talked to him about it yet.

"Where are you going to go?" she asked. "You guys could come to Indiana. In a few more months, Ray could build his first snowman."

"I might do that. Sounds as good as anything." His cell phone beeped and he glanced at the caller ID. "Well, I'm back on the clock. You be good for Aunt Lindsey, little man."

Ray nodded and hugged his father's knees. Tony leaned over and kissed his head.

"You two take care."

"Same to you," said Lindsey. She'd be leaving as soon as he did. Looking back at the house, she considered shuffling through the wreckage, maybe finding some undamaged trinket to take with her as a keepsake.

On the horizon, clouds marred the sky in an echo of the recent storm. Some memories were worth holding on to, Lindsey decided, but others were better lost in the rain.

All the Good I Could

Suzanne Johnson

Daniel

August come down on us like the fires of hell this year, and all we been able to do is pull the dried husks of the late corn and pray the fall rains get here in time to save the winter crops. I want food put away afore the cold moves in. Hard times is coming.

The boys seem to know something's about to change, even if they don't know what. Instead of cuttin' the fool and seeing who can do more playing than working, they been hunkering down to the job this summer, the sun turning their backs brown and changing their bodies from stringbean boys into the makings of strong men.

They're the oldest now, Frank at sixteen and Tom at twelve, and it would break my heart, knowing I won't be here to see them grow big and tall, if my heart wasn't so broke down already.

An old crow started coming close last week, hanging 'round the kitchen and porch. My grandda, who come from Galway and still held to the Irish ways, told me and my brother Moses how, back in the old country, everybody knew if a crow come to your door or window it meant your time was drawin' short.

I never held much to them old stories before, but that crow's made me think different. His evil eye pierces me like a slaughtering knife while his yellow claws dig for purchase in the old wood of the window frame.

I put that window in for Maggie the year before the war fell on our doorstep like the hand of an angry God Almighty. "Daniel, I don't need a window when the boys need shoes," she told me, but the light in her eyes said different.

Aye, I reckon that old crow's telling me my time's coming, and I'm half past ready. I figure that's selfish.

Preacher says a man who lives a long life is blessed. Says an old man can look back on his days on this earth and count each one a gift. I figure God'll smite me for it, but some of those gifts I want to throw right back in His face.

This morning, when I got out of bed, old crow wasn't there. I walked to the kitchen window and looked for his outline against the coming day, just starting to lighten the sky.

Instead, Henry stood at the edge of the woods on the north ridge, watching me. I thought my heart might stop as my eyes met those of my firstborn. He was tall, green-eyed, and auburn-haired like his mama, who died when he was a baby, and strong like Maggie, who brought him up.

I ain't seen Henry in eight years, since July of '62. But this is the summer for visions, I reckon. The heat and dry winds have stirred up old bones and spirits long gone and blown them in like dandelion wisps.

Eight years. In a different time and place, Henry would'a been married and give me grandsons – him and my other two older boys all – but their time and place was war, that blasted war. It didn't do nothing in the end but prove that prideful men fall and humble men are only prideful men hiding behind humility. I reckon I was one of those humble men.

Henry watched me for a right long time before turning and walking back into the woods, climbing toward the ridge. I knew where he was going.

Frank

I hand-rassled Tom for the last biscuit on the table and let him win. Then the fool started running round the kitchen like one'a them banshees Uncle Mose used to tell us about.

"Hush up, you want Papa to come and tan us?" I was tall as Papa now, but that wouldn't stop him from whipping me all the same.

Tom talked with his mouth full, something he'd never dare if Mama was still here. "He ain't gonna do nothing. He already left, heading up the ridge."

"He go huntin'? How come he didn't take us?"

"Ain't huntin'. Left his gun."

I looked out the window and didn't see nothing except that old crow been hanging around the last couple of weeks. "Reckon if that bird comes in the house, we can catch him and eat him?"

Tom didn't answer, and when I looked round, he'd gone. It was Saturday, so Papa let us take time off from field work unless it was harvest. The girls've done the house chores since Mama died, and I could hear them stirring in the back. If I didn't get out of the house, bossy old Lizbeth'd try to make me do girl work.

Used to be my job to milk the cows and water the horses in the morning, but the Rebs took the cows and the Yanks took the horses, so it didn't leave me much except to feed a few old ornery chickens and leave the eggs for Tom to gather.

I pulled on my boots – they used to be Henry's, I think – and walked outside. No breeze moved, and I stopped at the trough by the well and splashed water on my face. The sun was already blistering. I told Papa last night this had been the meanest summer heat I ever remembered, but he said I ain't old enough to remember much.

I picked up the bucket of corn, so hard and dry it ain't fit for people to eat, and scattered it around the dirt yard. Home Guard took all our chickens first time they come looking for Papa to hang him, but after the war, the Yanks give us money for General, the big gray horse they took.

Papa had to "testify," he called it, to get the money – Union dollars, not that Confederate stuff that won't buy nothing. I went with him, and he told them all about Henry and the others fightin' for the north. "I done the Union all the good I could," he said before making his "X," and it wasn't boastful, just the truth. I wanted to cry, but only babies and girls cry, so I swallowed it like a hard rock.

We went down to Jasper the next week and bought the chickens with that horse money. Made us a little better off'n our neighbors that was in the Home Guard, and made 'em hate us even more. Papa says it don't matter whether they like us or not, long as they leave us alone. There was plenty of folks like us that weren't Rebs, he said, and we knew who was our friends.

I finished with the chickens and noticed the crow done moved from the porch to the well, and it was looking toward the ridge. I ain't been up there since the war ended, after Papa didn't have to hide from the Home Guard anymore.

I always took him food that Mama wrapped up in a cloth, and I only slipped up once and ate some of the dried pork and cold potato myself. I was only ten or eleven, and scrawny. I reckon Papa knew I ate some 'cause I didn't know how to tie the cloth back like Mama had it, but he didn't say nothin', and I felt worse than if he'd fussed at me. We was all hungry then, but I knew him and Mama and the older boys didn't eat until all us little ones did.

The crow cawed its ugly noise and took off up the ridge, its sound making shivers run all over my arms. Henry used to tell us stories when the grownups weren't around, although he was 'bout grown hisself. He said a visitin' crow meant somebody was going to die. I didn't like it that the crow was flying after Papa. It sent a chill over my arms like I'd been dipped in water right out of the spring.

I decided he might need company.

Daniel

I followed Henry into the woods, headin' uphill. I knew he was going to the cave. He's the one what found it. When I needed a spot to hide from the Home Guard, he showed it to me.

He kept a steady pace ahead of me but didn't look back again. I figured he knew I was there.

Henry wasn't wearing what he had on last time I saw him – him and the other two older boys all had on their Sunday clothes that day. Maggie and the girls had washed everything and filled their saddlebags, along with some food to tide 'em over. I fixed them up with my best horses and rode up to Decatur with them, using most of the money we'd put back to buy them some guns and blankets. They didn't get to use them, not the blankets anyway.

Today, Henry's wearing the blue uniform the army give him. We was all forced to take a stand after the Secesh figured out they didn't have enough poor farmboys willing to fight their war. They said all the men between eighteen and thirty-five had to fight with the Rebs. Old Jim Webster told us about it when he come riding through in

June of '62. "'Course any man who ain't a coward's already signed up, I reckon," he said, loud enough for the boys to hear where they was washin' up after workin' the fields all day.

Jim's oldest boy was wearing the gray, and he didn't come home neither. God's got plenty of other things to forgive me about; I figure he ain't gonna mind adding the fact that I ain't sorry Billy Webster died.

"Papa, that ain't our fight," Henry told me the night we heard the conscription news. It was something we all agreed on. He was twenty-three, planning to get married to one of the county girls in the winter. "Me and Matthew and John gonna go up north," he said. "If we gotta fight, it ain't gonna be for them rich slave-owners down round Montgomery."

So they all went. The First Alabama Cavalry of the Union Army, they was called – a bunch of ragtag farmer's sons from Marion and Winston and Walker counties. I was proud of my three oldest boys, doin' what they thought was right instead'a what they thought was easy. Now I know it was devil's pride. It was the pride you pay for, the kind that conjures up ghosts on hot summer days to come and remind you of the bad choices you made.

But I reckon if the choice is between bad and worse, it don't matter much.

I didn't find out what happened to John and Matthew for more'n three years, when the Yankees who come to clean up the county told me they died of rubeola three months after I left 'em in Decatur. Twenty-one and nineteen, they was. They should'a had more to their lives than what they got, shoulda had more than graves in Tennessee away from their people.

I still didn't know 'bout Henry – only a bunch of stories I didn't believe, told by men who hate us because they lost the war. If anybody won that goddamned war, it sure wasn't me and my boys, but they tell the stories about Henry anyway.

Frank

The crow flew off somewhere and I couldn't see him anymore, but I kept climbing. It was cooler under the trees, and I figured it was a good day to visit the cave even if that ain't where Papa was going.

When he come home the last time, after living in the cave on and off for almost a year, he said he didn't want to ever go there again. By then, the Yankees had taken charge of the county and the Home Guard had quit trying to hang him and were trying to make do like the rest of us.

Then we found out my brothers died – except Henry, and we never knew about him. Papa got kind of quiet after that, didn't talk like he used to, not that he was ever a talky man. Then Mama got sick, and he didn't smile no more either.

But we kept on going, 'cause Papa says that's what people do. Just keep going till it gets better.

Some late blackberries called to me from a clearing, and I figured whatever Papa was up to could wait until I ate some. I crawled under the low branches and lay on my back in their shade, looking through the leaves at the blue sky and eating till my fingers was purple, and probably my mouth too. I wondered if that pretty Harris girl'd go walking with me next week. I mighta slept some.

Daniel

Even here in the piney woods, the sun was high and hot by the time I reached the cave. In the winter, when I was trying to survive the nights without a fire to give me away to the Home Guard, its wet cold would sink deep in my bones. Today, when I crawled through its narrow mouth, it felt good, like the hot and sticky sweat might cool on my body and give me some relief.

The sun slipped in at an angle from the outside, lighting up the front part of the cave. The back should've been black as night, but it wasn't. Henry stood there, and light shone around him like he was burning from the inside-out.

"I don't reckon you're real," I said, knowing not but hoping so.

"I reckon I'm real enough, in my way." His voice was deep and clear, just like it was eight years ago when I watched him ride away. It stole my breath, and I sat hard on the cave's dirt floor.

I had what seemed like a lifetime of questions, but couldn't find the voice to say them. Finally, "You know 'bout Matt and John?"

He sat facing me, legs crossed like an Injun, the way he always did as a boy. "They went fast. 'Measles' is what the doctors called it – it was all over the camps outside'a Nashville. Boys dyin' every hour."

We looked at each other a few minutes without talking. "Why'd you come back, Henry?" My heart was pounding out of my chest, and pain beat its way down my arm.

"Your time's coming soon, Papa. I wanted you to know I didn't do what they said. Wanted you to know what happened to me."

I don't know the last time I cried, but my cheeks were wet. "Tell me, son."

"I was on scout duty, me and a man from up in Illinois. Place called Cairo." Henry spoke soft, but his voice filled the cave, taking up all the extra air so breathing came hard. "It was a couple months after Matt and John died. We rode out ahead of the unit just before dark, and some Rebs ambushed us. Didn't ever see 'em."

His eyes were focused over my shoulder, as if he could see all the way back into those woods. "My scout partner's mount fell on him but mine ran off – you know that roan was always skittish."

"Except with you. You had a way with him," I said.

"Not that day." He smiled. "I lasted a while. Trapper found me later and buried me in the woods. But I wasn't a deserter, Papa. I know that's what some say, but it ain't true."

I rubbed my eyes and nodded. "I never thought you were, son. I knew – "

A branch snapped outside the cave, and I turned to see Frankie, his head stuck in the entrance, his purple-stained mouth hanging so wide open he could'a caught flies.

Frank

It didn't matter that nobody believed me. They all thought I was acting crazy cause I found Papa sick in that cave and 'bout had to carry him all the way down from the ridge. They thought because I was with Papa when he decided to die that I made up that part about seeing Henry.

But I know what happened to Henry, and there wasn't no way for me to know that without hearing it from him that day in the cave. I even think he said good-bye to me before he disappeared, but I can't be sure about that because Papa was having trouble drawing breath.

Now that fall's coming and the winter crops are planted, I wonder if I mighta got to Papa in time to make a difference if I hadn't stopped and ate those berries and fell asleep thinkin' about Bethany Harris. Prob'ly not, since we'd still have to get Doc Freeman, and Doc don't go nowhere fast.

We buried him next to Mama in the Smith cemetery, down on the edge of the land near the Fayette-Marion county line. I slipped out late yesterday and put up a new marker on an empty spot next to them.

I been working on it a few weeks, carving the marker out of a pretty piece of oak Tom and me cut last spring. I used Papa's whittling knife to etch in the names. I think he'd like it, knowing all three of my big brothers had a place, even if they wasn't there.

Matthew J. Smith, 19, private, 1st Ala. Cavalry, USV, Co. K, died 1862, Nashville

John M. Smith, 21, corporal, 1st Ala. Cavalry, USV, Co. K, died 1862, Nashville

Henry F. Smith, 23, private, 1st Ala. Cavalry, USV, Co. H, died 1862, Nashville

Papa was sixty-seven, and preacher says a man who lives a long life is blessed. I reckon, given his druthers, Papa'd just as soon have a few less blessings and a little more time. Or maybe that's just me.

EDITOR'S NOTE

It's all Ingrid's fault for asking, "Hey Jared, when are we going to do an anthology?" Or maybe it was Sean, who years ago planted the seed in my head of starting a writers' group at the Hoover Library. Maybe it was Larry for not telling me I was out of my mind, or Heather for being so gung-ho and tweeting the story call to the four corners of the known universe.

Most of all, I blame the contributors. Who knew there was so much raw talent bubbling under the surface of the Alabama literary scene, that so many writers would play along with this flight of publishing fancy, or that they'd work so hard to pen such varied, excellent tales with nothing but a "summertime ghost stories" writing prompt?

All kidding aside, many thanks to everyone who lent a hand in making this collection a reality. In addition to those who provided stories, I'd like to thank Haleigh and Meggan Huggins for their assist with the cover art, and my wife Lea for her all-around support.

My best hope is that others take as much pleasure from these tales as I've had in putting this collection together. And the next time you're walking alone on a warm summer night and hear a lost voice whispering in the breeze, be sure to give it a smile and a wave.

After all, you never know…

Jared Millet

March 2012

About the Authors

Michael P. Wines (My Best Girl)

Michael P. Wines is a biologist for the Environmental Institute at Auburn University who works on preserving eastern indigo snakes and Red Hills salamanders. He is a writer of children's fiction, a woodworker (www.wineswoodworks.com), and hopes to soon begin work on a Master of Biology degree with a focus on Herpetology.

Teresa Howard (Dead in Me)

Teresa Howard is often found at a corner table in a local bookstore working on her latest writing project. Her stories cover a wide range of speculative fiction and children's literature, and have appeared in *Sword & Sorceress*, *Neo-Opsis*, *Amazing Journeys*, and the iPhone anthology *Escape Clause*. Teresa is a member of the DC2K Writers Group that formed at A.C. Crispin's Dragon*Con workshop in 2000. For many years she was employed as a technology coordinator and computer lab instructor at an elementary school in Birmingham. She shares her home with SuzieQ, a loveable Tibetan terrier.

Ingrid Seymour (The Beaky Bunch)

Ingrid Seymour lives in the South with her husband and two kids, is a software engineer from 8:00 to 5:00, and a writer the rest of the time. She is fluent in Spanish, English, and French, and has won several writing competitions. Follow her publishing adventures online at fictionbound.com.

Lindsey Robinson (Sugar Baby)

Lindsey Robinson was born and raised in Bessemer, has a bachelor's degree in Journalism from the University of Florida, and has worked at newspapers in Alabama, Florida, and Georgia. Recently, Lindsey fell in love and moved to San Salvador, where she now teaches English. She will probably spend the next couple of years bouncing between San Sal and Alabama. All of her students have Southern accents.

Ray Busler (The Reproach)

Ray Busler lives in Trussville, Alabama with his patient wife of thirty-six years. He enjoys talking to writers and aspires to become one in the fullness of time. Ray can be contacted at ray.busler@gmail.com.

Sean DeArmond (Beachfront)

Sean DeArmond is a member of Write Club and cohost of the annual Flash Fiction Night. With his wife Sarah, Sean is a regular movie critic for HollywoodJesus.com, where he contributes needlessly long sentences to the spiritual reviews of team Brock & DeArmond. He wrote and performed in the two-act musical comedy *End of the World*, and can occasionally be seen performing standup at Birmingham's Stardome. Be sure to check out his first novel, to be released in early 2078.

Julia Jones Thompson (The Colors)

Julia Jones Thompson is an Alexander City native with degrees from Auburn University in Mathematics Education and Computer Science & Engineering. She is a software engineer in Auburn where she presently resides with her husband, Scott, and their cats. In her spare time, she enjoys cooking, gardening and writing.

Larry Williamson (Nancy's Jog)

Larry Williamson is a native of Tallassee, Alabama, a graduate of Auburn University, and a retired high school math teacher and football/track coach. He is the author of the historical novel *Tallapoosa* (NewSouth, 2001), the newspaper series *Over the River, Long Ago* (Tallassee Tribune, 2003-04), and the book of the same title (River's Edge Publishing, 2008). He is an instructor for Auburn University's Outreach Program, and a member of the Auburn Writers Circle and Alabama Writers Conclave.

Mary Brunini McArdle
(The House Near the Covered Bridge)

Mary Brunini McArdle is a member of the Huntsville Writers, has many publication credits, and has won numerous awards for her poetry, fiction, essays, and short plays. McArdle's work appears in Negative Capability Press's Alabama poetry anthology and *From the Sleeping Porch*, an anthology of Mississippi short stories. She has won several prizes in the Alabama Writers Conclave, including 1st place in Free Verse.

Megan Ingram (Wayward)

Megan Ingram has earned degrees in English from the University of Alabama and in Pastry Arts from the Gulf Coast Culinary Institute. When she isn't working or writing, she spends her days devising new dishes in her kitchen or slaying dragons in the backyard with her daughter. Married for thirteen years, she and her husband currently reside in Huntsville.

Larry Hensley (The Haunted House)

Number cruncher by profession, pencil pusher by obsession with a fondness for children's stories, Larry Hensley is married with two children (who've heard it all and read it some). When not hiking, fossil collecting, or chasing down numbers, he can usually be found curled around some book.

Bret Williams (The Apparition)

Bret Williams has been an Alabama resident since the age of eleven when his father was stationed at Redstone Arsenal. He now lives in the Birmingham area with his wife and three children and works as a software developer for a local company.

Margaret Fenton (Fourth of July)

Margaret Fenton grew up on the Mississippi Gulf Coast and received her Master of Social Work degree from Tulane. For nearly twelve years she was a child and family therapist at the Department of Human Resources in Birmingham. Her first novel, *Little Lamb Lost*, was published by Oceanview Publishing in June 2009. She and her husband own a cabin on Lewis Smith Lake and enjoy much of the summer there. She is the president of the Birmingham chapter of Sisters in Crime. Visit her at www.margaretfenton.com or find her on Facebook.

Lin Nielsen (Shades of History)

Lin Nielsen Cochran's first loves are science fiction and fantasy. A graduate of the Clarion West writers' workshop, her work has been published in two of the *Clarion* anthologies, as well as in magazines such as *Midnight Gallery* and *Southern Fried Sci-Fi*. In the mundane world, Lin designs engineering databases for the U.S. Army Aviation Directorate and lives in Huntsville with her husband Joseph, the drum king. Active in two writers groups, she also collects science fiction lunch boxes.

Joan Kennedy (Family Ties)

Born and raised in Ohio, Joan also lived in South Bend, Indiana and Pittsburgh before moving with her family to Birmingham. She received a BFA and has worked as an art teacher, photography assistant, and more than eighteen years as head of publications at the Birmingham Museum of Art, where she won numerous awards for her designs. Along with writing, she enjoys reading, drawing, and travel, and now lives along Buck Creek in Helena in her dream house, small enough to be comfortable, yet full of light.

Jessica Penot (The Exorcism of Mary's House)

Jessica Penot is a therapist and writer who lives in Huntsville with her husband, children, corgis, and other strange creatures. She is the author of *Haunted North Alabama* and *Haunted Chattanooga*, and is currently working on *Haunted South Alabama*. She writes a ghost column in the *Valley Planet* where she shares her love for stories that send shivers down your spine. Her new horror novel, *Circe*, was released in November 2011. Follow Jessica's ghostly pursuits at ghoststoriesandhauntedplaces.blogspot.com.

Tracy Williams (The Ghost of Bear Creek Swamp)

Tracy Williams was raised in Millbrook, Alabama, is a graduate of Auburn University with a degree in Sociology, and has been a lifelong resident of Georgia and Alabama. A participant of National Novel Writing Month, she currently works as a sales support specialist in the construction industry and lives in Calera, Alabama, with a miniature dachshund and a ragdoll cat.

C. M. Koenig (Feral)

C. M. Koenig, while still a student, is involved in painting, ballet, and robotic design. She aspires to become a genetic counselor who writes part time (though she'd love to do it for a living). Her work has previously appeared in JCIB's *Counterpane*.

Louise Herring-Jones (Earl and Bubba Save the King)

Louise Herring-Jones writes speculative and historical fiction as well as humor and nonfiction. Her science fiction and horror stories have appeared in a variety of anthologies, and she won the inaugural Charlotte Writer's Club Board Prize for fiction (2009-2010). Her historic baseball article "A Georgia Yankee: The Legend of Johnny Mize" appeared nationally in the *2010 Maple Street Press Yankees Annual*. She is a veteran reporter for *The Daily Dragon*, practices law in Alabama, and is an advocate for constitutionally protected freedoms. Visit her at www.louiseherring-jones.com.

Gruber, J. M. (Summer Forever)

J. M. Gruber lives in an attic in Avondale and writes mostly fantasy. He's a secret Yankee, born in Minnesota but Alabama-raised. He will accept gifts in the form of money, pie, or hugs, and thanks you in advance for your contribution. You can read more of his work at jmgruber.com or follow him on Twitter @jmgruber.

Jared Millet (Hurricane Season)

An expat from Louisiana, Jared Millet has lived in Alabama for ten years. Mild-mannered librarian by day, he moderates the Hoover Library Write Club and serves as Birmingham's municipal liaison for National Novel Writing Month. His stories have appeared in *Shelter of Daylight*, *Dreams of Steam*, and *Dreams of Steam II*. When no one talks him out of it, he edits short story anthologies.

Suzanne Johnson (All the Good I Could)

A native of Winfield, Alabama, Suzanne Johnson is a longtime university magazine editor, serving at six universities across five states. Her *Sentinels of New Orleans* urban fantasy series – inspired by her own experiences as a resident of the Big Easy during Hurricane Katrina – is published by Tor Books, the science fiction and fantasy imprint of Macmillan. Book one, *Royal Street*, was released in April 2012, with subsequent books to follow in fall 2012 and spring 2013. Suzanne currently works at Auburn University, where she is associate editor of *Auburn Magazine.*

ALABAMA WRITING GROUPS

Auburn Writers Circle
Membership by invitation only.
Contact: Larry Williamson (soosdog@gmail.com)

Coffee Tree Fiction Writers
Meets twice monthly at Coffee Tree Books and Brew in Huntsville.
Contact: James Frost (f.scott.fitzbeagle@gmail.com)

Huntsville Literary Association Short Fiction Critique Group
Welcomes all types of fiction. Meets monthly in members' homes.
Contact: Ginger Nelson at Yahoo Group: huntsvillewriters

North Ala. Science Fiction Writers & Cake Appreciation Society
Focus on SF, fantasy, mild horror, and general weirdness. And cake.
Contact: Lin Cochran at Yahoo Group: huntsvillewriters

Sisters in Crime (Birmingham Chapter)
Meets at Homewood Library and Little Professor Bookcenter.
Membership required. For information, visit www.southernsinc.com

Southern Magic (Romance Writers of America)
Meets at Homewood Public Library. RWA membership required.
For information, visit www.southernmagic.org.

Write Club (Hoover Public Library)
Open to the public, meets one Saturday each month.
For information, call Hoover Public Library: (205) 444-7800

WWW.SUMMERGOTHIC.COM

11826830R00170

Made in the USA
Charleston, SC
23 March 2012